Forcing Amaryllis

Louise Ure

New York   Boston

Copyright © 2005 by Louise Ure
All rights reserved.

Mysterious Press
Warner Books

Time Warner Book Group
1271 Avenue of the Americas, New York, NY 10020
Visit our Web site at www.twbookmark.com.

The Mysterious Press name and logo are registered trademarks of Warner Books.

Printed in the United States of America

First Printing: June 2005

10 9 8 7 6 5 4 3 2 1

Library of Congress Cataloging-in-Publication Data
Ure, Louise.
    Forcing Amaryllis / Louise Ure.
        p. cm.
    ISBN 0-89296-009-4
    1. Women lawyers—Fiction. 2. Women—Crimes against—Fiction.
3. Italian American women—Fiction. 4. Attorney and client—Fiction.
5. Trials (Murder)—Fiction. 6. Arizona—Fiction. 7. Sisters—Fiction.
I. Title.
    PS3621.R4F67   2005
    813'.6—dc22

                                                    2004010351

Book design by RLF Design

To Jeanne Ure,

who taught me that it's not real

unless you say it out loud.

And to Bruce, always.

Acknowledgments

Zane Grey wrote: "The preposterous luck of a beginner is well known to all fishermen. It is an inexplicable thing." Yes, as a writer I'm a lucky beginner, but with friends like these, there's nothing inexplicable about it at all.

First and foremost, my thanks to Judith Greber (aka Gillian Roberts) who taught me the basics and then encouraged me to write something longer than an e-mail. I would never have begun the book without her. And I would never have completed it without the passionate support of the Monday Night Writers' Group. Lisa Atkinson, Linda Blondis, Joyce Caulfield, Dianne Hales, Jude Hebert, Sylvia Marino, Joan Sills, and Imma Trillo: my thanks to you all for the critiques, the suggestions, and the endless encouragement. I expect to be remembered in your Acknowledgments soon.

My thanks, as well, to the folks at Book Passage in Corte Madera, California, for providing such a grand place to both meet authors and learn to become one.

I send love and thanks to the friends and family members who read the manuscript, re-read it, and then read it again. To Mike and AK Smiley, David and Sara Arnold, Ruth Smith, Amy Layman, James Buskirk, Fred Knipe, Lee, Jim, Olivia, and Robert Ure, and all the others who offered ideas, insights, and a smile.

I appreciate the experts who gave so graciously of their time and wisdom. Beth Bonora and Idgi D'Andrea of Bonora D'Andrea Trial Consulting in San Francisco. Gary Cortner, Don Hodges, and Lora Bailey–Van Houten, criminalists with the California Department of Justice in Fresno. Attorney Anna "Tina" Ortiz in Globe, Arizona. You provided sound advice and a briefcase full of ideas on all the trial consulting, forensic, and legal elements of the story. If there are errors here, they are mine.

I am especially grateful to my agent, Philip Spitzer, for having such faith in this novel. I have the luck of the angels to be working with him. And thanks also to my editor, Kristen Weber, for her great patience and expertise. She has breathed life into this work. A bow, too, to Susan Richman, Brigid Pearson, Tareth Mitch, Arlene Petzal, and all the folks at Time Warner's Mysterious Press for their fine work, and for embracing this book.

And of course, to my husband, Bruce Goronsky, who never for a moment stopped believing.

Forcing Amaryllis

To force amaryllis, place bulb in a cool, dark
place for two months, with no water. Then bring it to a
brightly lit place, increasing watering as leaves form. Feed
lightly every two weeks through flowering period.

Gardening tag for amaryllis (*Hippeastrum*)

Prologue

It's not real unless you say it out loud. At least that's what my mother always said. She usually meant it for bad things, like a spouse's infidelity or a child's worsening cancer. She wasn't duping herself, just adding some distance between herself and the tears.

But I think it's also true for good news. The cessation of war or an avowal of love has no potency until you say it out loud. Then it becomes real, etched into someone else's memory like initials carved into a tree. Then it has weight and substance.

What my mother didn't tell me is that not everything you say out loud is true. That sometimes, whether out of self-preservation or self-delusion, whole worlds can be built on the breath of a lie.

1

Half past six and you could already feel the heat. Summer mornings in Arizona hit like a telegraphed punch, and this one felt like it was going to be a knockout. I stripped off the U of A T-shirt and headed for the shower. Turning the water temperature from hell to limbo in recognition of the already hot day, I lathered with a sliver of soap and shaved my legs with a razor blade long past its expiration date. Who cares. Nobody would know but me.

At thirty-three I hadn't exactly come to terms with my body; rather, I'd decided to ignore it. I still had the strong, heavy-muscled build my grandparents had carried with them from northern Italy. My grandmother used to say, "Calla, you're not much for pretty, but you're sure good for strong." She thought it was a compliment. She counseled me to be a PE teacher, but I knew that wasn't the career for me. I admired the Australians in the '92 Summer Olympics who'd won gold medals in all the events you could enter sitting down.

In the last few years I had developed a fullness and

roundness to my breasts and belly that I tried to disguise with long jackets and loose pants. It was as effective a disguise as the exaggerated sideburns on the face of a man losing his hair.

I threw open the closet doors and grabbed three hangers without looking for a match. I hadn't bought anything new for a long time, and my clothes were all the colors of a bleak desert landscape: a field of sand and shadow and quartz. Like the evolution of female birds, I had learned to soften my sounds and my colors for survival.

I used to wear bright blue and vermilion, buttery yellow and hot orange. Now I dressed in mouse colors. I didn't glance in the mirror even once.

I stuffed the last of the notebooks and tapes into my briefcase and headed out the door. Last night's focus groups confirmed my original thinking on jury selection. I just had to write a summary of the group's discussion and put the finishing touches on my analysis for the Rondo case. Mr. Rondo was suing his employer because the combine machine that picked and cleaned Pima County's premier cotton crop did not have a safety guard next to the whirling blade, and he had lost most of his right arm. His lawyers had asked us to help select jurors for his trial: jurors who might look past some of Mr. Rondo's own peccadilloes, especially his drinking and neglecting to wear his prescription glasses when operating the machine.

I had conducted focus groups with typical Tucson jurors and realized listening to the participants that this case was riddled with hot-button issues: alcoholism, product liability, physical disability, and personal responsibility versus corporate indifference. It wouldn't be a matter of helping Mr. Rondo select the perfect jurors—it would be deselecting those who could do the most damage to the case.

I prayed for the Jeep to start without the aid of jumper cables from a neighbor. The car was over ten years old, but it was all I could afford. In a kind of minor miracle, it started at the first turn of the key, the radio already tuned to an old-fashioned Spanish-language station that featured the *baladas rancheras* and *corridos* I remembered my mother and stepfather singing to each other when I was a child. I didn't know the words to this one, but hummed along at the chorus and imagined a story of separated lovers and long hard days of work under a blazing blue sky. The *rancheras* always sounded sad to me. Aunt Giulia said that was why country music and *rancheras* would both be around two hundred years from now. "There will always be sad people."

I felt good about what we had learned in the focus groups but wondered why we had taken the Rondo case in the first place. Marley and Partners Trial Consultants almost always worked for the defense, both in criminal and civil litigation, and Mr. Rondo was the plaintiff in this suit.

It's not that my boss, Jessica Marley, thought one side was more righteous than the other, it was just where she had her strings of influence and friendship: big-ticket defense attorneys and businesses with deep pockets.

But the trial consulting business was slow this year, slower than the usual hundred-degree malaise that hit the industry every June here in the desert Southwest, and Jessica seemed to be accepting smaller, less credible jobs than I had seen her take before.

Rondo was a case in point. I usually tried to keep an open mind about each client, but I was having trouble with this one. Yes, Mr. Rondo had lost most of his arm, but I couldn't help feeling that it was his own fault and now he was trying to get somebody else to pay for it.

In any case, Jessica would make money on the Rondo work, and that would help cover some of the bills piling up. If it went to trial and they secured a hefty verdict against Mr. Rondo's employer and Thayer Combine, the success could generate more business for us from other plaintiffs in civil trials. Anything that would help keep my job secure sounded good to me. My own bills were doing more than piling up; they were claiming squatter's rights and making a home for themselves.

I turned east on Speedway, passed the redbrick structures of the University of Arizona, and headed to the office. Decades ago, a *Life* magazine article called Speedway "the ugliest street in America," with its run-down strip malls, parched desert landscaping, and faded billboards. Tucsonans took that comment to heart, not wanting to be the ugliest anything in America, and spent years sprucing

up the route. Now fewer billboards sprouted on the road-
side, and there were paloverde trees and beavertail prickly
pear cactus planted in the medians. But Speedway was
still the ugliest street in the city, if not the country.

After fifteen minutes of squinting into the rising sun, I
turned north on Wilmot and pulled into the parking lot for
the Redrock Bank complex. I hoped that if I arrived this
early I'd be able to find a space with afternoon shade for
the car, but everybody else seemed to have the same idea. I
steered the Jeep into a slot at the end of a shadeless aisle
and left the side windows cracked open.

I grimaced at the unmade-up face in the rearview mirror. Horn-rimmed glasses framing eyes that couldn't measure up in a staring contest. Skin too familiar with the
Arizona sun, and hair too disarrayed to even be called a
style. I considered making time for a trim but decided that
I had let it go so long now that the ends actually stayed behind my ears like they were supposed to. See? Six dollars
saved on the trim right there. I stopped at the little coffee
shack in the parking lot that used to house a one-hour
photo business and ordered a latte to go.

Redrock Bank took up the first two floors of the building. Marley and Partners shared the third floor with a real
estate office and a temp agency. We were on close terms
with the temp agency, since Jessica's tantrums ensured
that our receptionists only lasted a few months. I waved at
the latest receptionist, Alice, a veteran of almost seven

weeks, and headed toward Jessica's office. Alice hissed once and waved me back to the lobby.

"Don't go in there, Calla. She's on a holy tear this morning."

I hesitated at Jessica's door. "What's wrong?"

"I think it's the staff vacation time that did it. Watch yourself."

I nodded and opened Jessica's door. She prowled and paced the length of her office, her sun-streaked hair frozen upright, like the mane of a charging lion.

Before I could say good morning, Jessica launched into her complaint. "How could she do this to me? How could she decide to have her baby three weeks early? Doesn't she know I don't have anyone to cover for her?"

I dropped into the guest chair across from her desk, pried the lid off my coffee, and hoped to ride out the storm with polite conversation. I took a tentative sip.

"Susan's having the baby already? I hope everything's okay. She wasn't due for another couple of weeks."

"I *know* she wasn't due for another couple of weeks," she pouted. "She certainly wasn't scheduled for maternity leave until then."

In Jessica's world work was the first priority, nail salon appointments were second, and family or life-threatening illness came in a distant third. Her idea of "balance" had more to do with a monthly review of her bank accounts than setting life goals.

"We've got a big new assignment from Whitcomb, Merchant & Dryer, and there's nobody to put on it. God, if we can get the inside track at their place, we'll have it made." She clicked her nails against the polished wooden desk and chewed on the end of a pen, mulling over her options.

Ours was a small office, six of us altogether, including the receptionist. With Susan taking early maternity leave, it left Jessica and three consultants to handle the business. And one of the three didn't really count, since he only handled trial graphics, the audiovisual presentation of evidence for the courtroom. That left Jessica plus two.

"What's the case?" I asked.

"It's a criminal defense. Sexual assault and first-degree murder. You probably know the name from the news — Cates. His family has owned half the rangeland down in the south part of the state around Patagonia for almost a century. Big money. And they want the whole menu: jury selection, strategy testing, community attitudes, trial graphics. Even survey research in case we need a change of venue. Oh, God," she said, holding her head in both hands, "we can't screw this up."

I imagined visions of end-of-month bank balances dancing in her head. "This isn't the guy who killed the woman he picked up in a bar, is it?" Rape and murder? No way I could get close to that. The distaste I felt could be heard in my voice, but Jessica didn't seem to notice.

"That's the one. Gideon Merchant himself is handling the defense, so we can expect fireworks. This one won't be a slam dunk for the prosecution." She pawed through a stack of papers on the desk, looking for the information the law firm had sent over. I saw the ragged edge of the Santa Catalina Mountains out the window behind her. The monsoon clouds were massing earlier than usual today, leaving ominous purple footprints across the hillsides.

"You could handle it," Jessica said, as if all her problems had just been resolved. "Aren't you just about done with Rondo?"

"I'll have the pretrial Rondo work finished this morning." I wished I still had stacks of analysis to complete. I wished I had a stronger backbone. I wished I had learned how to say no like I really meant it. "But you know I don't do criminal defense work. We agreed to that."

More than half of our assignments were civil cases, so six years ago when I joined the firm, Jessica thought that was an easy gimme in negotiating my deal. And my performance since then had been good for Marley and Partners; the research skills I learned from years in advertising had paid off. I may have cut my teeth on target audience psychographics for buyers of low-calorie beer and kids' cereal, but those skills translated into solid recommendations of potential jurors and strategies for our legal clients. And I loved using those skills on something more important than choosing a long-distance phone company.

Our arrangement wasn't a formal contract, just a verbal understanding that I wouldn't be asked to work on the criminal cases in the office. Up till now Jessica had never tried to breach that agreement.

"I wouldn't ask you if I didn't have to. But Tim is handling the job in Phoenix for at least another six weeks, and I'm in the middle of that pit bull thing." The pit bull case involved two Mexican nationals whose fight-trained dogs had killed a six-year-old neighborhood boy. Our clients were trying to get the case moved to Flagstaff, where there wasn't as much publicity, but the county attorney's office insisted that Tucson jurors could be just as fair in their deliberations. The Pima County prosecutors didn't want to lose the control or the limelight of the case.

I saw how this was shaping up. We were now down to one option for handling the murder case.

"I don't do criminal-defense work," I repeated like a mantra and rose abruptly from my chair. I threw the remains of the coffee into the trash and headed across the hall to my office with Jessica close at my heels. Silence reigned in the lobby; Alice had quit typing to hear our argument.

"I know you'd rather not," Jessica said, standing in the doorway to my small office, "but I really need you to cover this, at least until I can get done with the dogs. If you just go meet with the defense team today for a briefing, they'll feel like we're on top of this case and we won't lose them. Please."

That final word told me how desperate the office finances must be. Jessica never said please. But she still didn't sound like she meant it.

"Jessica, I don't do criminal-defense work. I don't like this kind of case," I repeated. She hovered over my desk, and I scooted my chair back two feet to maintain a perimeter of privacy.

"What is it with you?" She looked around my office for the answer and fingered her hair back into a casual arc. "Is there some reason you can't represent Mr. Cates?"

"Rape and murder? I won't do it." I straightened a nonexistent mess on my desk. "I don't even like to be around criminal defendants, and that means I probably wouldn't do a good job for him." I couldn't meet her eyes.

I hadn't ever told Jessica why I wouldn't defend someone in a criminal trial, especially one like this. Perhaps she thought it was squeamishness on my part. Perhaps she was right. Squeamishness combined with terror.

It was all because of Amaryllis—Amy, as my childhood pronunciation had abbreviated it. It had been seven years since my sister was attacked and left for dead, but seven years wasn't long enough to push it out of my nightmares.

"Well, get over it," Jessica said, slamming the office door back against the wall. "Business hasn't been so good that we can afford to be choosy about our clients. If there's no genuine conflict of interest here, then this is part of the job description, Calla. And if you can't do this job, I can always find someone who can." It seemed that our agreement had evaporated into thin air. The sound of typing started up again from the lobby.

She hadn't attached a "please" this time. The real Jessica had returned.

"Hey, wait a minute!" I said as she crossed the lobby. "What about our deal?"

"What deal?" she tossed over her shoulder. As usual, Jessica was looking out for Number One. And Number Two was so far behind you couldn't even see if I was raising any dust.

Damn it. I needed the money from this job. When I left the advertising industry six years ago, it was mostly because I could earn more doing trial consulting. In advertising, the folks making the real money are in the creative department. The lowly researchers don't get much, and I needed the extra income for Amy's care. It also didn't hurt that trial consulting felt more real—more necessary—than anything I'd done in advertising.

If Jessica had just honored her promise to keep me away from criminal litigation, I would have been fine. Sure, I'd still be scraping for every nickel to take care of Amy, but I would have been okay.

"Get over it," Jessica had said. Easier said than done. I let out a long breath. Well, if I had to attend one meeting with a criminal-defense attorney, then so be it. For all I knew, this guy, Cates, could be cherubic, soft-spoken, and innocent.

I took another deep breath and turned to the recommendations for the Rondo case, hoping to push the upcoming meeting with Mr. Cates's attorney out of my mind. I didn't think it would stay gone for long.

2

It was late afternoon when I arrived at the offices of Whitcomb, Merchant & Dryer.

"Hello, I'm Calla Gentry," I said to the movie star–cum–receptionist. She gave me a megawatt smile through lacquered lips. The offices were plush and quiet, the lobby floor tiled with three-foot squares of leather. Oversized paintings of wild horses looked down from two walls. The third wall was glass, overlooking the mosaic tile dome of the old Pima County Courthouse. The receptionist continued the Western theme with her squash-blossom necklace and tight suede blouse.

I asked for Kevin McCullough, the attorney who would be handling the day-to-day work on the case with the master himself, Gideon Merchant.

"Please take a seat. I'll tell Mr. McCullough you're here." She used the eraser tip of a pencil to push the phone buttons, her heavy silver bracelets clanking in a contrapuntal rhythm.

I sank into a soft, dark gray couch, hoping I could find my feet again when I needed to get up. I had just managed to find a balance between prone and perched when his footsteps squeaked across the leather tiles.

He had dark, curly hair and a lean face with a strong jaw: a Clark Kent face but stretched longer. His eyes were attentive behind steel-rimmed frames. I thought he looked smart, confident, and kind. I was probably right about two of those.

"Thank you for coming over on such short notice. We're going to have to hurry," McCullough said.

I lurched off the couch, my purse strap slipping off my shoulder and my overstuffed briefcase pulling me to the right. "I'm happy to help, but I'm just going to be doing the preliminary work with you. Jessica Marley will be the trial consultant."

He gave me a quizzical look, then marched down the hall to the conference room. "But Jessica said you were the best," he said over his shoulder.

I silently cursed Jessica for the misleading and inappropriate buildup of my skills, especially regarding a criminal defense. "She's actually our specialist in criminal litigation. I'll just be covering for her until she's freed up from an earlier case."

We found seats across from each other at the lozenge-shaped conference table, and I kept my back to the window. I opened my notebook and clicked a ballpoint pen into position. I was willing to handle this first meeting for Jessica, but I had no interest in small talk or in finding out anything else about the law firm or McCullough or Cates, the man accused of murder. I was going to get the facts and get out.

"That may be a problem," McCullough replied, as if he were reading my mind. "I have the whole team waiting for us at the county jail for a strategy session today. I've got a few minutes to fill you in on the basics of the case before we have to leave to join them." He gestured to two tall stacks of files in front of him.

Damn. If I got introduced to the entire team as the Marley and Partners representative it was going to make my disappearance more difficult. Jessica probably knew this was more than just a meet-and-greet appointment and thought that hiding it from me was the only way to ensure my attendance.

I'd have to go through with the trip to the jail and try not to get stuck with any commitments that would keep me on the case.

"Give me the broad outlines and how you think we might be able to help you. If Jessica winds up taking over as point person, I'll make sure she gets all the facts."

"Sure." He shifted a stack of files on the table closer to him. "Sign this Letter of Confidentiality first. That way we can say you're part of Cates's legal team, and any conversation we have about the case remains privileged." He slid a one-page form across the table, and I scrawled a signature along the bottom.

He picked up the top file, opened it, and began reading from the first page. "Raymond Cates, thirty-eight, a Tucson resident, is accused of the sexual assault and murder of Lydia Chavez, twenty-two years old, also from Tucson, at Gates Pass on April first of this year. According to the sheriff's report Mr. Cates was seen talking to Ms. Chavez in the Blue Moon bar on the night in question. They reportedly left at about the same time, but no one actually saw them leave together."

He paused and looked up. "All the evidence against my client is circumstantial. Tire tracks found at the scene are consistent with his tires, similar cat hair was found on both their clothing, and the gun used is the same caliber as a gun Raymond purchased several years ago."

"She died from a gunshot wound?" I continued to take notes.

McCullough stopped reading, took off his glasses, and began cleaning them with a handkerchief. "Yes, he — someone — raped her with a gun, then pulled the trigger. Not our client, of course. Mr. Cates is innocent."

"Of course." I swallowed an unexpected lump in my throat. My God, what terror that poor woman must have felt. April Fool's Day. But it was no joke.

I couldn't do this. I couldn't even have an objective conversation about the crime without panicking at the scenes of horror appearing in my mind. It reminded me too much of Amy.

"But he really is innocent," McCullough protested. "He can prove he wasn't even in Tucson when she was killed."

Hoping to find a graceful way out of the case, I said,

"It's not that I'm trying to turn down business, but you may not need as much of our help as you expect. The evidence sounds pretty thin. With that and an alibi, I'm surprised that the State was able to make an arrest stick." I clicked the ballpoint pen to the retracted position as if our business was concluded.

"Well, there is the parking ticket."

"What parking ticket?"

"A sheriff's deputy gave Ray's car a parking ticket at Gates Pass within an hour of the time the coroner fixed as the time of death. That's why they focused on Ray so quickly when the body was discovered."

That certainly made his circumstantial case more substantial. Wasn't that how they finally caught the Son of Sam killer?

"It's not all bad news," McCullough continued. "He has no priors, and we've got a strong alibi and his family's reputation going for us. But even circumstantial evidence can look bad if you add it all together. We've got a lot of preparation to do. Cates demanded an early trial date, and we'll need lots of help to get ready."

I shrugged my halfhearted agreement and clicked the pen back into writing position.

McCullough did triage on the files in front of him and stuffed only the most critical folders into the slim briefcase at his feet. "C'mon, they'll be waiting for us at the jail. We'd better take two cars."

I had to trot to keep up with him on the way to the

garage. Two basketball-center-sized parking lot attendants brought the cars around, and McCullough gunned the engine on his Porsche as I repositioned the seat on the Jeep. An all-time record—the Jeep started right up twice in one day. I ran two red lights between the garage and the freeway just to keep McCullough in sight. He turned what should have been a fifteen-minute trip into a seven-minute demonstration of virility.

I had never been inside the county jail before; all of my previous clients had been defendants in civil trials. The multistory white building sat apart from its fellows in a wide circle of landscaped desert two miles west of I-10. It looked more like an airport hotel than it did a detention center, with fewer bars and less security glass than I expected.

We showed our ID and submitted to a pat-down and search of our briefcases, then were shown into a medium-sized conference room with a high horizontal window on the west wall. A rectangular metal table was bolted to the floor, and all but two hard-back chairs around the table were taken.

We hadn't interrupted any conversation. Everyone was busy with notes or a search through documents while they waited for us. McCullough apologized for our tardiness and greeted several of the attendees, but I didn't catch all the names.

He began the introductions. "This is Calla Gentry, from Marley and Partners Trial Consultants. Calla, the rest of the group is as follows. First, we have Gideon Merchant, the senior partner who will oversee our efforts here. . . ."

I nodded at the florid cheeks of the founder of Whitcomb, Merchant & Dryer. He was thirty pounds overweight and wore a conservative suit with thin white pinstripes and a bright red power tie. Tufts of white hair peeked from behind and below his ears, curling in the oppressive jailhouse heat. He was already scowling when the introduction began, so I didn't take it personally when he frowned at me. "Ms. Gentry," he said, stirring then tasting the coffee before him.

"Steffie is the paralegal working with me," McCullough continued. A strawberry blonde with a constellation of freckles across her nose smiled and waved from the end of the table.

"On your left is Anthony Strike, the firm's private investigator." Strike was tall and lanky, with black hair, a Zapata-style mustache, and a quick, lopsided grin. He slouched in the straight-backed seat as if it were a rocking chair in front of an Old West sheriff's office. His cowboy boots were worn down at their angled heels, and his pearl-snap shirt was rolled up at the sleeves. Definitely a Tucson character: the Wild West was still alive in him.

"Next to him is Dr. Marjorie Ballast. She'll be reviewing all the forensic evidence for us. And she'll either be our expert witness in those areas or she'll tell us who to get for specific forensic rebuttal." Dr. Ballast looked a little like George Washington and wore a severely cut olive green pantsuit. I double-checked to see if I'd missed an Adam's apple. She didn't even look up at the introduction, continuing to take notes in a black, fabric-covered day planner. She probably thought it was a waste of her time to come to a meeting this early in the game, before all the evidence was available for her to review. She was probably right.

"And right beside you, of course, is our client, Raymond Cates." Cates was on the short side of average and looked like a tennis player: trim build, long limbs, and an even tan. He wore orange scrubs with "Pima County Jail" stenciled on the back. Somehow he managed to make the jail uniform look pressed and tailored. It made Anthony Strike seem underdressed for the meeting.

Cates's sandy brown hair drooped over his forehead, and he threw his head back to get it out of his eyes, like a horse trying to rid himself of a bit and bridle. Not exactly the cherubic image I'd been hoping for, but I'd settle for soft-spoken and innocent.

He surveyed me from my forehead to my lap, then turned abruptly and faced Kevin McCullough across the table. I couldn't tell if I'd met with his approval or not.

McCullough ticked off one agenda item on the sheet in front of him. "Okay, this is June fourteenth, and since we have not waived the right to a speedy trial, we're scheduled to start with jury selection on August twenty-first. That leaves us less than nine weeks to get ready."

I counted back on my fingers. Cates had been arraigned at the end of May, and since capital murder is not a bailable offense, he'd already spent almost three weeks in jail. An August twenty-first date for jury selection meant that the State was barely inside their ninety-day window for a "speedy trial."

No one spoke up at the mention of the early trial date. Finally Cates threw up his hands in exasperation. "I know that wasn't your recommendation, Kevin, but I want to get this over with and get out of here."

What a fool. Preparation for any felony trial would be difficult in that short amount of time, and I couldn't imagine getting ready for a death-qualified jury in only nine weeks. On the other hand, it wouldn't give the prosecution time to fully develop its case either.

McCullough nodded as if he agreed with my mental argument and continued going around the table discussing each person's area of responsibility, asking questions about timing, and setting priorities. Dr. Ballast was already working on retesting the cat hair and tire patterns. She wanted to do a ballistics comparison on Cates's gun, but he'd told the police that he'd lost it years ago.

"A .41 Magnum, that's an unusual caliber, isn't it?" Merchant asked.

"Sort of," Cates replied. "There's less recoil than a .44 Magnum, and you have a better chance of hitting what you're aiming at. I left the gun at my father's ranch years ago when I moved to Tucson." It was the first time he seemed to take a real interest in the discussion around him. For the rest of the time he was doodling on the pad in front of him. It looked like a landscape with high-flying birds above the mountaintops. He must have been thinking about his freedom.

"It seems to me that finding the gun and proving it wasn't the murder weapon is in your best interest," Merchant said. "Have your father keep looking for it."

Cates nodded.

McCullough and Strike were going to spend time with the alibi witness, Hector Salsipuedes, who worked at the Cates ranch. He had told the sheriff's deputies that he and Cates were sharing a beer at the ranch near Patagonia, more than an hour away from Tucson, when the attack occurred. Strike was also going to investigate the character and life of the victim, Lydia Chavez, to see if other potential suspects could be suggested to the jury.

Merchant raised the issue of the parking ticket. "Can we suggest that someone else drove Ray's car that night? Or that the officer is mistaken? What do we know about this Deputy Niles? Is there any bad blood between him and the Cates family?" McCullough and Strike nodded to each other and jotted notes.

When my turn came, McCullough asked when we'd start doing research on jury recommendations. I tried to hedge my answer.

"I suppose that we could begin almost immediately, but it would only give us preliminary guidance. We should really base our selection on their response to our strategy and the witnesses and evidence we want to present. I can line up focus group respondents for the next several weeks, and then, as we finalize our strategy and presentation, we can conduct a mock trial with them."

"Why wait for a final strategy?" Cates asked. "They certainly aren't going to change how they feel about murder, are they?"

I waited for McCullough to answer his client's question, but he gestured for me to proceed. "No, but they may change how they feel about *this* murder. For example, if you said 'I didn't do it, you have the wrong man,' a juror may feel differently than if you said, 'I did it, but voices told me to.'"

"I didn't do it." Cates snorted once and gestured to the rest of the table. "I already told these guys. That's our strategy because that's the truth."

McCullough jumped in with a reply to put his client at ease. "I know, Ray. And of course, you're right. But we want to make sure that we're presenting our defense in the strongest possible light and that we've found the most receptive people we can for the jury." He paused and checked the tabbed markers in the notebook in front of him, then shut the book with a muffled bang.

"All right. That's all for today, folks. We'll plan to meet the middle of next week for updates."

We shuffled chairs, gathered papers, and stood to leave. I said good-bye to Dr. Ballast, who looked through me as if I were a dirty window with a dull view on the other side. Cates stopped me with a hand on my arm.

"I've been trying to place it, but can't come up with anything. Have we met before? Maybe at Presidio Grill?" he said, naming one of the better restaurants in town.

I glanced down and started to form a response, but nothing came out. My arm seemed suddenly hot where he held me, and I heard Amy's nightmare screams echo in my head. I swallowed the gasp building in my throat.

3

I don't know how I made it out of the jail without causing a scene. I remember Kevin's voice calling me to wait for him, but I ran out of the building and back to my car, stopping only for the obligatory searches by the officers. My fingertips were numb, and I shook with both chills and sweats.

What had happened back there? For just a moment—standing there at the table with Cates's hand on my arm—I pictured Amy's attack as clearly as if I'd been there. And I saw Cates's hand holding the knife.

Could Cates really be the Animal, as I had called him all these years? Amy hadn't known his name and didn't give me many details about the rape, and I had probably let my all-too-vivid imagination fill in the gaps with wild guesses and vapor-filled assumptions. Now, of course, she couldn't tell me anything, but I needed to be with her anyway.

I started the car and headed back to the office to clear my desk and get across town to my sister.

· · ·

S aguaro Nursing Home sat right across the street from the Tucson Medical Center on Grant Road. The proximity was only cosmetic; they shared no staff or medical resources, but I felt better having a world-class hospital this close to Amy.

It had taken hours before I was free of Jessica and her demands. I didn't arrive at the nursing home until the end of visiting hours, but the staff was used to me by now and let me in almost anytime. My heart pounded with the urgency of seeing her, but I still drove twice around the lot and searched for a space under a streetlamp and within sight of the front door.

"Ms. Gentry, when can we expect this month's check? . . ." Damn her. Why did the nursing home's business manager have to be working so late?

I waved at the woman as if she had simply called out a greeting and turned left down the first corridor. The marbled green linoleum usually gave me a peaceful and cool feeling, even in the heat of summer. Tonight it seemed dank and mossy, as slippery as my thoughts.

Amy's room was the fifth on the left, with a window looking out to a small garden area and the front parking lot. Sometimes I stood outside the window after a visit, calling quiet encouragement to her the way I'd done when we were kids sneaking out of the house at midnight to go toilet paper somebody's house.

I took a deep breath to calm myself, eased open the door, and breathed in the cool, antiseptic smell of the room. A small night-light glowed at knee level, casting soft shadows up the wall. The roses I'd brought last week from the back garden had died, forgotten, in a dry vase on the windowsill. Mrs. Pilker, Amy's nonagenarian roommate, rumbled a snore in the bed closest to the door.

I tiptoed to the second bed and looked down at my sister. A call button pinged at the other end of the hall, then rubber-soled footsteps moved that direction in response.

Amy hadn't changed. Her features were still relaxed into an exemplar of sleep: lineless brow, full, soft lips, and delicate shallow breaths. Her arms were outside the covers and had been positioned by her sides. The stuffed prairie dog and jackrabbit Aunt Giulia had given her were nestled close to her fingertips. Amy's closed eyes looked sunken—bruised—and her skin had a soft, bloated texture, as if she had been underwater too long.

She hadn't opened her eyes for more than two years now, but with each visit I still hoped her smile or grasp would welcome me. I brushed a strand of dark hair off her face and stroked her cheek with the back of my fingers.

"Amaryllis, my little Flower Bud," I said, using our mother's private nickname for her. "How are you this evening? We'll need to be quiet tonight. Mrs. Pilker is asleep, and you know she needs her beauty rest." I resettled the stuffed animals higher on the bed around her pillow and, careful not to disturb the IV, tucked her arms under the light blue blanket.

"Do you mind if we don't read tonight, Amy?"

It was an empty question. Except for two euphoric moments of semi-wakefulness, Amy had slept—like a space traveler on an intergalactic journey—for almost seven years. In homage to my mother's philosophy that possibility becomes fact when you say it out loud, I still insisted that Amy could hear me. We were in the middle of reading *Gulliver's Travels*, but I didn't open the book. The words would only swirl and blur before my eyes tonight.

"Let's let the Lilliputians have at him tonight, and we'll catch up with them later."

I leaned forward so that my forearms were cushioned by the edge of the mattress and stroked the shape of Amy's hand under the blanket. We sat silent for long minutes.

"Oh, Amaryllis, am I just jumping at shadows? Am I going to keep seeing him around every corner?"

There was so much I wanted to say to her, and so much I wanted her to say. I stared at the boxy weave of the cotton blanket, remembering the story of Amy's rape.

She was nineteen then and rich with the dark, Hispanic beauty of a ripe pomegranate. Amaryllis Del Arte had inherited her father's Latin coloring, while I carried my father, William Gentry's, lighter, English genes. She was quick to laugh or flirt and could twirl on one arched foot like a music-box ballerina. She was going to be a nurse.

My phone rang at two o'clock that morning seven years ago, two hours past the end of Halloween night.

"Come get me," Amy had whispered, and told me where she was.

I jumped into a pair of sweatpants, threw a denim jacket over my pajama top, and ran to the car. It took almost an hour to reach the No-Tell Motel on the outskirts of Nogales, sixty-five miles to the south.

I pounded on the door to room six. Two minutes passed like an eternity before Amy opened the door. Her right eye was sealed shut, and she clutched a bath towel to her naked body. Blood ran down between her legs.

"Oh, Amy, what happened?" I sat her on the bed and brought a glass of rust brown water from the bathroom.

"Attacked," she said. "Parking lot, leaving the rodeo. He tied me up." The strips of cloth were still wound around her wrists.

"He used a knife on me." She gestured to her lap, and I gasped.

She had lain in a black corner of the rodeo parking lot for hours, she said, fearful of the pain, the blood, and his return. Only in the early morning hours had she been able to crawl to her car, drive to the closest well-lit haven—a room at the seedy No-Tell Motel—and call me.

I couldn't find her purse anywhere. Maybe it still lay in a gravelly rut in the parking lot. Maybe her attacker had it.

"No doctors," Amy said between clenched teeth. I paid

no attention to her protests and drove to the nearest hospital with Amy's broken body braced by my arm, her head resting in my lap.

Amy wouldn't tell them what had happened, and after a while they quit asking. The attending physician, Dr. Sanji, was a brown, round-faced man with a thick accent that left his syllables as distinct and separate as the pickets on a fence. He knew these wounds were not self-inflicted, but without her help he could take no action. That night he cleaned and sutured and braced, but he couldn't touch the real damage, the damage to Amy's soul.

I brought her home and had the locks changed. Amy's listed address was different from mine, but she had carried a spare key to my apartment and I had an overwhelming fear that somehow her attacker would find her again.

After three days Amy could walk without help but would not leave the house. Bruises blossomed like storm clouds across her face and her rib cage.

I thought if she could talk about the attack, then we might begin to leach it out of her before her heart turned as hard as Tucson's limestone bed of caliche. But she rarely spoke, preferring to distance herself from that night by hiding behind a wall of silence. It's not real unless you say it out loud. We'd learned our lesson well.

I tried to coax her with her favorite foods: *albóndigas* soup with its light broth and savory meatballs, *pipian de gallina* with pumpkinseeds folded into the chile sauce. She shrank into herself, unaffected by hunger or the aromas of cooking.

Now, looking down at her sleeping form in the nursing home, I wondered again if I could have done something else. Could I have brought her back from the brink of that chasm with more doctors or more love or more time? On Thanksgiving Day, three weeks after the rape, Amy's near-perfect suicide attempt took all my options away.

4

By Saturday morning I had more of a grip on myself. Cates was no rodeo mugger who attacked women in parking lots. He was rich and well educated, and his lawyer was sure he was innocent of these current charges. I was letting my fears elope with my imagination.

Amy had been raped, but I was the one who now cringed and cowered. I had become the victim without the crime, violated by proxy. Suspecting Cates was another symptom of my disease. I knew that. I conjured up bogeymen behind every tree.

That still didn't mean I wanted to spend any more time with Cates. Come Monday I swore I would tell Jessica once and for all that I couldn't work on the case, and then I'd put him out of my mind.

But right now I needed someone to calm my jangling nerves. Someone granite-solid and soldier-straight, someone whose voice didn't go into a higher register when they talked to children or animals. I needed to see Aunt Giulia.

. . .

Try this one," Giulia said, handing me an empty crossword puzzle grid. "I think I've got a winner here. It's called 'To Err/Heir/Air is Human.' All based on homophones, but there are only ten real clues. All the others say 'sounds like sixty-one across' or 'sounds like three down.'"

Giulia had been supplementing her income for the last two decades by creating mind-numbing crossword puzzles. She was the only person I knew who could tell you the four-letter word for "bacchanalian orgy cry" and could use it in a sentence.

"Of course, it won't work on the East Coast," she said, referring to the new puzzle. "They pronounce one of those 'errs' like the sound a Rottweiler makes right before he attacks." She leaned across the mobile home's plastic dinette table and shuffled among bills and newspaper clippings until she found her package of Mores. She lit the tip of the thin brown cigarette and drew in a first inhalation as if it were a breath of the purest mountain air. She treated the lighting of a cigarette like a tea ceremony.

"Did you use *hoard* and *horde*?" I asked.

"And the third one. Here's another hint to get you started. I also used *gamble* and *gambol*."

"As if that's going to be any help."

Spinning the crossword puzzle around on the table in front of me, I described meeting Raymond Cates and told Giulia about my frenzied impression that he might be Amy's attacker.

"It was his hands," I said. "Oh, I don't know. Maybe it

was just the situation. He's accused of having killed a woman by putting a gun inside her and shooting her. That's not so different from what happened to Amy. I mean, it was a knife and . . ." I swallowed hard.

Giulia held her cigarette at chin level between her thumb and forefinger like a Frenchman, and watched my eyes. "What was it about his hands that made you think he was Amy's attacker?"

"He's missing the top half of the ring finger on his right hand." I pictured that shortened finger resting on my sleeve as the meeting at the jail broke up.

"So?"

"Remember Amy's nightmares those first few days after the attack? She kept saying 'day-doh' or something like that. And she never remembered it when she woke up."

Giulia rolled the tip of her cigarette in the ashtray. "I know you were trying to make something of it even then. It might have been a name or a street or something she saw that night."

I nodded. "But yesterday at the jail, when I saw his hand, it came to me—almost like a seasick feeling. I knew what it meant."

Her eyebrows hunched.

"*Dedo*. It's Spanish—finger. Maybe Amy was trying to tell us how to identify him."

Giulia sputtered her disbelief. "Why wouldn't she just have told us there was something strange about his fingers?"

"I don't know."

Giulia kept shaking her head. "And in Spanish? I know Amy's bilingual but—"

"You remember how Papa used to tease her about dreaming in Spanish when she was tiny? He said it was his special gift to her."

Giulia smiled at the memory. "Yes, but even if that's what she meant, there must be a thousand men in Tucson who have something wrong with their hands or fingers."

I thought about Mr. Rondo and his missing arm. Between the mines, the ranches, and the cotton crop, there are a lot of ways to hurt yourself in this town. And I wasn't even sure if Amy had meant a deformed finger, a burned or unsightly hand, or maybe a strong, evil one that held her by the throat. Maybe "day-doh" wasn't a word at all.

Giulia ground the butt of the cigarette in the ashtray and rose to pour me coffee. "We've had seven years to get used to what happened to Amy. I don't like it, but it happened. We can still love Amy and take care of her, but we can't let this rape incapacitate us. It can't define us. That would mean that he won," she said.

I sighed. It seemed so much clearer in my mind than in my explanation to her; so much more real. "This felt different. Maybe because we were at the jail . . ."

"Let's go back to the beginning," Giulia said, humoring me. "What else do we know about Amy's attack?"

We went over the details for the thousandth time. Amy was attacked leaving the rodeo. She said he had a black truck, but she didn't know what kind it was and she didn't see the license plate. His belt buckle was silver and shaped like a sun, with rays. Amy had thought he was a cowboy, with his boots and Stetson hat. She said she never got a good look at his face.

Giulia took notes with a mid-century penmanship that danced across the page like the Rockettes.

"She said the knife he used had the design of a snake on the handle," I continued.

Giulia grimaced, probably remembering Amy's shudder as she'd tried to translate her dark memories into darker words. "Coral and turquoise, right?"

"Yep, and she said he called her Sweet Thing."

Giulia paused. "Well, there's not much we can do about a nickname, a knife, or a belt, but I'll tell you what. I've got a friend at the motor vehicle division. I'll ask her to find out what kind of car Raymond Cates drove seven years ago. We'll find out that it wasn't a black pickup truck, and you can go back to a normal life, okay?"

I nodded. It was good to have Giulia's levelheaded thinking involved.

I picked up a faded photo of Amy and me taken in front of the house on Seneca Street when we were girls. Our house was pink stucco, with rounded archways and two cherry red steps leading up to the front porch. It looked like a piggy bank with lipstick on. We played jacks on that red concrete porch until we wore a gray divot in it and the mechanical bounce of the ball could no longer be counted on. Then we graduated to lipstick ourselves. In the photo those colors had faded to a gentle blush.

Momma had married Franco Del Arte less than a year after the divorce papers showed up. She knew from the first day of my father's absence that he wouldn't be back, that he had to seek softer climates and cooler passions. And she knew from the first day she met Franco that he was the man she would spend the rest of her life with. Amy was born that same year, and I found happiness in the role of big sister and six-year-old guardian angel. I was Socrates to a single pupil, a general whose troops numbered one.

Momma had expected to have a whole garden of children, but we were the only two flowers that grew before she lost control of the car on a stretch of sandy road outside of the aptly named Why, Arizona.

Aunt Giulia let us sleep through the night rather than come tell us our parents had been killed coming back from Mexico. "What could you have done at three o'clock in the morning," she said, "except be less prepared to face the day?" She took a leave of absence from her job at the *Arizona Daily Star*, moved into our family home, and set out to learn how to be a mother. She used to joke about acting *in loco parentis*, but never told us that loco had nothing to do with going crazy.

I gave Giulia a hug and took a copy of her new puzzle back to the house.

. . .

The rest of the weekend was taken over by mindless errands and time with Amy. I tried balancing my checkbook and gave up after an hour's hunt for a fourteen-dollar difference. What did it matter? That extra fourteen bucks wouldn't go far in paying for Amy's care this month anyway.

Our parents' small life-insurance policy had been just enough to pay for their funerals. Giulia still helped as much as she could with Amy's care, but without insurance it took the bulk of my salary to cover it. And I wasn't willing to turn Amy over to the state system, even though it would have cost less. There just wasn't enough hope there.

I did transfer the balance on my credit card to a new card with a low introductory interest rate. Maybe if I kept moving the money around to new, low-interest cards, I could keep paying for Amy's hospitalization without pulling more money out of my meager savings account.

On Sunday I took Giulia to visit Amy. We tucked her limp arms into a new pink nightgown, brushed her hair, filed her nails, and rubbed buttery kukui-nut lotion into her hands, all the while keeping up a running chatter of gossip and recipes and news about Giulia's co-workers.

Giulia never once looked at Amy's face, concentrating instead on the sleeve of the nightgown or the palm of her hand. Perhaps she saw too much of my mother in her. She missed her sister like a lost limb, even after almost ten years, and I thought of the terrible finality Amy's death would mean to me. I could always convince myself that my sister might come back to me someday. Giulia knew she'd lost her sister for good. She'd already had to say it out loud.

I stopped to pick up a pizza on the way back from the nursing home, then settled in to try the homophonic puzzle. Crossword king Merl Reagle would have been proud of Giulia; this one was Sunday *New York Times* quality. But after *perish, slay, pain, brute,* and *cruel* turned up as halves of five separate homophonic pairs, I put it down unfinished.

5

I had a flat tire on the way to work Monday morning, so it was almost ten o'clock when I arrived. The temperature was already over a hundred degrees, and the tire-changing exertions left me with dark rings of sweat under my arms. My hair was as wet as if I'd been swimming, and my glasses were sliding off my nose.

The receptionist handed me two pink message slips as I passed by the front desk. The first was from Mr. Rondo's lawyers with a question on jury selection; the second was from Kevin McCullough.

"Thanks, Alice. What did McCullough want?" I pushed my wet hair back off my forehead and glanced at Jessica's closed door.

"He wants to go ahead with some early focus groups. He said he'd give you the details when you call him back."

That was the last thing I wanted to do, so I headed into Jessica's office, intending to hand over the project. She had the phone set to "speaker" and was taking notes from voice messages that had been left over the weekend. She held up one long, manicured finger in a "just a sec" sign and waved toward the guest chair. When she finished listening to the last message, she hit number three on the keypad for delete and hung up the phone.

"Did you hear that?" she asked. "You'd think these lawyers couldn't go to the toilet without having their hands held." She checked the finish on her nails as if imagining the hand-holding she'd just been asked to do.

"What is it? Does one of our clients require a little TLC?"

"It's this pit bull case. We have the research in affidavit form, but now the attorney wants me to present the findings in court," she said. "What's on your mind?"

"Kevin McCullough wants to start focus groups on the Cates case right away." I dropped the message on her desk. It was only a slip of paper, but I felt as if a ten-pound weight had been lifted off my shoulders as I let it go.

"Oh, no, you don't." She waved off the offending note. "I can't possibly get involved with Cates yet. I'll be at the courthouse all afternoon on this dog research. You return his call. I'll be able to pick it up again next week." She turned back to the telephone, content with having delegated the project.

"Look, Jessica, you asked me to attend one meeting last Friday, and I did it as a favor to you." I heard Aunt Giulia's voice in my head, Don't let her push you around.

"Do you have a legitimate conflict of interest here, Calla, or do you just not like the case?"

I wanted to be honest with her. I truly did believe in our jury system, and I tried to keep an open mind about our clients. I didn't want to assume that Cates was guilty of this or any other crime just because he'd been accused. But I also owed it to Jessica to let her know that I had reservations about working on the case.

"It's personal. Nothing that I could really call a justifiable conflict of interest," I confessed. "But we had an agreement that I wouldn't have to work on criminal cases."

She waved off my complaint. "I've got a lot on my mind right now. We'll talk about it after I get back from court." She pulled a gold-toned compact from her purse, opened the lid, and smiled at herself in the small mirror to check her lipstick and confirm her best angle.

I headed into the break room and grabbed a bottle of water. Could I quit this job? No. The only other two jobs I had the skills for, advertising and market research, didn't pay as well. And I enjoyed the notion that I was working for justice, even if that justice was only on the civil side of the legal world. I had my answer. I had to stay at Marley and Partners, and for the moment that meant doing the best job I could for Raymond Cates.

I hadn't heard back yet from Giulia with any news about Cates's car from seven years ago, but I couldn't get that shortened finger out of my mind. I knew I was being silly, but I had to at least know he hadn't owned a black pickup to be able to work on his case. I sank into my chair and spun toward the window. They say the silhouette of the Santa Catalina Mountains looks like an elephant head, but I thought it looked more like a cowboy hat today, the kind with a little dimple, like a saddle, on the top. Cowboy hat. Cowboy. Ranch. Patagonia. How could I find out where Raymond Cates had been on Halloween seven years ago? At his father's ranch near Patagonia? Or was he thirty miles away in Nogales at the rodeo grounds near the Mexican border? Seven years is a long time. Nobody would remember where they were or where Cates was. But if I could somehow prove he was miles away from where Amy was attacked, it would make me feel better about helping select his jury in this murder case.

Raymond Cates probably wasn't Amy's attacker, but a little legal research couldn't hurt in any case. And it might help me get justice for Amy—no matter who her attacker was. Marley and Partners hadn't worked on any rape cases in the last two years, and I knew some laws had changed. Right now I wasn't even sure what the statute of limitations was for a rape in Arizona.

And what about attempted murder, for that's certainly what Amy's attack was. Whoever he was, he left her for dead, slashed inside and out, in the gravel lane of a vast, dark parking lot.

Not working on criminal cases at Marley and Partners had left me with a lack of expertise. I was going to ask Jessica about the statute of limitations, but that would have opened a Pandora's box of questions.

I may not have had much experience with criminal trials, but I surely knew how to do research. And I had a place to start: the Santa Cruz County attorney's office.

I called Kevin McCullough and told him an emergency had come up and we couldn't schedule a meeting until later. Then I told Jessica I was feeling sick and had to take the rest of the day off. I headed for Nogales.

The big towns of the desert Southwest are as modern as any other cities—full of biochemists and CPAs and personal trainers. But there's an echo of both the Old West and the Franciscan missionaries who settled the territory as well. Every man could be a cowboy, every day a miracle. The road to Nogales had some of both those influences.

It was a landscape riddled with denial and promise: dry riverbeds, dust-choked sagebrush, and the soaring white towers of the Mission San Xavier del Bac. I slowed back down to the speed limit as I passed the centuries-old church. From this distance you couldn't see the tiny mouse carved into one tower or the cat on the other. It was said that if the unfinished dome on the second tower was completed then the cat would catch the mouse and it would mean the end of the world, so the Indians and settlers through the centuries had left the church incomplete.

Was that what I was doing now by investigating Amy's attack? Was I finishing the construction of a tower that was never meant to be completed? I didn't know if I felt like the cat or like the mouse.

I was filling the gas tank at Tubac, halfway down the sixty-five-mile route to Nogales, when a more prosaic problem arose. I had signed a Letter of Confidentiality with Raymond Cates's legal team. I was sworn to hold his information in confidence and to do nothing that would infringe upon his defense.

Well, noticing an amputated finger could hardly be considered privileged communication, I chided myself. I wasn't really using any information I heard from his lawyer. And knowing that he'd been charged with a sexual assault was hardly confidential. Hell, everybody in Arizona knew he'd been accused of rape and murder, thanks to all the publicity. Maybe this wasn't a conflict at all.

Optimism doesn't sit comfortably at my table. I'd only driven thirty-five miles, and I'd already come up with two reasons not to go on. It wasn't a new trait for me. When I was a little girl, I wrote fables that always ended sadly. "The Ladybug who Lost Her Way Home and Her House Burned Down," "The Wildflower Who Grew So Tall and Proud That She Was Pulled Out by the Roots." I called it *The True Book of Fairy Tales*. I was a budding fatalist.

Now, more than ever, I was sure that those tales reflected real life. If I unfurled and stood tall like the calla lily I was named after, then I too could be cut down, ripped from my anchorage and discarded, like Amy had been. My own personal San Xavier del Bac–style Armageddon.

What could I do that might give me a chance to send the ladybug home in time, a chance to watch a flower blossom and unfurl? Maybe even a chance to wake a sleeping princess.

. . .

I reached Nogales thirty minutes later. It was a town holding its Mexican neighbors at bay with tall walls, barbed-wire fences, and green-striped Border Patrol trucks every few hundred yards. I circled three times past the offices selling Mexican car insurance to tourists just before they crossed the border but I still couldn't find the street I was looking for. I stopped a young border patrolman and asked directions. Alternating between Spanish and English, he pointed me north again, toward a newer, sand-colored building sprawled across the hilltop like a fat cat in the sun.

It was one story tall, with a peaked central roof and two long wings to anchor it to the hillside. I battled a hot, dry headwind across the parking lot, eased open the main doors, and crossed the herringbone-brick lobby. When I rang the buzzer for attention, a young Mexican woman shuffled from a hidden alcove and directed me through a glass security door and down the hall to the office of Margaret Lance, county attorney for Santa Cruz County, Arizona.

Room 300 was labeled with a black decal on frosted glass. I knocked and entered a small anteroom that held a secretary's desk and two chairs for visitors.

"May I help you?" said a young woman coming in from an interior office. She wore a polyester suit that must have been like the seventh circle of hell in this heat, and she had short, plain fingernails with no polish. Her arms were full of files, and she tripped as she rounded the desk, spilling the pages like pickup-sticks across the surface. I helped her pat the files back into a stack and asked to see Ms. Lance.

"I'm Margaret Lance." She smiled at my surprise and reordered the files. "My secretary is off on her lunch break. I'm just cleaning out old files for her."

I wished the shock hadn't shown on my face. Her eyes may have said Harvard, but the clothes said Kmart. I liked her at once.

She looked a little younger than me—maybe thirty— with soft, wavy brown hair worn down past her shoulders. When she escorted me into her office, a glance at the photos and degrees on the wall told me I was right about Harvard.

I sat across from her desk and put my purse and brief-case on the floor. "I'm here on behalf of a friend. She was assaulted here in Nogales seven years ago and wants to know if it's too late to press charges."

She waited, wondering perhaps if this was the same kind of "friend" who needs advice from doctors at cocktail parties.

"Assaulted as in raped?"

"Yes, but he also used a knife on her. She almost died."

"It may not be too late," she said. "It used to be that the State had to file charges within seven years of the offense. Sometimes that meant that we had to create a John Doe warrant—you know, no name on it, but using the DNA profile of the attacker that we'd recovered from the victim as the ID—just to get in under that seven-year time frame. But Governor Hull signed a bill just last year that eliminated the statute of limitations on sexual assaults. There could be cases from several years ago that we can solve now with new DNA techniques. Did your friend file a police report at the time?"

"No. She went to the hospital and then went home. You see, she was attacked in a parking lot on her way home, but she thinks she may know now who the man was." I picked up my purse and wound the strap around and between my fingers like a rosary.

"She's only just now recognized the man? How did that happen? It's been seven years."

"She saw him again and a . . . a . . . physical trait of his jogged her memory." I didn't want to give her any more specific information in case it could be tracked back to Amy or to Cates. Or to my Letter of Confidentiality. "Do you think there's any chance of filing charges now, rape or attempted murder, after such a long time?"

"Well, it's not easy. It's hard to find witnesses and corroborative evidence after such a long delay. Is there any physical evidence? The clothes she was wearing that night? Did the hospital collect evidence or do a rape kit?"

"I don't know." If the hospital had done a rape kit they hadn't told me about it, and they hadn't charged me for it on the bill. I still had the clothes Amy wore to the rodeo, but I didn't know if there would be any kind of evidence there, except for the shreds of tattered denim that remained from her skirt.

"Please have your friend come talk to me," she said, handing me a business card. "I don't know if we can help her with these charges, but we have a good victim assistance program if she wants to talk to someone."

I fought back an unexpected surge of tears. Oh, if only Amy could talk to someone. Or talk at all.

I had a prepaid cell phone with a minimum number of minutes on it, to use in case of a road emergency. This qualified as one. It was almost two o'clock, and the lunch rush would have ended by now. When I got back to the Jeep, I rolled down the windows and called Alphabet City in Tucson while I waited for the interior to cool off enough to sit down.

The restaurant would never be famous, but only a year after opening it was already infamous for its eclectic menu. Run by Selena Garza, my best friend from high school, Alphabet City was a tucked-away, ten-table, hole-in-the-wall on Fourth Avenue, with a menu that changed daily based on a letter of the alphabet. One day might be *C*, when they offered crab, corned beef, cabbage, and custard. Another day might be *M* with macaroni, mustard greens and mousse. *Ch* got its own day, because of all options it presented; *E* days were to be avoided.

"It's Calla. What day is it?"

"H."

"I'll be right there." I hoped the *H* did not include headcheese or herring. In truth, I would have gone to Alphabet City even if it had been an endive and eggplant day; I needed to see Selena's brother more than I needed the food. Enrique helped out in the restaurant when he wasn't assigned to Pima County sheriff's department duties. And since Selena's divorce in December, Enrique was spending even more time with his sister and her two boys.

When I arrived at Alphabet City an hour later, the departing lunch crowd had freed up three parking places in front of the restaurant.

"Hola, chica," I said, spotting Selena at the hostess desk. "I'm sorry I haven't been in for so long."

From across the room Selena was as shockingly beautiful as she had been in high school. Coal black hair, a trim waist, and bright white Chiclet teeth. But when she turned the right side of her face toward me, I could see the damage her ex-husband had done. The glass of her right eye stared straight ahead, a lodestar in the night sky of her face. She grinned, seeing me.

"It's been too long. How's Amy? And how's Aunt Giulia?" Selena wiped her hands on a damp towel.

"There's no change with Amy. Giulia and I are fine." I sank into a seat at the front table. "Any chance your brother is around? I need help on something."

"Sure, he's trying to fix the garbage disposal. I'll get him."

I glanced at the menu while Selena disappeared to the back of the restaurant. Thank God, they included both halibut and hamburger under the offerings for *H*.

When I looked up, Enrique was standing across the table from me. The laugh lines around his eyes deepened with his smile.

"You've always been able to sneak up on me." I got up to hug him.

He was a man of uncommon grace, even at two hundred and thirty pounds, and I'd had a crush on him in our high school days. That teenage yearning had translated over the years to a feeling of comfort and security; Enrique was the only man I would have trusted with my life—and my sister's.

He wore his black hair straight back from his forehead, like a resurrected Cesar Romero, and it gleamed in the overhead lights. At thirty-six Enrique carried a maturity and calmness that he hadn't possessed in his wild teen years. Maybe it was the dozen years of drunks, car crashes, and illegal immigrants he had seen while on patrol with the sheriff's department that had done it; maybe he had seen too much. He said that he could recite the exits off I-10 between Tucson and Phoenix as easily as he could the Lord's Prayer. And sometimes they sounded the same.

Enrique still had the heart of a big brother, railing against any injustice done to his family. I didn't have any proof about what had happened to Selena's ex-husband, but shortly after Selena lost her eye, the ex wound up in the hospital with both legs and both arms broken. He left town as soon as his injuries healed. Enrique never mentioned his name again.

Selena came back to the table with three tall glasses of sweet, creamy *horchata* and sat down. "Tell us what's on your mind. What can we help with?"

Swearing them to secrecy, I told them about meeting Raymond Cates and realizing that he could be Amy's rapist.

"He lived near Nogales seven years ago. He has a damaged finger, and now he's accused of a rape and murder that are similar to Amy's attack. It's not a lot, but he could be the one. And I can't go to the authorities because of this Letter of Confidentiality I signed, but I also can't sit back and do nothing."

"What did Amy say about his fingers that makes you think this is the guy?" Selena asked.

"Oh, hell, it wasn't anything specific. Those first few nights she had terrible nightmares and would wake up screaming. It sounded like '*dedo*,' and her hand would be arched into a claw shape. I'm guessing she remembered something about his hands or his fingers."

"Maybe she just remembered his hands coming at her," Selena suggested. "Or maybe your bilingual guess is wrong." Her glance at Enrique told me she thought I was nuts.

"Maybe. I've probably blown this all out of proportion, but I've got to know if he could be the one." I shredded the paper napkin that was already sodden from the cold glass of *horchata*.

Enrique spread hummus on a piece of bread. "You don't have to put your job in jeopardy," he said in the same tone of voice I bet therapists use with delusional patients. "Let's find out as much as we can about Mr. Cates and whether he could really be Amy's attacker. If he is, we'll find a way to take it to the authorities."

I breathed a sigh of relief.

"I have a friend who's a private investigator," he continued. "If he's free, I'll bring him over to your house this weekend. You explain the situation to him, and we'll see if he can come up with more evidence one way or another."

I stayed for a hamburger with Havarti cheese, and we talked about families and days gone by. I didn't realize then that Enrique's help was going to make matters even more complicated.

6

By Wednesday I couldn't postpone a response to Kevin McCullough any longer, and we arranged to meet at his office at eleven o'clock. When I arrived at Whitcomb, Merchant & Dryer, the air conditioner panted with exertion but the lobby was still so warm you could almost smell the horses in the paintings.

I enjoyed a restful twenty minutes on the deep couch until the receptionist showed me into his office.

"—and I'll confirm that with Calla, now that she's here," McCullough said into the phone, and hung up.

"Confirm what?"

"A question about pretrial publicity that I was discussing with Mr. Merchant. We may want to make use of the media, see if we can use it to get our side of the story out."

I didn't let the distaste I felt show on my face. I knew that lawyers and trial consultants often used the media to influence potential jurors. They called it "presenting a balanced picture of the defendant" or "educating the community," but it all boiled down to trying your case in the streets and not in a courtroom. Not my way of doing business.

"I'd be happy to discuss the pros and cons with you." The words were more enthusiastic than my tone of voice.

Clients usually get their own way, but I could at least lay out the options for him before he threw himself headlong into this publicity effort. We talked for a half hour, but I'm not sure McCullough heard any voice but his own.

At the end of the discussion he asked me to deliver some papers to Cates at the jail during lunchtime. "Your rates are cheaper than a delivery service." So much for being perceived as an integral part of the legal system. I stuffed my ego back down under my wallet and agreed to the errand.

Wednesday didn't seem to be a big visiting day at the Pima County Jail, so I found a parking place in the front row. The same sheriff's deputy from my first visit was also on duty today and nodded to me with familiarity. This wasn't a first-name relationship I really wanted to encourage. Prison guards are not high on my list of potential boyfriends, although they'd probably have a healthy respect for law and order.

Who was I kidding? There was no list of potential boyfriends. In seven years I hadn't been able to shake the specter of Amy's attacker. Any man could be a monster.

Except for Enrique, that is, and he had taken on the contours of a guardian angel. I spent my nights alone.

It took ten minutes for them to bring Cates to the small attorney-client interview room. I sat across from him and slid McCullough's file across the table. It wasn't sealed; the jailer had exchanged its original manila envelope for a lighter-weight envelope without a metal hasp closure.

"It's hotter than hell in here," Cates said. "If it's this bad in June, imagine what August will feel like this year."

If he was guilty of killing Lydia Chavez, then I hoped that by August he'd be facing life in prison or the death penalty, and I wouldn't care how hot it was while he waited. I tried to regain my objectivity, but I couldn't take my eyes off his right hand; it was as mesmerizing as a rattlesnake.

As if in response to his comment, I said, "When did you hurt your hand?" If it had happened since Amy's attack, then he couldn't be the Animal.

"Oh, this?" He waggled his finger toward my face like a tongue. "Long time ago. I was just a kid." He still looked fairly boyish. No gray in his hair and a smirky kind of grin that I bet some women found attractive.

I stared into his eyes to see if the vagueness of his reply was done on purpose, but there was no telltale flicker of deception. He hadn't said exactly when it happened or how it happened. Could I have taken the silly coincidence of a damaged hand and a murder charge and built a whole

city of lies around them? I nodded at his response and left
the county jail without the answer I really wanted.

M cCullough had left me a phone message to say that he
was set on doing the early research we'd discussed.
"Let's get our side of the story out there," he said when I
called him back. You mean, let's contaminate the jury pool,
I thought.

In the end, I agreed to recruit potential Tucson jurors
for a focus group session to find out their attitudes about
the case. Then McCullough could decide where to concentrate his efforts for Cates's publicity campaign.

I didn't like this part of the business. Trial consultants
have a bad enough reputation as it is, and I didn't want to
add to it. I'd heard all the comments about the industry
offering "the best verdict money can buy," and sometimes
that was true. A trial consultant's recommendation on strategy, presentation style, or juror selection could often make
the difference in the final outcome of a trial.

I preferred to concentrate on the parts of my job that
leveled the playing field between the parties—the parts
that clarified the evidence, not those parts that clouded the
truth.

But it didn't look like I was going to get out of this
image-building research until Jessica was free, so McCullough and I worked out the final details on the timing and

demographic makeup of the focus groups, and I contacted a local research facility to begin the recruiting.

Cates, the county jail, and the summer heat had wrung me out like a sweat-soaked handkerchief. At home that evening I took a glass of iced tea and an old puzzle of Giulia's out to the patio and turned on the misters to cool the air on the open porch. Rainbows caught between the droplets of water and the setting sun, creating a jewel box of colors around me. Easing back in the canvas chair, my mind drifted away from the Civil War theme of the crossword puzzle.

If I was going to get any answers about Amy's rape, then I had to start taking action. I picked up the cordless phone and called Enrique.

"I saw Cates again today, and he didn't tell me exactly when he damaged his finger." I explained about his vagueness. "God, I don't even know if I ought to be looking for something wrong with a finger at all."

"We can find out about the date. Check with his family. Friends. People who knew him growing up. We'll find out when it happened." Enrique paused. "But I don't want you to pin your hopes on this."

A baseball game growled in the background. It sounded like the D-Backs were losing.

"Here's something else to think about," Enrique continued. "It's one thing to dig into Cates's background. But maybe we can do more than that. Amy's rape was never investigated. We never looked for other similar attacks.

But I'll bet that whoever attacked her has also gone after other women."

"You're right," I said. "If we can find another woman who remembers what Amy said—the black truck or the cowboy hat or the knife or the belt buckle—" I spoke faster with each item.

"Don't get carried away, Calla. If there was something obvious that tied several attacks together, the police or sheriff's department would have spotted it. But it can't hurt to double-check. I'll do some investigation here and see if anything comes up."

I thanked him and started to hang up, when I remembered the real reason for my call. I told Enrique about the Santa Cruz County attorney's suggestion that we look for DNA evidence on Amy's clothes.

"I've had those clothes in a paper bag for seven years now. I couldn't bear to touch them—not even to throw them away—after the hospital gave them back to me."

I thought about the ruffled white blouse that could be pulled down over her shoulders on hot days, about the short denim skirt that showed off Amy's smooth legs. Although they represented a vile, despicable moment in Amy's life, I couldn't bear to lose them. I needed to hold on to any part of my sister I could.

"We use the Department of Public Safety's crime lab here in Tucson, but there are a couple of good private DNA labs that I can recommend. I'll get the names for you," Enrique said. "Oh, I reached my investigator friend, and he's free Saturday morning. How about ten o'clock?"

I agreed to the time and crossed mental fingers that my new credit card could bear up under the expense of the DNA testing. Maybe I'd get the testing results back before they found out I couldn't pay for them.

The lab work probably wouldn't show anything, but I felt good about having taken at least a small step. And when I filled in the crossword answer for "farthest west site of a Civil War battle" with Arizona's Picacho Peak, I felt a real sense of accomplishment.

7

On Saturday I woke early and took a walk around the neighborhood to enjoy the double-digit temperatures before they soared again. The university area was always more active, so I headed that way. I passed the handmade-sandal shop with the smell of rawhide and leather leaking out into the street, an oddly quiet fraternity house, and a Starbucks. I stopped to get a cup of coffee and perused the obituary section of the newspaper to see what Aunt Giulia had been up to.

Except for that leave of absence when my parents died, she'd been with the *Arizona Daily Star* for almost forty years, all of which time she'd spent in "the Morgue," as they called the library. One of her jobs was to keep updated obituaries on the famous and near famous, in case they died unexpectedly. She said once that she'd written Richard Nixon's obituary twenty-nine times, "always hoping this one would take." Nobody famous had died today.

When I got back to the house, there was a strange dark car in the driveway. I hesitated at the sidewalk, thinking about turning back to a more populated street, when Enrique opened the driver's door and got out.

"Nice wheels," I said, saluting him with my cardboard cup. The shiny new sedan was a big improvement over the ten-year-old white van he usually drove. I gave him a quick hug and turned to unlock the front door when I was stopped by his voice.

"This is the investigator I told you about. My friend, Anthony Strike. He's about the best in the business, and we've known each other for years."

I spiraled around, spilling coffee all over myself and the front stoop. Oh no. Standing in my driveway was the mustachioed, lazy-smiling investigator from Whitcomb, Merchant & Dryer.

"Howdy," he said, tipping an imaginary hat in my direction. His eyes lit with complicity, as if he knew there was a game going on, and he liked it.

I pushed my glasses farther up the bridge of my nose and turned back to Enrique.

"I know you're trying to help, but this isn't going to work. Mr. Strike is employed by the same law firm that hired me."

Enrique looked back and forth between us, clearly confused by this development. Strike seemed to enjoy our discomfort.

"I didn't tell him anything about the case, Calla. I just said I had a friend who might need his investigative skills."

Enrique shuffled his toe in the dirt like a young man too shy to ask for a date.

"So far that's still all I know," Strike said. "Here's a lady who may need my help."

I sighed. "Let's go inside."

Over coffee and day-old, sugary churros from the bakery down the street, I showed Strike Amy's picture and told him about her rape and current condition. I also told him why I thought Raymond Cates might be her attacker.

"You knew the minute you saw me that this would be a conflict, Mr. Strike. I'm sorry to have wasted your Saturday."

"Wait just a minute," he said, setting down his coffee mug. "I'm not sure that I've decided it is a conflict. From what I've heard so far, you're a lady who's interested in getting as much information about her sister's attack as possible. I don't see a conflict there with any other case I'm working on."

"But you know that I think Raymond Cates could be her attacker. And we're sworn to confidentiality regarding his case." Why couldn't he see what was so patently clear to me?

"I never go into a case with any assumptions," he said, wiping sugar off his fingers, then taking a sip of coffee. "Even if you told me you knew for sure that Cates was your sister's attacker, I'd still start the investigation with a clean slate and see if the evidence proved it. They're separate cases in my mind."

I rolled my eyes at his circuitous logic.

"Look," he said, "I'd like to help you find your sister's attacker. Right now I'd say it's probably not Raymond Cates. It's just a coincidence that you met somebody charged with a similar crime who has something wrong with his hands, and that might not be what Amy even meant about her attacker. So whether I'm doing it to clear Cates's name or to help you find out the truth doesn't matter. Let me dig around a little bit, and we'll see where it goes." He rolled up the cuffs on his long-sleeved shirt as if he was ready to start that digging right now.

I nodded. "I don't know how I'm going to pay for this, but go ahead and give it a couple of days." I watched him take a sip of the cooling coffee. "But I want to go with you."

He almost spit. "That's not the way it works, lady. I work better by myself. Just let me do my job."

I held my ground. "If you want to help me, this is how you can do it. I can't find these things out on my own, but I've got to be there, see it with my own eyes." He didn't look convinced. "It would mean a lot to me. And maybe I can help with something." I knew I was pleading, but I couldn't stop myself.

He shook his head. "You remind me of that story about the man who goes out and buys a dog and then does all the barking himself."

"Woof."

Strike smiled. "You remember the legend of the Arizona Robin Hood?" Enrique and I shook our heads.

"He put the shoes on his horse backwards so the posse couldn't tell which direction he was going."

"And . . . ?" I waited for the punch line.

"That's the same way I do my job. It's going to look like I'm going backwards for a while before I find anything new. You can come with me, but you can't tell me how to do this job. No assumptions, right?"

I nodded.

As I walked them back to the car, Enrique passed me a note with the name of a DNA testing lab in Phoenix.

"What ever happened to that desert Robin Hood?" I asked as Strike folded himself into the passenger seat.

"Oh, he got killed. The guy who put the horseshoes on for him turned him in." He grinned and tipped his invisible Stetson again in farewell.

I didn't understand why Strike was willing to help me. There wouldn't be a lot of money in it for him, and it could jeopardize his job with Whitcomb, Merchant & Dryer if someone found out. Maybe it was better not to look a gift horse, in this case a pay-by-the-hour horse, in the mouth.

And there was something about that droopy mustache — something that made me comfortable and warm. It had been a long time since anyone but Enrique made me feel that way. First Amy, then Selena's fate at the hands of her brutal husband. The damage to both of them had built a wall of fear around me. Could this man or that man be a batterer, a killer, a rapist? How would I know?

When Enrique and Strike had gone, I went out to the storage room off the open carport and pulled out the three cardboard boxes labeled "Amaryllis." I had gathered all her belongings from the university dorm room, but I'd never had the heart to go through them before. I pictured the dorm room exactly as she had left it to go to the rodeo that Halloween afternoon—clothes strewn over chairs, nursing textbooks splayed like dropped handkerchiefs on the bed. It was a room held in mid-sentence, waiting for someone who would never return.

The first box held clothes, mostly lightweight cottons and T-shirts, the kind of thing a student could get by with for most of the year in an Arizona climate that rarely reached freezing. I refolded two sweaters and Amy's jean jacket and put them to the side. The second box had toiletries—desiccated now into lumpy, fragrant blobs—and a small black velour bag with a drawstring. In it I found a hammered silver ring with a chunk of black-veined turquoise in the middle, carved into a flower. Franco Del Arte had made it as a gift for our mother when Amy was born: a gesture of welcome for his almost new wife and brand-new, flower-named daughter. To Amy it was a milky blue manifestation of our parents' love, and she had worn it with pride. I brought it to my lips for a quick kiss, then tucked it into my pocket.

The paper bag holding Amy's clothes from the night of

the rape was on the bottom of the box, still crumpled closed at the top the way the hospital had given it to me. I sat cross-legged on the floor with the bag in my lap and uncurled the brown paper. Nestled at the bottom were the strips of cloth he'd slashed to bind her, some of them speckled with rusty brown dots. If that was blood, then it was probably Amy's, and I didn't think that information would help us. Sighing, I rose to my feet and went to find a mailing box big enough to contain all the clothes for the DNA lab. There wasn't a box big enough to hold all my lost illusions.

8

Since I had to do focus groups Monday night for McCullough, I decided to take Monday morning off as partial comp time. After all, it was June 24, the Saint's Day celebration for San Juan Bautista. Thanks to the Indian influences on the town, there are two other—less Catholic—ways that Tucsonans mark the day: pray for rain and get a haircut.

When I was a child, my family honored this onset of the rainy season by gathering at the Santa Cruz River to wash our hands, sometimes carrying a bucket of water back to splash on the garden at the house. In the last few decades the water table had dropped precipitously with increased use, and now even digging deep in the dry dirt of the riverbed wouldn't get you any water. These days a shower, a bath, or a lawn sprinkler had to do the ceremonial work that the river had done long ago. I hung a branch of creosote in the shower and celebrated with both the water and the smell of a desert deluge.

The haircut part of the tradition made less sense to me. The locals said that if you cut your hair on San Juan Day, it would grow back lush and full and shiny. I wasn't willing to turn down any offer of help right now, so on my way to mail the package to the DNA lab I took a detour to the walk-in, unisex hair salon on Broadway for that six-dollar haircut I had put off. I'd wait to see what kind of magic San Juan could work, but if his power had dried up like the Santa Cruz River, I might have to come back to the salon for highlights.

Strike called at ten thirty.

"I've got some work to do on Cates's case today," he said, "but I thought I could also stop at the No-Tell Motel in Nogales, see what they remember. Do you trust me on my own, or do you still want to come along?"

I wasn't looking forward to seeing the No-Tell Motel again. "I'll be ready in twenty minutes."

If the trip to Nogales didn't take more than a couple of hours, I could still get to the office after lunch. If it took longer, I was going to have to come up with something creative as an excuse for Jessica.

When Strike pulled into the driveway, the roar of the engine set off my neighbor's car alarm.

"Wow, not just a muscle car—a muscle car on steroids," I said. Strike made sure the car was in neutral, then revved the engine, and I watched the tach climb to 6000 rpm. I felt the vibration in my spine. I stepped back to admire the car, as I knew he expected me to. Black with gold stripes and tiny black and yellow Hertz insignias on the wheels. He revved the engine again.

"It's a '66 Shelby Mustang, one of the original thousand or so that Ford sold to Hertz for use as rental cars. Most of 'em were automatics, but not this baby."

"Have you had it a long time?"

"Almost fifteen years. I don't drive it much. For some jobs, like when I have to follow someone or do a stakeout, it stands out too much. Then I borrow Enrique's van."

Traffic was light, and he pushed the speed up to eighty as we headed south on Highway 83 toward the border.

"What do you have to do for McCullough today?"

"Meet with Salsipuedes. I want to make sure we've got all the details for his testimony." He passed a slow-moving truck as if it were a turtle in the road, and I watched the dusty, olive green hills of San Rafael Valley's cattle country pass by in a blur.

"You seem to understand what this is like for me, Mr. Strike. Somehow I never expect men to understand. Do you have sisters?"

"No, but I have an ex-wife."

"Tell me about her."

At first I didn't think he was going to answer. "She looks a lot like that picture of Amy you showed me."

Now I understood why he was willing to help me. Amy's picture made it personal for him. Made it too easy to imagine the same thing happening to his wife.

"What's her name?"

"Maria. We've been separated about ten years now, but we're still friends." He huffed a short laugh. "The only

thing I didn't give her as part of the divorce was this car."
He tapped the steering wheel with affection.

We were quiet for the rest of the trip, but a couple of
times I caught him looking at me as if there was something
important he wanted to ask. For my part, I was hoping
this detour to the Cates ranch didn't take too long, and I
could still get back to work this afternoon.

We slowed and pulled up to the entrance of the Cates
ranch. Two vertical timbers as thick as telephone poles
supported an arch over the entrance. There, a wrought-
iron design two feet tall celebrated Cates's Sleepy C
brand: a recumbent letter C with small caret marks, like
distant mountain peaks, on either side.

The gate was closed but unlocked. I got out and swung
it open, and Strike drove over the cattle guard. I shut the
gate again behind him.

A half mile of dirt road stretched between the gate and
the main house. Strike was cursing under his breath at the
abuse the Shelby was taking. He probably should have
thought about these ranch roads before he pulled the car
out of the garage. He downshifted to first gear and gin-
gerly released the clutch.

The sprawling house on the hill was visible all the way
from the main road. It was two stories tall in the center
where the original part of the house stood, with newer
wings branching out on either side. One massive cottonwood shaded the front door and porch, and feathery-

leafed mesquite trees dotted the landscape like surviving chess pieces near the end of a match.

A barrel-chested, bandy-legged man appeared on the porch as we approached. He looked as though his voice would be a bellow.

"That's George Cates," Strike said. "Ray's father."

His jeans were cinched tight under a bulging stomach, as if his legs belonged to a smaller, less strident man. He strutted to the porch railing, his angled, cowboy-boot heels punishing the wooden slats at every step. He took a short hit off an unfiltered cigarette and ground the butt out under his heel.

"Good morning, sir," Strike said. "I'm working with your son's lawyers, and I've come to see Hector Salsipuedes." I nodded at Cates as if I was part of that introduction.

"Good man, Hector. Lost his father when he was fifteen. Been like a son to me since then." Cates senior spat to the side. "What do you want with him?"

"I need to go over his testimony about the night he and Ray were drinking together."

"He already talked to the lawyers about that night. Leave him alone." He turned to go back into the house.

Strike narrowed his eyes and brushed the sides of his mustache with his thumb.

"You'd probably rather have him talk to me than the police, Mr. Cates. He's important to your son's case, and we've got to make sure that he can answer any question the prosecutor puts to him at the trial."

Cates senior stopped short of the front door and pulled another cigarette from the stubby pack in his shirt pocket. "He's down at the barn. Keep driving around this side of the house." He motioned with his free hand.

Strike nodded his thanks and nursed the car around to the left, careful to raise as little dust as possible and to avoid stones that could chip his pristine black paint job.

"I don't get it," he said as we rounded the side of the house. "Salsipuedes is his son's ticket out of this murder charge. George Cates should be parading him around like a Heisman Trophy."

"Maybe he's not such a prize after all."

A new, bright red Ford F-350 pickup was snugged up next to the open barn door, and a rhythmic hammering came from inside the dark building. A round-faced Mexican in his late thirties came out, wiping his hands on an oil-crusted rag. He had a light, arc-shaped scar on his cheek. Like Cates senior, he wore his jeans tight under a rounded belly. The back hem of his pants dragged in the dirt.

"Are you Salsipuedes?"

"That's me."

Strike turned to me. "Wait here. This won't take long." He opened the car door and approached Salsipuedes. I got out to stretch my legs but didn't stray far, aware that my low shoes offered no protection from the all-too-present snakes in the area. The men's voices carried to me clearly.

"My name is Strike. I work for Raymond Cates's lawyers, and I wanted to talk to you about that night you and Ray were drinking beer out here at the ranch."

Salsipuedes looked from side to side as if checking for avenues of escape, then gave a sigh of resignation.

"Come on, then. I've got work to do on this truck." He retreated to the building and knelt next to a round-fendered, rusty blue pickup truck that was sticking halfway out the barn door.

McCullough had said that Salsipuedes had been with the Cates family for almost twenty years. His mother and siblings were still in Oaxaca, and Hector sent money down regularly, but he'd decided to settle into the life of a cowboy and ranch hand in Arizona.

"About that night with Raymond. What do you remember?" Strike asked.

Salsipuedes dug his fingers into a tin of dark grease and continued to pack the wheel bearings. "It was a Monday, I think. I spent the day moving the cattle to the south pasture. I hadn't seen Ray all day. I was finishing my chores about nine thirty at night when he pulled in. We grabbed a couple of beers and drove over to where the herd was."

"How do you know it was nine thirty?"

"I don't know for sure; I don't wear a watch. Anyway, we just sat on the hood of the truck, had a couple of beers, and watched the moon. It couldn't have been much later than nine thirty because it was only midnight when I got back to the bunkhouse." That tracked with what he'd told McCullough and Merchant. Salsipuedes kept working, his eyes on the rusty parts in front of him.

"How come you're trying to fix up this old worn-out truck when you've got a brand new one out there?"

Salsipuedes jerked his head up and looked at Strike before glancing at the F-350 and then back to the mechanical task at hand. "Ranch gotta have more than one truck to get the job done," he mumbled.

"That one's kinda fancy for ranch work, isn't it?" Strike asked. "Leather seats and all?"

"That's none of your business." Salsipuedes swatted his thigh with his hat as if ridding himself of a pesky gnat.

Strike said he had a few more questions, and I walked back around the new Ford, keeping an ear cocked for the leathery passage of a snake. When the ranch hand turned his back to me, I jotted down the license numbers of both trucks, and the long vehicle identification number from the metal tag on the dashboard of the new truck.

After a few minutes Strike thanked him and returned to the car. He pulled out his notebook, looked back toward the barn where Salsipuedes sat hunched over the disassembled car parts, and started to write down the plate numbers.

"I already got 'em." I waggled the paper with the numbers under his nose.

His mustache curled up with his smile. "That's my girl. How'd you know to do that?"

I waited until we drove over the cattle guard. "Did you see the Sacred Heart scapular and the fuzzy dice hanging on the mirror of that new truck? That's no ranch vehicle."

Strike smiled. "And if it belongs to Salsipuedes, I wonder how a hired hand can afford the payments. That truck would have run close to fifty thousand the way it's tricked out."

When we reached the main road, I closed the gate behind us again and got back in the car. "I know how we can get some more information about who owns that truck." I fanned myself with the notepaper.

"I've got a few ideas, too. How about some air-conditioning and a burger to get us started?"

It took twenty minutes to get from the ranch to the tiny town of Patagonia and the air-conditioned Old Gringo Bar.

P atagonia has always been cattle country, but up until World War II it had also been a town full of hard-digging and hard-drinking miners from the surrounding hills. The Old Gringo Bar looked as if it might still carry the echo of their drunken shouts.

It was a small building with tiny, barred windows, a red brick base, and wooden slats from knee level up. I followed Strike inside, letting my eyes adjust to the darkness as the door shut behind me.

Six round tables with mismatched chairs squatted to my left, and there was a long wooden bar on my right. The men at three of the tables looked up as we entered; then, not seeing anything to amuse or intrigue them, returned to their food. Not another woman in sight except an elderly waitress in a short, hot pink skirt.

We each ordered a draft beer and a cheeseburger, then Strike asked for the pay phone. Luckily, it was at the far end of the room from the diners and tucked into an alcove with a three-legged stool.

I excused myself to go to the restroom. After I washed my hands and grimaced at the too-sallow face in the mirror, I heard Strike's voice just outside the door. I waited there, with my hand on the knob, to eavesdrop.

"Wells Fargo?" he said. "Molly Trenchant, please."

Then a moment later, "Molly? It's Tony Strike. . . . I know. I've been busy. But I'll make it up to you."

He paused to concoct his lie.

"There's a guy who owes me money, but he says he's broke and can't pay me back. I need to find out if that's the truth or if he's been spending the money on something else. He lives in Patagonia, and you're the biggest bank in town, so he's probably got an account with you. Can you help me?" A heartbeat later, he added, "Please, honey."

Strike gave her Salsipuedes's details, then I heard the scratchy-pencil sound of his note-taking.

"Uh-huh. That's not much in savings. Uh-huh. And that's how often? Every two weeks. Got it." There was a moment's silence. "No big deposit or withdrawal recently? . . . Uh, no, I gave him money months ago."

I left the restroom and brushed past Strike on my way back to the bar. When he finished his call and joined me, he ignored the cheeseburger and gulped down half of his beer.

He told me about the call to Wells Fargo, and I pretended I didn't already know.

"Was that the part you couldn't hear over the toilet flushing?" Strike asked with a straight face.

The color rose on my cheeks.

"I guess you really don't trust me to do my job alone." He nudged me with a denim-clad elbow, then continued with his report.

"Salsipuedes deposits two fifty every two weeks," he said. "That's probably his paycheck from Cates. His room and board is already paid for at the ranch, but that still only gives him about sixty-five hundred of income annually. Not nearly enough to afford a down payment on that truck with all the extras it's got and still send money back to Oaxaca. Maybe the truck's not his."

"That's one thing we can check right now," I said. "Let's see if there's Internet access at the library." We finished the onion-laden burgers and walked three blocks to the city library on Duquesne.

The young woman behind the desk wore a nametag that

said "Nicole. Library Volunteer." She looked as if she might still be in high school herself. She collected a credit card from Strike and showed us to an available computer.

I logged on to the VIN search site I had seen my insurance company use when we had to track down the car that had dented my Jeep in a parking lot. It would only take a second before the information I entered was matched to the current owner.

I tried the license number for the old blue truck first. The listed owner was George Cates. Then I typed in the long string of vehicle identification numbers for the new F-350.

"Marta Veracruz? Who's that?" It showed her address as a PO box in Patagonia.

I logged off and went in search of a local phone book. There were lots of Veracruzes listed, but no Martas.

Strike took my notes up to the desk. "Nicole? Where would I find this post office box?"

"There are a couple of mailing places in town, but I guess I'd start with the post office on Taylor." She gave him directions through a wad of spearmint-scented gum. We paid for the small amount of computer time we'd used and headed back outside.

At the post office, I pretended to fill out international mailing forms while Strike approached the clerk, a middle-aged man with thick glasses and comb-over hair.

"Hi there. I need to pick up my mail, but I forgot my

key. Can you check box 1825 for me, please? The name's Veracruz."

The clerk squinted and pushed his glasses back up with the middle finger of his right hand. "Veracruz? Are you sure? Mr. Salsipuedes already picked up his mother's mail today."

Strike thanked him and hustled me out of the building before I could squeak in surprise. When we reached the car, I opened the door and leaned across the roof, waiting for the interior to cool.

"Marta Veracruz is Salsipuedes's mother? So if this sweet old woman in Oaxaca needs money from her son in Arizona, how do you suppose she can afford a new truck like that?"

"I think I know how to find out," Strike said. "Did you see the license-plate holder on that truck? Jim Click Ford in Green Valley. We'll ask the guys who sold it to her. Let's head to Nogales first, then on the way home, stop in Green Valley and pay a visit to the Ford dealership. And for that one you get to play my wife."

9

I squinted against the blowing dust and debris. Arizona summers were not flattering to Nogales. It was mid-afternoon, and the temperature had soared to a hundred and nine. Buildings shimmered in the heat waves rising from the asphalt. I'll bet Strike was mentally kicking himself for driving the Shelby today. I would have preferred any car with air-conditioning. My shirt made a wet, sucking sound when I leaned forward in the seat.

Three of the bigger structures downtown had new white paint jobs that contrasted with the neglected, ill-used buildings around them like dentures in an old man's face. We looped through downtown and headed east.

The No-Tell Motel was on the outskirts of town near the rodeo grounds. It didn't look like it had changed much in the seven years since I'd last been there. Two stories of concrete and rebar with vaguely Mayan designs on the burnt orange walls. The sign out front still said they had "rooms to let by the half hour" for those who didn't think much of their staying power.

Weeds sprouted through the cracked concrete in

front of the office, and a dust devil swirled through the parking lot. I watched Strike push the heavy glass entry door and heard a small bell ping to alert the desk clerk that he had a customer.

The man who came out of the back room looked like a desert tortoise, his long neck and leathery skin shown off by a sleeveless white undershirt. Wife-beater underwear, Jessica called that style. His hairline had retreated to a U-shape at the top of his head, and tufts of gray hair waved in the breeze from the window air conditioner. I was willing to bet this was the only working air conditioner in the motel.

The conversation between the desk clerk and Strike was a pantomime to me. Strike seemed to be asking questions and not getting many replies. He opened his wallet and pushed a bill across the desk. That's when the conversation got serious.

The heat was becoming oppressive. After twenty minutes I gave up and went to join Strike in the air-conditioned lobby. He saw my approach, came out, and turned me back toward the car.

"What is it? What did he say?"

"Let's stop over there and cool off for a minute," he said, motioning to the Palomino Bar across the street. "I'll tell you everything on the way back."

The Palomino Bar was a squat, dark wood building, deeper than it was wide, with no windows on the front.

We left the Shelby where it was, dodged the one car coming from the right, and trotted across the street.

The heavy door opened with a squeak. It was dim and cool inside, and a plaintive country-and-western song on the jukebox asked Ruby not to take her love to town.

I dawdled as the door squeaked closed behind me and scanned the long wooden bar. Three drinkers, one a female, leaned on the bar for support. One short Indian-looking man had spurs on his boots. At least this town had the horses and cattle to go with the spurs. When you saw spurs in Tucson, it just meant it was a tourist staying at a dude ranch.

We took stools at the near end of the bar, away from the other drinkers. A jar of pickled eggs and a rack of packaged potato chips hugged the corner. The smell of bacon and decades-old frying grease permeated the air.

The bartender, a well-worn gray-haired woman in her sixties, stubbed out her cigarette and approached with a bar rag in her hand.

"What'll it be?"

"Tequila. No ice," Strike said.

"Just water for me." I looked around at the beer mirrors, the posted business cards, and the dusty array of bottles behind her.

When she returned with the drinks, Strike said, "Nice place. Have you been here long?"

"Donkey's years. My husband bought this place back

in the seventies." She polished a circle on the bar in front of him.

"Is your husband still around?"

"Now why would you want to know that?" She reached for something under the bar. The timbre of her voice had attracted the attention of the drinkers at the other end of the bar. I put one foot on the floor in case we needed to make a quick getaway.

"No need for that baseball bat," Strike said as if calming a growling dog. "I'm just looking for someone who might have been working here seven years ago."

"Well, you'd probably have been looking for me instead of that lazy-ass son of a bitch anyway," she said, relaxing. "He was around, but he didn't do much work."

Strike moved his shot glass in front of me and unfolded pictures of Cates and Amy on the bar. "Do you recognize either of these folks?"

"This one I know," she said, tapping the picture of Cates with a long forefinger. "That's Ray Cates. I don't recognize the woman."

"You know Cates well?"

"Not really. His family has a ranch outside of Patagonia, maybe thirty, thirty-five miles from here. He and his crew used to come in on weekends."

I watched her eyes, but they gave no hint of any affection or distrust of Cates.

"When was the last time he was in?"

"Oh, Lord, it's been years, now that I think about it.

They used to come in a lot, but I haven't seen him since my husband passed on, and that was more than six years ago."

"And you're sure you've never seen the woman?"

"Nothing's sure in this life, mister. But she's not a regular, I can tell you that."

Amy was only nineteen when she was attacked—too young for legal drinking in Arizona—so I had never thought of her as a "regular" at any bar, but the woman's words brought tears to my eyes anyway. I imagined a life for Amy that included meeting friends after a long shift at the hospital, the pulsing of a two-step country-and-western song on the jukebox, a sip of beer on a summer night. It was a dream that could never come true.

Strike left a five-dollar tip, and we returned to the car. The side trip to the Palomino had proved nothing. No one could place Cates and Amy in the bar together seven years ago. But it was interesting that Cates seemed to have changed his favorite drinking spot soon after Amy's attack. Or maybe that was when he moved away from his father's ranch and took up residence in Tucson.

We stayed quiet until we reached enough speed on the highway for the rushing air to have partially cooled the car's interior. Strike stared straight ahead as he spoke. "You know, I told you Saturday that I start every investigation from the beginning, without any assumptions." I nodded. "That's what we're doing here, too, going back to the motel to see if there's any record or any memory of

Amy being at the motel on Halloween or early on November first, seven years ago.

"You wouldn't expect that kind of place to have much paperwork, and they don't. But the motel manager has been there for fifteen years, and he said he would have been the one on duty. He remembers because his third child was born that year on November first, and he was worried that he'd have to find a replacement to take over the desk in case he needed to take his wife to the hospital on Halloween night." He paused, as if trying to find the right words. I watched the road. I couldn't look at him either.

"He said no one of Amy's description came in that night. He would have remembered a young girl, all beat up like that, who came to the desk for help or who checked in by herself.

"I asked him if he remembered a room back then that was pretty messed up with blood. He said that happened all the time. Cowboys, bar fights. He doesn't keep track of it."

I swallowed my first reaction: you must be wrong. Then I paid more attention to his news. Why hadn't I ever checked with the motel, even to see if they had seen someone fitting the Animal's description someplace in the neighborhood? When I found Amy, I rushed her out of that room and straight to the hospital. I hadn't given it a moment's thought, except to be happy that she'd found someplace safe to hole up until I could get to her. I never even approached the front desk when I went back two days later to get her car.

In retrospect my assumptions seemed as flimsy as a three-year-old's lie. Why would Amy, bloody and broken and still bound by strips of denim, have gone to the front desk of a motel and offered cash or her credit card for a room, when all she needed was a phone to reach me or the police? Wouldn't she just have asked for help? Especially if she didn't have a purse or any money with her. And if she was that confused or hysterical, then it was even more likely that the manager would have remembered her.

"Does he have any information on the people who did check in that night?"

"No. Almost all their business is done in cash. And he doesn't get many single women except a couple of neighborhood hookers that he knows by name." Strike sounded as disappointed as I was.

I wasn't sure what it meant, but I knew now that there was a big, black, eight-legged lie sitting in the middle of the web of Amy's story.

The Ford dealership in Green Valley was just off La Cañada Drive. Green Valley is best known as a retirement community, and the number of residents buzzing down the street in golf carts gave proof to the rumor.

"Just follow my lead," Strike said. He pulled the Shelby into a space marked for visitors and revved the engine once before he shut it off. A half-dozen people in the glass-walled lobby looked our way. Well, nothing like making a quiet entrance.

A trim young man with pomaded hair and a striped polyester tie approached the car as we got out. "Howdy, folks. Can I help you with something?"

"I'm interested in a new truck."

The salesman nodded with glee at Strike's directness. No pussyfooting around. No "I'm just looking."

"A friend of mine bought one from you and she loves it. The new F-350 . . ."

I nodded as if I loved it, too.

"It's a fine truck," the salesman replied. "Let me show you what we have in stock." He gestured to the front parking lot, where the trucks shouldered together like the Cardinals' defensive line on fourth down.

"Oh, it's more than the basic truck. She added all kinds of things—leather interior, a rack of roof lights—"

"I'll bet she got the big engine, too, honey," I said. All I could think of was Amy in that motel room. I was having trouble keeping up my end of the charade.

The salesman bobbed his head like a dashboard doll. "Oh yes, I remember selling a truck like that—a red one, right?—not more than a month ago. We don't get a lot of call down here for really hot trucks, you know." He looked around to see if any Green Valley retirees had heard him disparage their taste in vehicles.

"The thing is," Strike said, "the wife here won't let me

buy it unless we can get the same kind of great financing my friend got. One toy too many, you know what I mean?" He nodded at the Shelby.

The salesman glossed over Strike's comment. "I'm sure we can make it work for you. Let me check out the details on that other truck. Will you be using the Mustang as a trade in?"

Strike paled. "Uh, I don't know yet. Let's see what you can do for us."

The salesman ushered us into a small cubicle with two guest chairs less than a knee's length away from his desk. He sat down, spun his chair sideways, and clicked several times on the computer keyboard to bring up the data he wanted. "Ah, here it is. Red, F-350, purchased four weeks ago." Then he furrowed his brow. "I'm sure we can do a good deal for you, but your friend ordered it months ago and paid in cash."

"Marta Veracruz paid cash?" Strike asked.

"No, sir. That's not the name—"

Strike reached across the desk, pushed the salesman's arm away, and swiveled the computer screen to face us.

"Patagonia Development Corporation?"

I preceded Strike into the house, flipped the switch on the swamp-box cooler, and opened the back door to get a draft going.

"Let's see exactly who this Patagonia Development

to the discussion. His black hair was still long on top, but the white sidewalls that showed around his ears suggested that he, too, had indulged in a San Juan Day haircut after leaving my house. My own haircut seemed days ago instead of just this morning.

"We have to talk," he whispered to McCullough. They moved to the back of the observation room so their hushed conversation wouldn't leak out to the group on the other side of the mirror.

I knew what was coming, but I didn't know how McCullough would take it.

"Cates's alibi is starting to stink," Strike told him. "Cates senior bought a new truck four weeks ago, with cash. Then three weeks ago he signed it over to a Marta Veracruz."

McCullough raised his hands to his shoulders in a "so what" gesture.

"Marta Veracruz is Salsipuedes's mother. It looks like a payoff for his alibi. And if I can find a payoff, the cops can, too."

I lost McCullough's reply in the conversation coming through the speakers from the other room. Strike nodded twice and went out.

What would that revelation mean for McCullough's defense of his client? Would he focus on a case of mistaken identity? Concentrate on refuting the scientific evidence? Or would he push for a guilty plea and a plea bargain? I was more worried about the black Dodge truck that Cates had owned seven years ago.

McCullough's attention was back on the focus group participants. A young woman with a blue polyester scarf tied tight around her neck said, "I'd never leave my child alone so I could go to a bar. She got what she deserved." Several others nodded their agreement.

McCullough leaned toward me and whispered, "Maybe it's time to put the victim on trial."

The second set of focus groups on Tuesday night only whet McCullough's appetite for a pretrial publicity campaign. He had called in a public-relations firm Monday night after our first research and started a barrage of leaked information that painted his client as a victim of mistaken identity, and Lydia Chavez as a reincarnation of the whore of Babylon.

The Wednesday morning *Daily Star* bore the first fruits of his labors. One article was an op-ed piece about the ineptness of the sheriff's deputies for not looking more closely at Ms. Chavez's lifestyle and associates. There was also a letter to the editor about the good works of the Cates family through the years. I noticed that when McCullough was quoted, he was not emphasizing Cates's alibi witness quite as much as he had before.

Strike called at noon and asked me to meet him for lunch. I crunched the phone between my ear and shoulder and lowered my voice to a whisper. "I'd better not. Jessica's hotter than forty dogs about my taking Monday off. I need to put in some face time around here."

"Okay. Want me to come by this evening?"

"Sure." I doodled a row of asterisks and pound signs on the notepad in front of me. "What are you doing today?"

"I've got some work to do for McCullough. Background, details on Lydia Chavez," he said.

I added ampersands and exclamation points to the doodle on the page, turning it into a comic strip version of cusswords.

"Make sure you remember which one's the victim here."

There was an ocean-wide gap in the conversation. "I'm doing what I'm paid to do," he said into the silence. Great. Kevin McCullough pays for your time, and you jump to his tune.

I sighed. "Sorry, I'm just being crabby. See you tonight about seven?"

"Okay." He hung up with a quiet click that sounded like the severing of a lifeline.

The storage room behind the carport was cool, even though the rest of the house retained the day's heat. I pushed aside the cardboard boxes that held Amy's clothes and schoolbooks and opened the last box. After finding the bloody clothes in the other carton, I hadn't looked any further. Maybe this box held the answers I needed.

At first there didn't seem to be anything promising in it,

just Amy's past income tax information and paperwork that she'd had stored at the dorm. As I flipped past manila files labeled "Education Expenses" and "Income," I found a pocket-size notebook, bound in rust-colored parchment paper and secured with an elastic band. Most of the pages were empty. I turned to the inside front cover. There, in proper Catholic schoolgirl script, it said, "Diary, Amaryllis Del Arte." I slouched down against the cool concrete wall with my knees bracing my arms to read.

The diary covered two and a half years, beginning with Amy's sixteenth birthday. It ended more than a year before the rape. I pictured her teenaged face scrunched with concentration as she penned the opening pages, careful not to make a mistake. As she filled in later pages, the pen had moved more quickly, trying to keep up with the rush of emotion and thought she was trying to get down. A prayer for our parents. Reflections on anger and selfishness and the impermanence of life.

Later pages were crowded with what I thought were fantasy stories. A bareback ride in the moonlight. The straining of a taut denim thigh thrust against her. Had Amy confined her promiscuity to the fantasy stories in this diary? Or had she purposely lived out the erotic and dangerous deeds our parents had forbidden when they were alive?

Amy wasn't a virgin on the night she was attacked. I knew that. She was as showy and lush as her flower name-sake and had attracted the attention of one boy after another growing up. She seemed to go through men like they were trial magazine subscriptions.

I knew now that Amy had not checked into that motel alone. What did that mean? Had she been looking for the fantasy lover she wrote about? Did she go there with him or meet him there? And what had happened to change that fantasy to a nightmare?

I ran a mental slide show of my own romantic history. While it wasn't as littered with broken hearts as Amy's, it was certainly as colorful and sincere.

It was Michael Hawke who taught me how to be a woman. Curly brown hair as soft as a spiderweb, and when the sun was behind him it looked like a halo. We were sixteen, and I had just gotten over my crush on Enrique Garza. I grew to know the backseat of Michael's Nash Rambler like the contour of my own face.

He had a way of holding close without confining, ties that didn't bind. I remembered the evening that we spread a blue serape on the desert ground to watch the sun go down. Michael's tall champagne-colored Afghan hound, Sedona, threatened to run each time he picked up the scent of something interesting on the wind. Michael placed a rope in a wide circle on the ground and the dog settled down. It wasn't a leash or a wall; it was a protective circle, like soft arms around us that comforted us in our freedom.

All that ended when Michael died at the age of twenty, the victim of an untended strep-throat infection. It was the first time I ever heard the phrase "only the good die young." Giulia, overhearing that well-meant banality, turned to the speaker and said, "Horseshit."

The doorbell rang. Strike was right on time. I wondered which Anthony Strike it would be today. The one who worked for Whitcomb, Merchant & Dryer? Or the one whose eyes grew soft at the thought of the damage that had been done to a little sister.

11

B y Wednesday I still didn't have any more news about Cates or about the investigation of Amy's rape, but I got a new assignment from one of our current clients, a local chemical manufacturer who needed posttrial interviews of his jury.

They'd recently lost a case where their tanker truck crashed and contaminated the groundwater in a small Arizona community. Unexplained rashes and infections had blossomed in the area, and one baby died. Since there was every likelihood that other suits would now crop up, they wanted to know how the jury had reached its verdict. How did they react to the lawyers for each side? What evidence did they find most compelling in reaching their decision? The company planned to be better prepared for the next lawsuit. I jotted down the questions I would ask when I phoned the jurors.

Every time I tried to get rid of the Cates file, Jessica had another reason that she couldn't handle it. It seemed that she even scheduled dental surgery to be unavailable. In truth, my attempts to hand over the file were now all for show. I needed to stay close to the case to find out as much as I could about Raymond Cates.

Selena, Enrique, and I had agreed to meet at Aunt Giulia's on Thursday for a Fourth of July barbecue. I pulled into the trailer park late in the afternoon, raising a scorpion tail of dust in my wake. Fifteen trailers huddled together, radiating heat like giant loaves of freshly baked bread.

The two trailers next to Giulia's had tiny white picket fences around their bases, a plaintive reminder of the Ozzie and Harriet houses they emulated. In true Arizona style, one had a six-foot lawn of Astroturf and the other a gravel forecourt that had been spray-painted green. The proud but dusty marigold outside Giulia's trailer door was a vanquished queen in a conquered land.

I had marinated a flank steak, and the Garzas were bringing salmon, salsa, and summer squash, in keeping with the S theme of the day. Giulia was in charge of dessert and was making strawberry shortcake "with one blueberry on top, so it will look flag-colored." Even the oleanders, those perennial don't-worry-about-me-I'll-be-fine plants, were drooping in the heat. We draped ourselves on bench seats and folding chairs inside the trailer and downed cold beers and tortilla chips until the sun set and it was cool enough to go outside and light the grill. Jorge and Carlitos, Selena's twin boys, played cowboys and Indians in the bedroom.

Although we talked about everything from day care to

dieting, the conversation kept returning to Raymond Cates. Giulia had done a computer search at the *Daily Star* for information about Cates and his family, and she had turned up innumerable good works by Cates senior. There wasn't much information about Raymond Cates except one story that declared him one of Tucson's most eligible bachelors in 1994. The story described his wealth, his trim good looks, and his skill as a cowboy on his father's ranch. Was there a tie to the Nogales rodeo there? Maybe I could talk to some of the rodeo organizers, find out if they knew Cates.

Enrique's information was more disturbing. Because he hadn't found any specific information about Cates, he decided to investigate attacks similar to Amy's in the area. Almost three hundred rapes were reported in and around Tucson each year, but his search of sheriff's department records found eight women in the last ten years who were assaulted and raped by an object or a weapon. All eight cases were unsolved.

Enrique flipped through his notebook and tapped his finger at several of his scrawled notations. "They used a variety of weapons on these women: knives, guns, bottles, a broom handle, and in this—oh, geez—a plastic statue of the Virgin Mary." He took a final swallow of beer.

"Let's go talk to these women. Find out if they have anything in common," Selena said.

"Don't you think they've been through enough?" Enrique said, slamming the notebook closed and covering it with his hands. "If we find any similarities, I'll take it to my boss, but otherwise we leave these women alone."

Selena and I nodded, ashamed that we were so willing to put our own needs before those of women who had already been hurt so badly.

"Start with the gun or knife attacks," I said quietly.

Enrique summarized the details he'd copied from the police files. The first victim was a thirty-year-old single mother from Sells who was raped in a grocery store parking lot. His notes said that she saw her attacker, but I didn't know how much good that would do us. The attack was almost ten years ago.

The second was a preteen who was kidnapped while walking home from school and who escaped after two days of savage abuse. We probably shouldn't even be talking to her without her parents' permission, even though she would be an eighteen-year-old now.

The third was a University of Arizona coed attacked on campus in December four years ago, and the fourth was a tourist from New Mexico who was attacked in her first-floor hotel room. All four were raped with a gun or a knife.

"There's no clear pattern," I said. "The cities and kind of locations are varied. Two rapes were in warmer months, the others in November and December. Even if we include Amy's attack on the same time line, the attacks aren't evenly spaced apart—or even on the same day of the week."

In two cases the women got a good look at the attacker, and Enrique had photocopied the sketches. To me, all police sketches look like Mr. Potato Head, and these were no different. The eyes, nose, and cheeks were graceful generic arcs. Be on the lookout for a benign alien race.

"Maybe there's some other common denominator that we've overlooked. Maybe he didn't use a knife or gun every time," I said.

Enrique protected his notebook from my prying eyes and flipped another page. "Here's one. A student nurse from Marana who was picked up in a bar and attacked by a man who had given her a false name. He raped her with a beer bottle." He kept his eyes down while he read, unwilling to face us with the brutal facts.

"And this one, the victim of the broom-handle rape. She's from Phoenix. Came to town for the International Mariachi Conference a year ago May and said her attacker wore cowboy boots and a Stetson hat."

He ran his finger down the page of notes. "Oh, yeah, and this one. A stripper who was attacked as she left work."

It was a long shot that any of these cases could help us find or confirm the name of Amy's attacker. I'd heard that only one rape in four is even reported. What were the chances that I'd find someone who was attacked by the same man who had tried to kill Amy? But I had to start somewhere, even if it meant invading these women's privacy. Oh, God, I didn't want to hurt them. They'd already been through so much.

When Enrique went out to grill the salmon, I replaced his black spiral-bound notebook with a similar one that sat next to Giulia's telephone. Each time he glanced through the half-open door he saw that notebook, undisturbed, right where he'd left it. I surreptitiously jotted down the details from all eight attacks and passed the list to Selena. In his typically diligent fashion Enrique had included their addresses and phone numbers in his notes as well. Maybe we could find them. I knew Enrique was right. We shouldn't bother these women. But I convinced myself that if their rapists could be found and made to pay, they'd thank me for it.

I replaced Enrique's notebook, and we took plastic lawn chairs outside to watch the fireworks that were set off from "A" Mountain. Since Giulia's trailer was almost at the base of the mountain, we had to look straight up past the white-painted boulders forming the massive letter *A* that gave the peak its name to see the brightest, highest displays. Jorge and Carlitos clapped for each burst of light and booed at each thunderous dud. When the show was ending, I gave Enrique and Giulia a hug and walked to the Jeep. Selena, under the pretext of carrying leftovers, came with me.

In hushed tones we agreed to split up the list of victims and start our interviewing the next day.

I craned my neck to admire the final burst of pyro-
technics overhead and thought about the investigation
we were starting. Maybe I was lighting the fuse on my
own fireworks with this. Or maybe the fuse led to dyna-
mite.

❧ 12 ❧

Selena arrived early the next morning with squealing brakes. Gravel sprayed like buckshot from the tires. She had dropped the twins off with her mother. The car must have felt lighter—faster—to her, unencumbered by motherhood.

"How are the boys this morning?" I asked.

"We had to have another discussion about why their daddy can't live with us, but I think they're going to be okay."

The seven-year-olds would probably be all right, but I wasn't sure about Selena. She had married Travis in her early twenties, and this was her first year away from the wrath of his fists. Over the years, I had watched him isolate her from her family and friends but was helpless to provide the support she needed to leave him. Selena, too, had cowered in his presence and tried to patch things up even after he incinerated all her clothes in an effort to keep her at home. She found the strength to leave him only when his anger cost her her right eye.

Since the Fourth of July fell on a Thursday this year, a

lot of people would be off work Friday, enjoying a longer-than-usual holiday weekend. Maybe we could find some of these woman at home.

We sketched out a grid of the eight attacks based on as much information as we could remember from Enrique's notes. We filled in dates, locations, circumstances, what weapon was used in the rape, and any details about the attacker that the women had reported.

There were three cases we decided not to pursue at all. The young girl who had been kidnapped and held for two days said that her attacker was definitely a Latino, and she'd helped with an artist's rendering that looked nothing like Cates.

Another attack looked so dissimilar, and so sad, that we couldn't imagine following up on it. Beatrice Bonair, a seventy-two-year-old winter visitor to Tucson, had been attacked at the Benedictine Chapel in December of 1998. She was the victim raped by the plastic statue of the Virgin Mary, and Enrique had made a note that she had committed suicide a few months later. I didn't think her family could provide any more details, and this didn't feel like the same man who had attacked Amy, anyway. Clearly, evil came in more than one shape and size.

We also gave up on the tourist from New Mexico. She was still listed in the Albuquerque directory, but the person who answered the phone said she was traveling overseas and would be gone for the next three months. I'd come back to her later if I had to.

That left five possible cases that could help us. When we divided the list between us, Selena volunteered for the Sells and Marana interviews, although that meant she would have to drive a hundred-mile semicircle west of the city. I agreed to take the Tucson victim and contact the woman from Phoenix.

I didn't want to bring the rape back to life for these women, but they might be able to remember something they hadn't told the police.

I also wanted to know if Raymond Cates might have been their attacker and for that I used a black-and-white photo of him. I was enough of a researcher and close enough to the legal profession to know that simply showing them Cates's picture would never stand up in court as a positive identification. So Selena and I pawed through two weeks' worth of newspapers and clipped photos of other men we could include in this makeshift photo array. We created two cards with five photos each. All the pictures were of white men between twenty-five and forty-five, with no facial hair. Cates's picture was in slot number four.

I didn't want to phone ahead in case these women chose to leave or not answer the door once they knew what my questions were. But my first interview was with Mary Katherine Carruthers, the U of A coed who had been attacked on campus four years ago, and I didn't know where she lived now. Enrique's notes had shown her address as a residential dormitory on campus, but that address wouldn't still be good four years later.

I started in the most obvious place: the phone book. An M. K. Carruthers was listed on Fort Lowell. I tried the number, and when a young woman answered, I asked for a fictitious Dr. Brewer. I thanked her politely when she told me I had the wrong number. The age of that voice sounded right. It was a good possibility that M. K. Carruthers was the Mary Katherine I was looking for.

I've always thought that using only initials is a dead give-away that you're a woman living alone. My college friend Lynette Grissom, a wispy, blond, single woman from Alabama, lists her address and phone number under the name Rocco Trujillo. She never gets any heavy breathers.

M ary Katherine's current house was almost ten miles from where her attack had taken place, but you could see that it was not that far away in her mind. Intricate wrought-iron bars and boulder-size bushes of thorny cholla cacti covered the windows. A menacing growl became frenzied barking when I rang the doorbell.

I took an involuntary step back when she answered the door. She was short, with rolls of fat threatening even her man-size T-shirt and shorts. Eggplant-colored bags sagged under her eyes, and her gaze skittered from me to the sidewalk to see who else was there. I recognized a rape survivor.

"What do you want?" she asked from behind the wrought-iron safety gate. A Doberman pinscher quivered with restrained power at her side.

"I've come about something that happened to you four years ago. . . . "

"Who are you? Where did you get my name?" Her alarm was building. I had to talk fast before she shut me out.

"I've been talking to the police." Well, Sheriff's Deputy Enrique Garza, anyway. It wasn't a total lie. She started to close the door.

"I'm trying to find my sister's rapist. We can't let them get away with this."

She started to dissolve. Tears welled up in her eyes, and her shoulders hunched into a shape I could have recognized in the mirror. Depression as anger turned inside out. She gave the dog a complicated hand signal and opened the door.

The room was coal-mine dark, with curtains blocking both the sunshine and the view of barred windows. She waved me toward a couch and sat in a straight-backed chair with her hand on the back of the dog's neck. Her solace of choice was Cheetos; a half-eaten Costco-size bag of the orange worms graced the coffee table.

"I don't talk about that time," she said.

"I understand. I'd feel the same way. But I really need your help."

She looked down as if the answers were to be found in her lap. "He hurt me, you know. He did things to me that will never go away." She stopped, then heaved a sob. "I'll never have children."

A briny smell of regret rose from her in waves. I crossed the room and knelt at her feet, stroking her hand and keeping a wary eye on the silent and attentive Doberman.

"Did you get a good look at him? Did he say anything?" I needed to prompt any memory she might still have of that night. Maybe something she forgot to tell the police.

She continued to shake her head, either weary of the burden of her sadness or in negative reply to my questions. My photo array would do no good here. I said a quiet good-bye and left. The dead bolt slid home before I stepped off the porch.

I decided to visit Amy on the way home and followed Grant Road to the east. I snuck in without anyone asking about overdue bills and promised checks, and heard a baby in Amy's room. Amy's roommate, Mrs. Pilker, had her whole family visiting.

"Hi, little one." I smiled down at the baby, who was playing at the foot of Mrs. Pilker's bed.

"This is Emily, Nana's great granddaughter," a young woman said without introducing herself.

"She looks just like her," I said, hoping this was a compliment. I'm sure Mrs. Pilker would have loved the visit, but she slept through it.

A few moments with Amy and the Pilker family brought the comfort I needed. A little life and love after dipping into the dark world of rape.

. . .

The second woman on my list, Miranda Lang, lived in Phoenix, and she would have to wait until tomorrow. I took a quick shower and put on an oversized white shirt that draped longer than my shorts. Selena was due back within an hour, so I brought in the gallon jar of sun tea I'd left to brew in the backyard and clipped a fistful of mint from under the bedroom window. I was laying out a plate of *nopalitos* when I heard Selena's car pull up outside. The vinegary strands of pickled cactus were her favorite snack, and I owed her for all the driving she'd done today.

"Hold on, I'm coming!" I called in answer to her knock. I had the plate of *nopalitos* in my left hand and used my mint-laden right hand to open the door. The crushed leaves gave a fresh, green fragrance to the air.

Selena leaned against the doorjamb, rivulets of sweat framing her face. She did a fake stagger into the room as if she had been wandering in the desert for three days, then inhaled deeply of the herbal aroma and crossed into the living room. Her huaraches squeaked with every step across the tiled floor, the thin braids of rawhide contracting in the cool room.

"Take your shoes off and come sit under the misters," I said, guiding her outside to the ocotillo ramada, where the misters were going full blast. "How about a big glass of iced tea?"

"Yes to the tea, but that's just to take the edge off. What I really want is a beer."

I went back inside for the beer and a bucket of ice. Selena was fanning herself with a palm-size notebook when I returned.

"I only found one of the three women I was looking for," she said. "But she said that Cates might have been her attacker."

I pressed the bottle of beer to my forehead but felt a shiver that was caused by more than the cold glass. "Tell me."

"Well, I started in Marana. I thought I'd start in the north and then head south to meet the others. The Marana victim is Christie Parstac, the student nurse. She's an RN now, married, with a two-year-old boy and another on the way. She didn't want to talk to me—said she was trying to put it all behind her. But she seemed to understand that we were trying to catch someone who might still be out there hurting women.

"Her attack was at the end of the school year six years ago. Geez, after six years you can still see the scar of rope marks around her neck. She'd gone out with two girlfriends and met this guy at a bar near campus. She told her friends she was going to stay for a while after they left. She had another couple of drinks with him, then he drove her out past the airport, strangled her, and raped her with a beer bottle."

I cringed. "If she spent time with him at the bar, then she got a good look at him and maybe her friends did, too. What did she say about his picture?"

"Hold on, I'm getting there. Before I showed her the

pictures, I asked her what she remembered about him. She said he had introduced himself as Philip Harms or Harns—she wasn't sure. She said he had light hair and was good looking. He didn't look threatening."

"Did she say anything about his hands or fingers?"

Selena shook her head, then took a slug of beer and pushed her hair off her forehead.

"The sad thing is, I think Christie still blames herself for coming on to him in the bar. She still thinks she should have realized he was dangerous.

"In the end, she wasn't sure about the photo. She said it could have been him, but she also said that picture number two could have been him. You know, the PR photo we cut out of the paper about that lawyer who had just been given a judgeship?"

My spirits sank. Christie might have been our best lead. A student nurse, like Amy, and she got a good look at him. The circumstances were at least similar: two women out celebrating in a public place. If she couldn't confirm Cates as her attacker, then who could? Maybe the real rapist was someone who vaguely resembled Cates. I jotted a note to follow up with the friends she'd been with at the bar. Maybe we'd get lucky and find someone with a photographic memory or an amateur video from that night. Right. Fat chance.

We decided to continue the conversation over dinner, and Selena followed me into the house and perched on one of the kitchen barstools while I worked. I would have loved to put chicken or strips of beef in the quesadillas, but after splurging on steak for the Fourth of July party, chiles and cheese were all my budget could afford.

"What was your next stop after Marana?" I asked, crumbling the *queso fresco* and Monterey Jack.

"I went to Sells, but no luck there." Selena said. That was another sixty-five miles to the west and south of the city. No wonder she looked hot and tired when she showed up.

I didn't remember many details about the Sells victim from my cursory review of Enrique's notes. "She was attacked in a parking lot, right?"

"Right. A grocery store parking lot in Sells. But the family's moved away. The neighbors think they went back to Mexico, but they don't know which city."

"Almost ten years ago. She probably wouldn't have been able to help us anyway." I sprinkled green chiles and cheese on a tortilla.

"I can keep looking if you want," Selena said.

I shook my head and plopped the tortilla in the hot pan. Selena got tomatoes and guacamole out of the refrigerator, and I chopped the cilantro.

"What about the third one?" I asked, flipping the quesadillas.

"No luck on that one either. That was Sharon Hamishfender, the stripper who was attacked leaving work. She's moved from the address that was shown in the phone book, and none of her neighbors has a forwarding address for her. But I haven't given up on her. One of the neighbors said that she came from Patagonia, like Cates did."

"She did?" I grabbed the chart of victims and crimes that we'd prepared and added the notation "Patagonia" under Hamishfender's name. "Let's see, she'd be thirty-four now, four years younger than Cates. They probably didn't go to school together."

"Maybe not. But Patagonia's a small town. They might have known each other."

"Let's see if there's any family left there. And try an Internet search for her," I said, placing the plates on the table. "With a last name that unusual, we might be able to track her down."

"Unless she's changed her name or gone underground as a result of the rape," Selena answered, cutting into the warm quesadilla. Molten white cheese oozed out on the plate.

Selena was right. Many of the women on the sheet had unlisted phone numbers now or were only listed as initials or under their husbands' names. Without cribbing from Enrique's notes, we wouldn't have been able to find most of them.

When we finished eating, I walked Selena out to her car. "Thank you, chica," I said with a good-bye hug. "You've done me a world of good today."

"I'm not sure these women we talked to would agree

with you. Christie Parstac, the nurse, wasn't even sure she wanted the guy caught. Didn't want to bring it all back."

"I know." But sometimes looking under the bed is the only way to know the bogeyman's gone.

13

On Saturday morning I decided to travel to Phoenix without first phoning Miranda Lang. I didn't know if she would see me, but if not, the four-hour round-trip still wouldn't be wasted. I could use the thinking time. I slid a cassette of the Mariachis Cobres's twenty-fifth anniversary album into the Jeep's tape player and listened to the sweet duet of the Carillo brothers on "Maria Elena" as I joined I-10 and drove north.

When I was growing up, the road between Tucson and Phoenix was a vast and empty landscape defined only by car-size tumbleweeds and barbed-wire fences. Now both cities were edging in from the north and south, but it still left almost a hundred-mile stretch of Indian reservations, six-foot mesquite trees, and isolated saguaros, like lonely sentries, in between.

I passed the airplane graveyard not far out of town; the bodies of the abandoned planes on the horizon looked like an unsuccessful alien invasion. Ten miles beyond that, at the base of Picacho Peak, was an ostrich ranch whose long-legged inhabitants could have been the stunned passengers from those downed alien crafts. I don't know how they were tolerating the one-hundred-and-five-degree day; there wasn't a patch of shade in sight.

By the time I reached Tempe, on the outskirts of Phoenix, I had put most of the gruesome details of my conversation with Selena behind me, but Phoenix traffic was driving my blood pressure up instead. Even on a Saturday morning, six lanes roared thick with chrome and steel and exhaust fumes. I exited on Seventh Street and headed toward the center of town.

Miranda Lang lived in a small group of tidy, two-story condominiums on Central, only a mile or so from the high-rises downtown. Faux-Mexican beams stuck out near the roofline, and a small metal sculpture of an owl perched on the roof to drive away over-friendly pigeons. Eucalyptus trees and shoulder-high palms had been planted between the condos for shade and privacy. Open carports took up half of each unit's ground-floor space, and concrete steps led up from the sidewalk to the entryways.

Her door opened just as I raised my hand to knock. She had her backpack strap over her shoulder and her car keys in her hand.

"Oh!" She stepped back into the entryway. "I didn't know anyone was there."

Miranda Lang was chiseled, with a face like a clenched fist. She was a small woman with spiky black hair and a sharp nose. The sports bra and Lycra shorts she wore left no question about the rock-hard state of her conditioning.

Her calf muscles were well defined, divided like the heart shape of a cleaved apple, and her stomach muscles rippled and tightened into ropes. Even her fingers looked strong.

"Ms. Lang, I'm Calla Gentry. I've come up from Tucson to talk to you."

She cocked her head but didn't respond. When she juggled her keys from her left hand to her right, I noticed the small atomizer of mace attached to the key ring.

"I need to talk to you about your rape last year. The same thing happened to my sister, and I'm trying to find the man who did this." I waited for a response. A bead of sweat dripped down my temple.

She hesitated for so long that I thought I'd lost her. Then she pushed past me and headed down the concrete steps. "Follow me."

She got into the black Saab in the carport and gunned the car out of the parking lot. I had to hurry to get my car backed out before I lost her at the corner. She didn't go far, turning into a strip mall a half mile down the street and waiting for me at the entrance to a Jamba Juice.

"Wait here," she said, gesturing to the small wrought-iron table on the sidewalk. "Can I get you something?"

The place looked far too healthy for me, so I asked for bottled water. She came out a few minutes later with my water and something deep green and frothy for herself. Kryptonite, probably. With a booster shot of Invincibility.

She dropped the backpack from her shoulder to the

ground. The chained connection between the wooden dowels of a pair of nunchucks stuck out from the top.

"Nunchucks?" I asked. "You're into martial arts?"

"I'm into anything that will protect me," she said. The muscles around her eyes and mouth tightened.

She didn't look anything like the photo Enrique had included with his notes. That woman had dark hair that swooped under her chin. Her lips had shown a trace of tawny lipstick, and she had worn teardrop-shaped turquoise earrings. Of course, in that photo she also had a split lip and a raw cut under her eye. Miranda Lang had made herself over, in more ways than one.

I explained the circumstances of Amy's attack. "I don't know if this is the same man who assaulted you. Right now I'm trying to get as much information as possible. Anything you can tell me about that night will help. Even the smallest detail might be important."

She stirred her drink, then gave a powerful suck on the straw, but the thick green slush didn't make it all the way to the top. She stirred it again.

"It was thirteen months and twenty-two days ago," she began. But who's counting.

"I own an art gallery here in town. I thought I'd mix business with pleasure and go to Tucson to meet with one of my artists, then go to the Mariachi Festival downtown." The International Mariachi Conference was well known in Tucson. It had promoted and fostered the traditional *sones* and *canciónes rancheras* style of mariachi music for almost twenty years, and it drew appreciative crowds from all across the country.

"The concert ended about ten thirty at night, and I was alone walking back to my car. I had arrived late and was parked almost a half mile away." She measured her words like a metronome.

"A thunderstorm was brewing—kind of unusual for that time of year—and it started bucketing down rain. I had started to sprint to my car, when a man pulled up in a Lincoln Town Car and offered me a ride." She stared into her drink as if it held the next sentence in her story.

"I don't usually take rides from strangers," she said, looking up at me. "But it was a nice car, he was well dressed and friendly—you know, not giving me a come on, just being helpful—and it was raining hard. I got into the car."

"What happened then?" I didn't want to break the spell of her narrative. She seemed to have to tell this in her own way, at her own pace. My questions could wait.

The sunny sidewalk, the Jamba Juice, and the nun-chucks had disappeared. Miranda was back in the Town Car on a rainy Saturday night in April.

"I told him where my car was parked, and he turned in that direction. When we got there, he asked if I'd like to join him for a drink. He seemed nice enough, so I said yes." She paused while she tried to figure out how to ex-plain her actions. "I don't know Tucson very well, so it was several minutes before I realized that we were headed out of town and not toward any lighted area or bar."

Enrique's notes said that she, like Lydia Chavez, had been discovered at Gates Pass, a saddlelike route through the Tucson Mountains that leads to the Arizona-Sonora Desert Museum and the Western movie location, Old Tucson. It offered breathtaking views of the city lights as well as the darkness and privacy to commit just about any heinous act. Dozens of bodies had been discovered at the pass over the years, mostly the result of drug deals gone bad.

"I still didn't get too worried. He said he wanted to show me the lights of Tucson, and then we'd head to a bar he knew out that way." She shook her head, marveling at her own naiveté.

"He waited until we got out of the car. Then he hit me in the face with his fist. I was so dazed—I don't think I lost consciousness, but my reactions were slow. He tied my hands behind my back with his belt. I remember the buckle digging into my spine. It was both rounded and sharp. Like a fan. Then he raped me."

She stopped. It wasn't the end of the story. It was the end of the part that was easy to say out loud.

"I was told he used a broomstick on you."

She gave a grunt. "Is that what it said? Maybe they were just being polite. Or maybe they didn't know when the officer filled out the form." She waited until a triad of teenagers pushed past us on the sidewalk, chattering like birds.

Her voice lowered to a whisper, and she hunched toward the table. Her finely developed muscles, grown to protect her in times of attack, were covered in goose bumps.

"It was an ocotillo cactus."

I held myself still. Didn't breathe. Didn't react. I pictured the ocotillo branches: stiff, whip-like stems that grew over ten feet long and were covered with thick, brittle thorns. I'd always imagined that they used an ocotillo for the crown of thorns at the Crucifixion.

"Did he rape you himself as well? I mean —"

"No. He stood over me giving himself a hand job. But I don't think he ever got hard. He grunted once, then turned away and broke off the branch from an ocotillo."

I leaned across the table to put my arms around her shoulders. She started to shrug them off, then buried her head in the crook of my neck and started to cry.

"Damn," she said through the tears. "I promised myself I would never cry again. I've worked so hard. Nobody was ever going to hurt me again."

"I'm so sorry to bring this all up for you again." I meant it. What was I doing? Finding Amy's attacker wasn't going to help my sister get better. All I was doing was bringing the pain back for a lot of women who were trying to get on with their lives.

And what was it doing to me? I knew now that my sister had lied to me. That she hadn't had enough faith in me to tell me how the attack had really happened. What would have been wrong with saying that she had been attacked and forced into the motel room? That she had maybe even gone willingly into that room? I wouldn't have thought less of her, and the crime would have been no less vicious.

Miranda dried the corners of her eyes with the sweatband on her wrist and struggled to compose herself.

"Have you talked to anyone?" I asked. "Any professionals, I mean. This must have been a terrible thing for you to go through. Maybe somebody can help." I wasn't a big believer in therapy, but there were some things the human mind couldn't be expected to get through without help.

She hiccuped a small laugh. "Oh, yeah, I've talked to professionals. Talked till I'm blue in the face. Then I decided to take matters into my own hands and joined a martial-arts studio. It may not help, but at least I have an outlet for my aggression."

"You obviously got a good look at the man. Can you tell me what he looked like? What he wore?"

"Most of my impression of him is from when we were in the car, and he had a cowboy hat on, so I'm not sure how tall he was. But he was slim, in his thirties. I think he had light-colored hair and eyes, but you couldn't see much underneath that hat." She sniffled a couple of times, but the boxing-weight-lifting-martial-arts Miranda was coming back now.

"You mentioned the belt buckle. Do you know if it had the rays of a sun on it?"

She drew her hands behind her, the muscle memory of her fingers retracing the shape of the belt and buckle that had held her tight.

"It could have."

"What about his hands? Did you notice anything unusual about his hands or fingers?"

She closed her eyes to travel back to that time and place. "Nothing specific. He did wear a sharp-sided ring on his right hand, but I don't know which finger. When he punched me, it left a corner-shaped cut under my eye." She pointed to her face.

I looked more closely. There was a light, right-angled scar near her cheekbone. I took a final sip of water, screwed the plastic cap back on, and looked around for a trash can.

"There was something else," she said. "He called me Sweet Thing."

My heart thudded in my throat.

14

Someone had called Miranda Lang "Sweet Thing" and raped her with a cactus. Someone had also called Amaryllis "Sweet Thing" and raped her with a knife. I knew now that we had two victims of the same man. But I didn't know who that man was.

And what about this ring? Cates didn't have a ring on his right hand, but of course, he wasn't allowed jewelry in jail. Anyway, it would have been difficult to get a ring sized properly to fit over the bulbous, mashed end of his ring finger, and then not be too big to fit the finger itself. Maybe the Sweet Thing rapist wasn't Cates at all.

At the last moment I decided not to show Miranda the photo array that Selena and I had put together. Her description of the man could have been Cates, and she might have been able to identify him right away. But the legal researcher in me balked. Miranda might be able to file charges against him, and I didn't want any jury to think she'd been prejudiced by this informal, pre-lineup photo.

I was also afraid of the Letter of Confidentiality I'd

signed. It was a sure bet that finding someone else to testify against Cates would be considered a breach of that agreement.

When Miranda saw my reaction to the words "Sweet Thing," she grabbed my wrist. "You know who he is, don't you? It's the same man who attacked your sister. Who is he? You have to tell me."

"I don't know anything." I stood and prepared to leave.

Now that it was possible that Miranda could take a measure of revenge on her rapist, she wasn't about to let go. "Think about what he did to me," she said. "Give me his name. No one has to know it came from you."

I shook my head. I couldn't do it. I still believed in the justice system. I believed that accusations should come from evidence. That you're innocent until proven guilty. I couldn't serve up Raymond Cates as the Animal until I had proof. And right now I had none.

I settled for a middle ground. "Did you work with the Tucson Police Department or the Pima County Sheriff's Office when this happened?"

"Both. But my primary contact was Detective Giordano at the police department," she said. "The attack was outside the city limits at Gates Pass, but they called it a kidnapping and that happened inside the city limits, so the Tucson PD took the lead."

"I'll tell you what. Go back to the police department. It's been over a year since your attack, and they're probably not pursuing it actively anymore. Remind them about it. Ask them if there have been any occurrences since you last spoke to them that might resemble your attack."

"But you said your sister was attacked seven years ago."

"Just ask them."

That left my conscience clear. Miranda would not have been following the Cates trial, since it was a hundred and twenty miles away. And for some reason the police department and the sheriff's office hadn't linked the two crimes. I would think that Gates Pass and the violent thrust of a weapon inside the women would be quite enough to tie the attacks together. Maybe they'd already looked into it and Cates had an alibi for the night of Miranda's attack. Maybe they had no reason to look at him before at all and it was just his proximity to Lydia Chavez in the bar that made him look guilty.

At least this way Miranda could move ahead, and I wouldn't be fired.

So much for looking under the bed. All I had managed to do was prove that the bogeyman was still there.

On Monday, Jessica's hard stare and tapping foot reminded me that I had clients other than Raymond Cates. The Rondo case was going to trial, and we had to begin jury selection next week. In the meantime, I also had work to do for Azchemco, the chemical company that had lost its polluted groundwater suit. We had worked with Azchemco from the very beginning, conducting focus groups, preparing trial graphics, planning strategies. They weren't pleased when they lost that first lawsuit.

I started the phone interviews with the jury foreman from the Azchemco trial. Was there early agreement in their discussions, or had there been great debate to reach a verdict? What was the most pivotal piece of evidence in his mind?

"Well, I can't remember specific pieces of evidence, but I can give you a pretty good idea about our thought process," he said. He proceeded to give me a thorough summary of the plaintiff's case against Azchemco.

"What about the defense case from the chemical company?" I asked.

"We had a hard time sifting through all the data and all their charts." Damn. I was afraid that was going to be the answer.

Three more phone calls confirmed my suspicions: Azchemco's lawyers had been so in love with all the scientific data from the chemical company that they hadn't concentrated on the most important points of their argument and had instead left a scattered and ineffective impression with the jury. TMI, as my computer-savvy friends would say—too much information.

Juries do the best they can. And they usually get it right. Sometimes they can find their way through a rambling presentation or shoddy trial graphics. Sometimes they can even ignore the words of the law to reach the heart of the law. But this wasn't one of those cases.

I had seen Azchemco's data. It was impossible that their spill caused all the problems cited in the lawsuit.

"Remember, you're talking to a bright twelve-year-old," Jessica always counseled our clients when she described jury dynamics. They didn't always listen.

She had pleaded with them for simplicity, but they felt the overwhelming amount of scientific evidence would work to their advantage. It didn't.

I summarized my conclusions in a report for Azchemco. This was not the kind of news that Jessica liked to give a client. We should have fought harder to keep the message simple. But at least we knew how to improve their odds at the next trial.

A nthony Strike was waiting at the curb when I arrived home that night. He looked good in jeans. There were lighter colors on the denim creases where the pants met his hips, as if they'd been bleached by countless hours riding horseback in the sun. I lifted the bag of groceries from the cargo area to my right hip and balanced it there while I dug for my keys.

"Thought you could use a pick-me-up," he said, bringing a bouquet of wilted white daisies from behind his back.

He was six or seven inches taller than I, and my nose

was even with the pearl snaps on his shirt. I breathed in the sweet, musty smell of sagebrush.

"Oh, you're right about that, Mr. Strike. I'm thinking that just about anything else would be a better career option right now."

"Call me Tony, please, or Tonio. Mr. Strike sounds too old." He held the screen door open as I worked the key into the dead bolt on the front door.

"Tonio? That sounds too soft for you." I rummaged through a cupboard for a vase.

"Ah, that's because you don't know me well enough yet."

Without asking his preference, I mixed lemonade and iced tea in a big pitcher and added the remaining sprigs of mint from my evening with Selena. I took the tray outside to the patio.

"Have you given any more thought to the fact that Amy didn't check into the No-Tell Motel?" he asked.

I hadn't been able to think about much of anything else. "It's not that she didn't check in," I said. "It's that she didn't check in alone. So either she went to the motel with someone or someone attacked her and forced her there."

I poured more tea over the melting ice in my glass. "Amy would have told me if she'd been forced into that motel room." I left the other half of the option—the possibility that she'd gone willingly—unsaid.

He stared at a spot someplace between the rosebush

and the mulberry tree by the back fence. "You know half of all rapes are date rapes?"

I looked down at my lap and shook my head, both in answer to his question and in disbelief. "Fifty percent?"

He nodded, still focused on that patch of crabgrass in the middle of the yard. "It doesn't mean that Amaryllis did anything wrong. She just met up with someone who did."

I brushed a tear from my eye. Stop it, Calla. This is nothing to cry about. This is nothing worse than what you already thought happened to her. It doesn't change the rending, the tearing, the horror that occurred. If you're going to feel bad about something, feel bad that Amy didn't have enough faith in you to tell you she was attacked by someone she knew. Who might she have met? Who became a rapist instead of a date?

Strike lounged against the kitchen wall while I cooked. First he told me about his progress on Cates's current case.

"McCullough has got me jumping through hoops. He's looking for ammunition against Lydia Chavez. Wants to make it look like she brought this on herself, and deflect the attention from Cates."

"He's thinking about those comments we heard in the focus groups. 'She got what she deserved, She shouldn't have left her child alone.' I know McCullough's only doing his job, but I hate this part of it—blaming the victim." I opened a package of corn tortillas and pulled tomatoes, lettuce, and leftover rice out of the refrigerator. "Did you ask McCullough what George Cates said about giving Salsipuedes the truck?"

"Oh, he said it was more like a loan than a gift. Said Salsipuedes has been a good employee for years and was going to pay him back over time. He didn't know why Salsipuedes had registered the truck in his mother's name."

"Yeah, right, pay him back over the next forty years or so, based on his current salary."

Strike smiled. "Yeah, wish I could find a banker like that. There's no way the prosecution can refute the story of a loan, but if they ask him about it on the stand, it'll probably look fishy to the jurors."

I agreed with him. "What else did McCullough have you doing today?" I abandoned the dinner preparations and took the stool next to him.

"I wanted to get to know Lydia Chavez better. See if we could come up with other suspects for her murder. Her next door neighbor, Sandy Lyle, seems to have known her best."

"What did she say?" I refilled the lemonade/tea mix in our glasses.

"Nothing bad about Lydia, that's for sure. They used to babysit for each other's kids on a regular basis, and she found a note from Lydia on her front porch the next day, saying she was going to meet a potential new boss at the bar."

"Chavez just left a note and left her baby alone?"

"I guess she thought her neighbor was going to be home within a couple of minutes, and she was, but the note got blown off the door. She didn't find it until the next morning. She heard the baby crying about ten o'clock that night and went over. That's when she started getting worried about Lydia."

I imagined the lonely wails from the Chavez baby coming from the house. What had happened to that little boy now that his mother was gone?

"But nobody really said anything bad about her, huh?"

"Not the neighbors, not her ex-boyfriend."

I had seen a picture of the ex-boyfriend, Bobby Minor, a small-time ex-con who now worked in an auto-body shop on Grant Road. Strike had told me that Minor had been picked up on a DUI charge the evening that Lydia died. It was probably the luckiest arrest of his life: sitting in a drunk tank is a great alibi when your ex-girlfriend gets killed.

"What did the boyfriend have to say?"

"Oh, he's a piece of work. Claims that Lydia used to be a party girl but just wasn't any fun after she had the baby. I think his words were, 'She really changed. She really got *old*.' Imagine that. After twenty hours of breast-feeding and changing diapers she doesn't want to go clubbing with him." Strike shook his head at the foolishness.

Bobby Minor sounded too young and too selfish to be a father. "I'll bet he had lots of excuses for why he should fund his own drinking habits and dance club evenings before he paid any child support, too."

Strike nodded. "But get this. Right at the end he says, 'When they get this bastard, I'm gonna sue for emotional distress. He killed the mother of my child.'"

I shook my head. I could dismiss Minor's rantings as those of a selfish young punk, but he'd probably win the case.

I warmed up refried beans along with the rice, stacked the tostadas, and turned our conversation to the investigation of Amy's attack. I told Strike about the grid I'd worked out for the other rapes.

"Enrique's not going to be happy about you going to see these women."

"I know, but I think he'll understand." I remembered Enrique's own ability to bend the rules when his baby sister was involved.

"I've got two 'maybes' out of this group," I said. "Christie Parstac, the student nurse, and Miranda Lang at the Mariachi Festival. They don't have much in common, but they were both raped by an object—a bottle or a cactus branch." I shuddered, remembering Miranda Lang's interminable night of pain.

"And in both cases they were attacked by someone they'd just met. Someone who picked them up." Maybe three cases, if I added Amy to the list.

I put a bottle of Tabasco on the table along with the

salads and gave him the rest of the details from the investigation Selena and I had been doing.

After a first big bite Strike grunted his thanks and spoke around the food in his mouth. "It sounds like there are a couple of things I can follow up on for you. I can track down Christie Parstac's friends from the bar and see if they remember the man who picked her up. And I can try to find Sharon Hamishfender. Her case may not be as relevant, but I think it's interesting that she's from Patagonia, like Cates is."

"I appreciate the offer, but I'll follow up on those leads. It might be difficult to explain how an investigator got their names, and I don't want to get Enrique in trouble." He nodded and continued eating as I spoke. "And maybe they'll be more willing to talk to a woman."

If these witnesses were going to be scared off by rampant virility, this guy could do it. He radiated masculinity like a steroid stove. But somehow it conveyed warmth and confidence rather than the fire of his sexuality. Hmmm.

"You know, I appreciate everything you're doing." I cleared the plates and tried to rid my mind of the image of Strike bare-chested.

"You mean you actually trust me to do my job without you tagging along?"

"We'll see." I smiled back at his grinning face.

"Oh, speaking of doing my job without you, I forgot to tell you about the Blue Moon."

"The bar where Cates and Chavez supposedly met that night?"

He nodded and swirled the melting ice in his glass. "The bartender says it was really busy that night. He didn't recognize the picture of Lydia Chavez but says he remembers Cates. Says he was acting like a big shot, buying lots of drinks and then accusing the guy of shortchanging him."

"If it was Cates, it sounds like he made a pest of himself. But it doesn't confirm that he was sitting with Chavez that night, does it?"

"No, but it gets worse. The bartender is a big basketball fan, and the NCAA finals were on TV. Cates was making a scene about getting his bill, right when the guy wanted to watch the game."

"So?"

"The guy can peg the time right down to the minute. Eight minutes to go on the clock. Maryland had just pulled ahead of Indiana. I checked. That happened at nine thirty-five. It means that Cates was in Tucson at nine thirty and not near Patagonia like Salsipuedes says."

My dinner dropped in my stomach like a stone. "So Salsipuedes is lying?"

"Not necessarily. Maybe we can prove that it wasn't Cates, that the bartender misidentified him. I'm going back over his credit card receipts from that night to find other witnesses—see what they remember."

We knew that Chavez had arrived at the bar at eight o'clock to meet the mysterious new boss. Did he ever show, or did she wait impatiently for an hour and a half? Who had she been sitting with if it wasn't Cates?

When I walked Strike out, he hesitated in the doorway, one arm braced on the doorjamb. He reached back with the other hand to cup me at the waist.

"Thank you for dinner," he said. "And for keeping an open mind on my trustworthiness."

His kiss was slow and gentle. I'd finally found something soft enough about him to merit the nickname Tonio.

⁓ 15 ⁓

I didn't hear back from Strike on Tuesday, but when I got home, a small white card was tucked into the front door, right next to the knob. I half hoped it was a note from him, maybe checking to see if he could come by that night, and I practically skipped up the front walk to retrieve it.

It wasn't. It was a business card from a Detective Giordano, with the Tucson Police Department. His handwritten note on the back gave a cell phone number and asked me to call. My guess was that Miranda Lang had contacted the Tucson PD immediately after my departure, and now they wanted to know where I fit into all of this. I turned on the swamp-box cooler and decided on a shower before I called him back.

He answered on the third ring and agreed to come by at seven thirty that evening. At exactly half past the hour a beige Taurus rolled into the driveway and parked behind my car. I had the feeling he'd been waiting down the block for the right time to arrive.

Giordano had the squat, sturdy build of a barrel cactus,

and wore a bolo tie and a bad hairpiece. None of it did much for his image. The string tie, held together at his neck with a black square of onyx or plastic, looked like a relic from the airport souvenir shop. And the toupee, several shades darker than the gray at his temples, reminded me of a tree dying from the roots up. He blew his nose into a white handkerchief as he shambled up the walk.

"Sorry," he said, stuffing the handkerchief into a back pocket, "it's all this back and forth from air-conditioned buildings to the heat outside and back again. You'd think I would have gotten used to that after all my years in Chicago." He sniffled once.

"You're from Chicago?"

"Oh, I've been here almost ten years already." He waved away the years. "Shouldn't keep calling myself a Chicagoan."

I ushered him inside. "You didn't say what you wanted to talk about. How can I help you?"

He looked around the room for his seating options, and seeing only two, chose the armchair in front of the TV. I sat on the rump-sprung couch.

"It's about Miranda Lang. She says you came to see her over the weekend and that you may have some information about her rape last year." He dabbed at his nose.

Thirteen months and twenty-*five* days now, but who's counting.

"She says you may know of a similar attack."

I'd have to be careful. I couldn't disclose any information about Cates or my association with his trial. But I could certainly tell Giordano about Amy.

"I don't know anything specific. My sister was raped and maimed in an attack in Nogales seven years ago. She attempted suicide soon afterward and had head injuries that have left her in a coma. She never filed a police report, but lots of the details she told me about were similar to Miranda's." I clasped my hands in front of me, the perfect example of a helpful citizen-witness, then took a sip of water.

"How did you know about Ms. Lang?" He held a pen poised above a small spiral notebook.

I almost spit out the water. How could I have known about Miranda? I didn't want to get Enrique in trouble, but I couldn't say I read about it in the paper. They never use the names of rape victims in the news. I wiped at the drop of water at my lip to buy myself time.

"I don't remember. I think someone at a bar told me about her. It was a friend of hers, or a friend of a friend. Something like that."

He raised one eyebrow and jotted a short note that could have been a checkmark or a question mark or the first line in a game of Hangman.

"And why have you started this investigation now? Has your sister's condition improved? Or have you learned new facts? After all, it's been seven years."

What could I say that wouldn't lead back to Cates? I hesitated, then gave him the truth.

"It's hung over me like a shadow for seven years. I feel like I was the one he tried to kill, and I'm tired of living like a victim. I want him to pay for this, and if that means I have to go after the facts in Amy's rape, I'm ready to do it now." I nodded twice to demonstrate my resolve and sat up straighter. It may not have been the whole truth, but it was certainly a big part of it.

He waited three long beats, then, satisfied with my answer, flipped to a clean page in his notebook. "Tell me as much as you can about your sister's attack. I don't know if we'll be able to do much with it after all this time, but it can't hurt to take a look."

I forgave him for the plastic bolo tie and the bad toupee.

When I got to work the next day, I shut the office door for privacy and made two phone calls. The first was to the hospital in Nogales to see if they had run a rape kit the night I brought Amy in. It took a lot of cajoling to get them to agree to look up seven-year-old records and then to provide that information to someone other than the patient herself. I explained about Amy's comatose condition and then referred them to the "person responsible for payment" line at the bottom of their form. I guess they decided that if you provide the money, you're entitled to the information.

They said it would take hours to look up the records

and agreed to call me back when they were available. I hoped there was something to find. If they had done a rape kit, it would be invaluable. The information it contained, and the doctor's supporting statements, could verify that an attack had taken place. And if there was a semen sample and it matched Cates, I could prove he was the rapist.

The second call I made was to the DNA lab where I'd sent Amy's clothing. They had completed the test and confirmed that they had two separate DNA profiles from the material.

"Let me get this straight. Traces from the blouse and the skirt have the same DNA as the hair in the brush I sent you." I had included Amy's brush from the nursing home, thinking that it was one way we could match at least one sample of the DNA. Okay, Amy's DNA was on all three items: skirt, blouse, and hairbrush. Makes sense.

"Yes," the lab technician replied. "But we found a second DNA from saliva on the denim strips as well."

I gave a silent cheer. Maybe this was the real proof I needed. I pictured the squalid Nogales motel room. If Amy's attacker had pulled on the strips of cloth with his teeth as he was tightening them, or even if he'd drooled on them, it might have trapped saliva or skin cells in the denim.

"I don't know much about DNA. Is it a clear profile? Is there enough there to analyze?"

"It's a small sample, but that's fine. We use a process

called PCR—it's kind of like molecular xeroxing—to complete the sequence. Glad the cloth was stored in a paper bag and not plastic. It hadn't deteriorated to a point where we couldn't use it," he said. "What we don't have is a person to match it to."

I knew how to fix that.

16

C ates was in jail, so I had no real reason to be afraid of going to his house. But sometimes the lion's den is just as frightening without the lion in it.

I took a deep breath for courage. If I had a prayer of finding out whether Cates had been in the hotel room with Amy, I had to get a sample of his DNA to the lab.

His Tucson house was on the near north side of town and was buffered from the city's noise and traffic by several acres of desert vegetation. I turned into a narrow driveway that was marked by a galvanized tin mailbox and followed the meandering dirt road between creosote bushes for about a hundred yards.

It was one of the original, rammed-earth adobes with small graceful windows set almost three feet deep in the earthen walls. It was a house that would stay cool in the summer and warm you all winter long. I coveted it.

Beams as big around as my waist protruded from the roofline, and a scarlet bougainvillea ascended the wall like a wisp of red smoke to meet them. Crickets chirped in the bushes, and a sprinkler ratcheted a watery spray someplace in the back; otherwise the house was silent. I opened the screen door and knocked three times on the heavy timbered front entrance. No response. I reached for the knob and jiggled it. The door was unlocked. Maybe there was someone in the back of the house, near that sprinkler.

I turned the handle and opened the door enough to stick my head in. It was a small parlor with a fireplace, a love seat, and two straight-backed chairs. The only thing moving was the pendulum on a grandfather clock on the mantel. I eased the door open and took one step inside. "Hello?"

"What are you doing?" The voice came from behind me. I jumped, whacked my elbow on the doorknob, and spun around. It took me a minute to place him.

"Mr. Salsipuedes, isn't it? I was with Tony Strike the day he came down to the ranch to talk to you. I'm Calla Gentry. I'm with the legal team defending Mr. Cates. I didn't think anyone heard my knock."

"Then why did you go in?" There was no curiosity in the question, just a deadpan delivery.

"Mr. Cates's lawyers asked me to come by and pick up something. But now that you're here, maybe you could help."

He shrugged and took off the heavy work gloves he'd been wearing, then reached past me to open the door all the way. Still hearing Amy's plaintive nightmare cry of "day-doh," I surreptitiously checked out his hands. Salsipuedes' nails were dirty, but his hands were otherwise ordinary looking.

I preceded Salsipuedes through the parlor to a large kitchen at the back of the house—a kitchen built for a gourmet cook. Unglazed Mexican tiles on the floor, a solid granite countertop, and Wolf and Viking appliances that cost more than my annual salary. A separate pantry for countertop appliances and pastry preparation was tucked into an alcove at the back of the room. It was a kitchen Emeril Lagasse would have been comfortable in.

He dropped the gloves on top of a handwoven red and blue runner on the table. "I'm just here fixing the fence out back. I don't know how I can help you."

The air had a touch of lemon, an undertone of furniture polish, and a lush, rich floral smell like frangipani. Since Cates had been in jail for almost six weeks, I was sure someone else was in charge of household maintenance.

"Does Ray cook?" I asked, gesturing to the pristine surfaces.

"No, it's Mercedes, his housekeeper. She does most of the work around here. What are you supposed to pick up?"

I stalled for time. "May I have a glass of water, please?" He filled two tall glasses with cold water and waited for my reply.

"I'm supposed to look for his gun," I ad-libbed. "Smith & Wesson Model 57, I think he said." I pawed through my notebook looking for verification. "Mr. Merchant thought it might be helpful for a new pair of eyes to check for it. Make sure that Ray's father hadn't overlooked it in a cupboard or something."

"I think I'd better check with Mr. Cates first," Salsipuedes said. "Ray doesn't like people getting into his things."

"I understand. But if he's innocent, then finding the gun can only help him, don't you agree?" I couldn't help thinking about the bartender's memory that Cates had been in Tucson at nine thirty.

Salsipuedes braced his arm across the archway to prevent me from moving further into the house. "Mr. Cates said the gun isn't here."

"At least we haven't found it yet. Shall we call his lawyer right now?" I bowed my head toward the telephone as if it gave direct orders from God. "I'm sure he won't mind taking time away from Raymond's defense to make his request a second time."

Salsipuedes's deference to the bosses was clear. He wasn't going to make Cates's lawyer ask twice to have a simple task performed.

"Don't mess up anything," he warned. "Mercedes will kill you if Ray doesn't."

"May I use the bathroom?" I hadn't seen anything in the kitchen or entryway that I could use to get a sample of his DNA, but the bathroom was likely to have something.

"Down the hall. Last door on the left."

I followed a gray and black Navajo rug down the cool

hall and ducked into the bathroom. I turned on the taps to disguise my movements, then opened drawers and cupboards looking for my sample. No toothbrush. No hairbrush. No dirty drinking glass. Damn that housekeeper. And damn my luck for having used the guest bath instead of the one off his room. But I could use the ruse of searching for the gun to find my way back to the bedroom area and look for both a hairbrush and a sun-shaped belt buckle. I returned to the hallway.

Salsipuedes was on the phone in the kitchen. I didn't know whom he was talking to, but if he was checking on me, I'd have to move fast. I traveled farther into the house instead of back to the kitchen. The room across the hall looked to be a study or guest room, so I turned left, toward the room at the end of the hall.

Yes. The master bedroom. It was a symphony of deep green, tan, and black. A Nile-green leather chair and footstool anchored the left side of the room, along with a stained-glass reading lamp in shades of pearl and cream. The bed was a four-poster, with thick, round-top newels like fence posts.

There was a four-drawer dresser against the wall, and I hurried across the room to search it. The top drawer held more ties than any self-respecting cattleman should own. The second drawer had an array of belts, curled up like cinnamon buns in a baking pan. None of the buckles was sun-shaped and silver.

Chrome faucets glistened from the next room. I scooted around the bed and into the bathroom.

Nothing. It looked like the finest hotel bathroom awaiting a new arrival. No personal toiletries on the countertop. Even the bar of soap was new. I created a couple of new cusswords in my frustration and reentered the bedroom just as Salsipuedes came around the corner.

"Are you done now?" he asked, glancing behind me to the open bathroom door.

"I was just admiring the house."

Then I saw it. There, just to the side of the bathroom door, was a small semicircular hall table with an arrangement of dried flowers and a palm-size porcelain ashtray tucked under a trailing stem of lavender. An ashtray with two cigarette butts. Camel. Non-filter. I had never seen Cates smoke, but he lived alone, so they might be his. Would the tidy Mercedes have overlooked this little ashtray for six weeks? I didn't know, but I had to take that chance. I leaned against the small table, palmed the butts, and gestured back to the bedroom.

"I'm going to start looking for the gun in there."

"You're not going to start anywhere. George Cates said to throw you out."

"Come on, Hector. You know Ray couldn't have killed anyone. He was with you. How can the gun possibly hurt him?" Unless Cates was in Tucson at nine thirty and not at the ranch like you said he was.

He leaned closer and reached to pinch my collarbone between work-hardened fingers.

"Get your hands off me." My voice was neither as loud nor as threatening as I'd hoped. I wrenched my shoulder out of his grasp and quickstepped to the door.

Once I was safely in the car, I looked back to see Salsipuedes glowering in the doorway. For a small man he sure was good at looming.

{ 17 }

I mailed the cigarette butts to the DNA lab first thing on Friday morning.

When I got home after work, Giordano was parked in my driveway. He got out of the car and stopped to blow his nose, then tucked away the handkerchief and ambled toward my front door.

"Good afternoon, Ms. Gentry. I have just a few follow-up questions."

"Come in, Detective. How's Miranda's case going?" I held the screen door open for him and deposited my brief-case and purse on a dining-room chair. The room felt closed in and dead, too much hot air trapped inside all day. I opened the sliding-glass door to encourage a breeze.

"We've been busy. Ms. Lang said you wanted us to compare her rape to any recent attacks that had happened in Tucson." He waited for me to fill in the uneasy silence. I didn't.

"We looked back at all the cases that had occurred within the last twelve months," he continued. "You know what we found? Another date rape where a man picked up a woman, a Miss Chavez, and raped her with a weapon. Also at Gates Pass, like Miss Lang." It was about time he noticed the similarities, I thought. I tried to look interested without looking like I knew anything about the Chavez killing. A mourning dove called a pitiful refrain from the yard.

"Here's the funny part. We've got the perp on this other case; he raped her with a gun and then killed her." He waited to see my response, then asked, "Do you know the name Raymond Cates?"

"Cates? I think I've heard the name before. He's going to trial soon, isn't he?" I regretted the words as soon as they were out of my mouth. If Giordano didn't already know about my trial consulting role for Cates from his own research, then he would find out in a few short weeks when the trial started, and it would look as if I'd been lying to the police.

"What do you know about all this, Ms. Gentry?"

I held my lips together to prevent a spurt of information. I didn't want to mislead him, but I couldn't start talking about working on Cates's case. If I did, I wouldn't know where to stop. My suspicions, my doubts, the grid of other victims, Amy's information, the details on Cates's current case—it would all come pouring out, woven with suppositions, hypotheses, wishes, and regrets.

"I'd like you to come downtown with me," Giordano said, pulling his car keys from his pocket.

"What for?"

"I had Miranda Lang come down from Phoenix. She's going to attend a lineup for us and see if she can identify anyone."

I looked back into the dining room, where my notes from the interviews with all the other women were spread across the table.

"Just let me get my purse."

I locked the sliding-glass door and placed a wooden dowel in the metal trough to secure it. Then I picked up the shoulder bag from the dining-room chair, straightened the incriminating papers into a stack, and placed the morning paper on top of the pile.

He let me ride in the front seat so I didn't feel as if I were under arrest. "Detective, I can't possibly help you with a lineup. I never saw my sister's rapist and, except for calling him a cowboy and a possible reference to his fingers, she never described him to me. I don't understand why you want me there for Miranda's lineup."

As much as I wanted to catch my sister's attacker, I couldn't get involved in Miranda's case. If Cates was her rapist, she was going to have to prove it with her own information and not from anything I told her. Otherwise it would put both me and my job in jeopardy.

"You may not think you know him, but maybe he was stalking her. Maybe you saw somebody hanging around."

He wheeled into a parking space and came around the car to open my door. He must have had a history of gentlemanly behavior; the politeness seemed to come naturally.

Or maybe he was just used to transporting felons in the handleless backseat. We crossed the parking lot, and I looked up at the three-story, gray concrete ribs of the building. They looked like bars. I followed Giordano down a well-lit hallway to the elevator.

The detectives' area was not divided into cubicles, just metal desks back-to-back, bristling with telephones, computer terminals, and stacks of paper. Only two of the twelve desks were occupied, and those detectives glanced up and then continued with their work. Giordano sat me in an armless chair at the side of his desk, then excused himself. When he came back, he had Miranda Lang in tow.

"I think you two know each other," he said as introduction.

Miranda gave me a tight smile and gripped my right hand with her left, like we were two schoolgirls whistling in the dark. She looked less like a warrior today, wearing a dark cotton skirt and blouse with a thin ramie sweater tied over her shoulders. Giordano told me to wait while he took Miranda into the viewing room for the lineup.

I fidgeted at the desk, crossing and uncrossing my legs and trying to read his papers upside down. Ringing phones went unanswered, and one detective tried to calm a hysterical caller on another line. "Listen to me, Ella. Just slow down and listen to me for a minute." It didn't seem to be working.

After several minutes a group of four men exited from a

door halfway down the hall on the right. I craned my neck around the corner to see them. All were about five eight or five nine, with sandy hair, and in their twenties or thirties. One man had short hair on top, but kept it long around the back so it cascaded over his shoulders. He brushed a lock of hair behind his ear, and I stared at his hand. The thumb and index finger and the web of flesh between them were bright red, as if he'd dipped his fingers in strawberry jam. Was he part of the lineup?

I stood and had turned toward the ladies' room when Giordano and Miranda came around the corner from the other direction.

"I'm sorry, I'm so sorry," Miranda said, wiping the tears from her eyes. "I was positive I could recognize him, but I'm just not sure." She walked to the window and stared down at the street.

Giordano toyed with his empty coffee cup. "Don't worry, we'll get him." The disappointment was obvious on his face.

Two more doors opened and closed farther down the hall. I asked Giordano if he still needed to interview me, but his reply was cut short by a shout from the corridor.

"Hey! What are you doing here?" Cates said. His voice was full of indignation and threat.

Like a dog picking up a scent on the wind, Giordano turned to face me. "I'm sorry about that. I should have kept you both in the viewing room until the lineup partici-pants cleared out. But now that you mention it, Ms. Gentry, I may have a few more questions for you." His glance swung from Cates to me and back again.

A short, dark-haired officer cuffed Cates's hands behind his back and prodded him farther down the hall for his return to the county jail. Miranda took Giordano's offer of another officer to walk her to her car. That left the detective with all his attention on me.

"How do you know Ray Cates?" he asked.

"His lawyer hired my firm to help with his jury selection." I didn't elaborate.

"How does he fit into Miranda's rape?"

"I don't know that he does." I wasn't trying to dodge the question, but I didn't know if pursuing Cates for other attacks would abrogate the Letter of Confidentiality I'd signed.

"Look, the only way I know Raymond Cates is that I was hired by his defense team. That's why he recognized me and why he was probably surprised to see me here. I don't know anything else about Miranda's attack, but if I did, I couldn't say anything because of my legal relationship with Mr. Cates."

Giordano looked like he'd heard the punch line but didn't get the joke. "There's something else you haven't told me," he said, then waited for me to fill in the silence. When I didn't, he gave a deep sigh. "You're walking a very fine line here. And you're bound to make more enemies than friends by doing it. I'd be careful if I were you."

I nodded. "Who was that other man? The one with the red mark on his hand?"

Giordano looked at the group of departing men. "The guy that's got the mullet going?" He saw the question on my face. "The hair. Short on top, long in the back. White trash–Brad Pitt–wrestler style."

I smiled at the description. "Yes, who is he? What's he doing here?"

He sorted through a stack of loose papers on his desk and tapped twice on a line at the top of a page. "Terrence 'Red' Blanken. He matched enough of Miranda's description that we brought him down for the lineup, too."

"Did she describe his hair like that? I thought she only remembered the cowboy hat."

"She didn't say anything about the hair, but he wasn't wearing it like that last year. We picked him up when Miranda first reported her rape, but he had an alibi. I thought we'd try again today and see if we could shake that alibi loose."

I waited until Giordano turned away to straighten the other papers on his desk, then scanned the rest of Blanken's rap sheet. Twenty-eight. Tucson address. A dozen Peeping Tom convictions, then he finally escalated to house invasion and attempted rape when he was twenty-one.

"What about his car? Does he have a black Lincoln Town Car like Miranda remembers?" What I really wanted to ask was if he used to own a black pickup truck.

"He's worked off and on for the last ten years at We Park—that big long-term parking lot out by the airport. He might have had access to lots of different cars."

Giordano picked up Blanken's file and tapped it on the edge of the desk. One loose sheet cartwheeled to the floor. I swooped down to get it and turned it over in my hands. It was the photo of a knife, with the sinuous design of a snake on the handle, writhing and ready to strike.

"Is this turquoise? And coral? And ivory?" I pointed at each of the snake's scaly dimensions. He flipped the photo over, read the notes on the back, and confirmed it.

A turquoise snake knife? A shiver raced between my shoulder blades. Maybe Blanken was the Sweet Thing rapist and this was the same knife he had used on Amy.

Now I had two men who had been accused or convicted of a sexual assault, who owned or had access to black trucks, and who had something wrong with their hands. And one of them had a turquoise snake knife.

"What's that on his hand? Is that a burn?"

"No, it's a birthmark. Makes him easy to ID, unless he wears gloves." So easy that Miranda would probably have noticed it if Blanken was her attacker. Maybe not, between the darkness and the terror that night.

"By the way," I asked, "did Cates own a Lincoln Town Car a year ago?"

Giordano frowned. "Not registered to him. But his father has one."

Two men with probable access to the right kind of cars

for two different attacks. And one of them had the right knife.

I headed for the front door, hoping I'd be able to flag one of Tucson's small fleet of taxis for a ride back home. "Red" Blanken was unlocking the door to a blue-gray Taurus in the public parking lot down the block. He glanced back at me and nodded, then got in the car. Despite the heat, a chill went up my spine as I watched him drive off.

It took twenty minutes before a tattered yellow taxi arrived. As I waited in front of the police station, my eyes traveled from the lacy white structure of St. Augustine Cathedral on my left to the drive-thru liquor store across the street. If you couldn't get justice on one corner, a couple of other options for solace were available here as well.

18

Selena and I met Saturday night after the crowd at the restaurant had thinned. I had a glass of Perrier and a slice of peach pie, in keeping with the theme of the night. Late diners still lingered over coffee at two tables, but Enrique had turned off the outside lights to discourage any new arrivals.

After leaving bills on both their tables, Enrique sat down to join us. I told them about Miranda's lineup and about Terry "Red" Blanken.

"I'll look up his record," Enrique said. "See if he was doing time on either a peeping or home-invasion charge when Amy was attacked."

"Could you also check if Blanken was in prison when that other student nurse was raped? You know, the one you told us about?" Selena had broken the news to him that we had, in fact, contacted some of these women. She said his reaction had ranged from furious to curious, then finally to supportive.

"Will do. But remember, his alibi doesn't have to be just prison time."

"It's a place to start."

Selena poured more water in my glass. She had asked the student nurse, Christie Parstac, for information on the two friends who had been with her in the bar. Although her attack was six years ago, I still had high hopes that her friends, also from the adult education program at the community college, might remember her drinking partner in the bar that night. One girl had moved to Chicago, and we'd have to wait until tomorrow to phone her. The other was still in Tucson, and I planned to see her in person.

Selena looked tired. Between her boys and the restaurant, her days were long. I kissed her on the cheek, yelled good-bye to Enrique over the sound of the dishwasher, and went home.

I wouldn't have noticed the car except that he kept his lights off. I had just turned off Fourth Avenue and headed east on Speedway, savoring the dry, dusty air as it cooled the night. The SUV's engine started as I drove past, and its boxy, dark shape took position a half block behind me. I flicked my own lights off and on twice, thinking the driver might notice that his lights were off, but he maintained a dark and ominous presence behind me. Three turns later it was still on my tail.

I picked up my cell phone and tried to find the buttons for Alphabet City as I rounded the corner. It rang three times before Selena answered.

"Is Enrique still there? I need help."

Selena must have run outside with her cordless phone;

her voice carried over the sound of an engine starting up. I had just caught him. When she handed Enrique the phone, I explained my concern.

"It's a black SUV, a big one, like a Suburban, and it's been on my tail for the last three turns with its lights off." I wondered what kind of car Cates owned these days and whether the police would have given back his car after comparing tire treads. Unless there had been a jailbreak, it couldn't be Cates behind the wheel. But my run-in with Salsipuedes had convinced me that Cates still had plenty of loyal friends on the street.

I couldn't imagine that I would have attracted the attention of Red Blanken at the police station, so I didn't think he was the likely driver of the big black car, and I had seen him the day before in a Taurus. But he did have access to other cars from the airport parking lot.

And I couldn't think of anybody else I'd pissed off recently, except for Jessica because of all my absences.

I glanced at the green street sign on the corner to give Enrique my latest location and signed off. I kept going straight so that he could find us, hoping that he'd get there before the black car made a move. Although we were still on city streets, there was no other traffic in sight, and the houses I passed weren't lit. Everyone was asleep or enjoying a warm summer night on the town. Ignoring my own advice, I speeded up to lose the big car, turned off my headlights, and ducked into an alley.

The black car approached as silent as a hunter, tapped

my rear bumper, and sent the Jeep's steering wheel shuddering. I gripped the wheel and accelerated. Then a second wrenching crunch, this time sending the Jeep in a sideways slide as the alley crossed a larger street.

An engine behind me revved high, but I didn't realize it was Enrique until he pulled up even with the giant black SUV.

The windows were darkened; I couldn't see who was in the car. Suddenly the SUV braked and reversed in a semicircle to head back the way we'd come. Enrique slowed to check on me, then turned back in pursuit. I waited, my pulse racing like the end of a sprint, and the night settled back, quiet and dark, around me.

When Enrique returned, the frustration was clear on his face. "I didn't catch the car or get the plate number. Are you okay?"

I lied. I said I was.

We made a two-car parade back to my house, but Enrique wouldn't let me go in until he'd checked inside and made sure the doors and windows were secure.

"If you're going to get involved in tracking down a rapist and would-be murderer, you're going to need more security than a cell phone. At least an alarm system. And maybe a guard dog or a gun."

He was right. Up until the time of Amy's attack I thought I could talk my way out of any situation. Language—words, the power of reason—held all the answers for me, whether they were the persuasive words I'd researched for thirty seconds of advertising, the solution words to crossword puzzles, or the comforting words of the psalms I'd read as a child. Words were truth, somehow. And they were all I needed to rise above any trouble that came my way.

From the moment I saw Amy's broken body, I knew I could no longer rely on the power of those gentle swords. Language alone didn't save Amy, and it couldn't save me. Words had lost their strength.

After I brought Amy home from the hospital, I had changed the locks, put a peephole in the front door, and beefed up the locks on every door and window. Walks were now taken with my house key or car key thrust between the two middle fingers of my right hand like a short spike. I wore a whistle around my neck. But none of it really made me feel safe, and I couldn't afford the guns or big security systems that would.

These days my trust in words only extended as far as crossword puzzles and menus. Puzzles allowed me to feel a bit of order in the universe—gridded squares, exactly the right number of letters, only one possible right answer. I still loved them for the same reason I loved Selena's menus. They gave protected, finite borders to the options in my world. They had black-and-white clarity. They were my truth and my comfort, my new psalms.

I wrote myself a note to look at Cates's file for information on his car. If the police had matched his tire tracks to the Chavez killing, then the information on make and model would be listed. I wondered if he still favored large black cars. And whom he trusted the keys to.

Could Cates have been mad enough at seeing me in the police station yesterday that he used his phone privileges at the jail to tell someone to follow me? To do what? Scare me? Well, whoever was doing it, it was working.

I closed all the curtains and called the nursing home to check on Amy. With an ear tuned to the sounds of cars on the street, I watched three TV cooking shows in a row, then treated myself to a package of Kraft macaroni and cheese.

Sunday morning I took advantage of the time difference and called Ellen Dunlop in Chicago. She had been with Christie Parstac the night of the attack and might remember what the man at the bar looked like.

She was breathless when she answered the phone. I explained who I was and why I was phoning, and that gave her enough time to catch her breath.

"Sorry, I just came in from a run," she panted. "I felt so bad about Christie. We never should have left her, but everything seemed to be okay."

"What do you remember about the man?"

She paused to pull up the memory. "He had sandy brown hair. I thought he was really handsome until I got up close."

"Why do you say that? What was different up close?"

"He kept his mouth shut most of the time. Kind of a thin-lipped smile, you know? But when he did smile, you could see he had really bad teeth. Yuck." That hadn't been in the police report.

"Bad teeth? Like someone who doesn't take care of his teeth or someone who needs braces?" Cates didn't have bad teeth. I tried to remember if Blanken's photo on his rap sheet had showed him smiling. Probably not.

"They weren't misshapen. Just yellow. That really turns me off." I imagined Ellen: a runner-thin twenty-seven-year-old with a brilliant smile and perfect skin.

"Did you notice anything about his hands?" Missing finger? A birthmark the size of an Idaho potato?

"Just that he wasn't wearing a wedding ring. That's the first thing we always looked for." I promised to fax the photo lineup, and she said she'd call back with her reaction.

It was only a short trip to Kinko's, and there was no one in line ahead of me. I keyed in her fax number and watched the paper coil through the machine, then went to meet Christie's second friend, Lola Uribe, at Tucson Medical Center.

I didn't know how much good this description of yellowed teeth would be. Christie Parstac hadn't mentioned it in the police report or when she talked to Selena. And Amy hadn't said anything about her attacker having yellow teeth.

Lola Uribe was a small woman with large, strong

hands. After nursing school she had decided on a specialty in pediatric oncology and was on the seven-to-three shift in the cancer ward at TMC. She held a thin, quiet baby over a basin with her left arm and sponged his hair with her right.

"We call them our Pantene babies," she said with a smile, massaging the shampoo into his scalp. "Sometimes just the water, the rocking, and the silky hair can make them feel better." Sometimes it made me feel better, too.

"I hope you can remember that night six years ago. Can you help me identify Christie's attacker?" I asked after I explained my mission.

"Maybe. I've sure thought about him a lot since that night." I showed her the five photos I'd put together with Selena. I wished now that I had a picture of Blanken to include. She craned her head to get a better look without having to readjust the baby in her arms.

"He's not there. I'm sure." My heart sank.

"Ellen mentioned that she remembered his yellow teeth. Does that sound familiar?"

"I never got close enough to him to notice. But I sure got close enough to see his face. He's not one of these," she said, indicating the photos with her chin.

"Did you get close enough to notice anything unusual about his hands?"

"His hands? Except for the fact that they were all over Christie, no." I guess I didn't need to come back with

Blanken's picture. She probably would have remembered seeing that birthmark.

Christie said the photo of Cates was a maybe. Lola said definitely not. I'd wait to see what Ellen thought of the fax before I'd cross this student-nurse attacker off the list. But Lola Uribe struck me as the kind of woman who would notice the leaves and not just the trees. If she hadn't recognized Cates's face from the photo lineup or said anything about a birthmark or a missing finger, then it probably wasn't either one of them. Damn.

19

I still had work to do on the Rondo case. The citizens who had been called for jury duty were due in at nine, but the courthouse was bustling by eight thirty on Monday as lawyers, witnesses, clerks, and potential jurors vied for a last cup of coffee and a Danish before the court sessions began. Our courtroom door was already open, and I took a seat with Mr. Rondo and his attorneys at the plaintiff's table, closest to the jury box.

Mr. Rondo was playing his victim status for all it was worth. In previous meetings he had pinned his shirt or coat sleeve over the stump at the end of his missing arm. Today he wore a short-sleeved shirt with a tie: professional and pitiful. I was surprised he hadn't painted the stump lime green.

The jurors' experiences and attitudes were going to be more important in our decisions than their demographics, so I had a host of questions for us to pursue during voir dire, the part of the trial where the lawyers get to know the jurors. I wanted to hear about their work history, gauge their respect for authority, and find out if any of the jurors were related to someone with a disability. That would give us a sense of how they viewed Mr. Rondo and whether they could appreciate the life-changing circumstances that a missing limb could cause.

There's no scientific way to know how a person is going to vote on a jury. You could look at demographics, lifestyle, background, political affiliations, clothing, and occupation and still not see a clear picture. You could ask them if they'd ever done jury service before and how that trial had concluded. You could probably use a Ouija board and have the same success rate.

I'd heard about a lawyer in Globe who asks potential jurors a question about the bumper stickers on their cars. "Save the Whales: Collect the Whole Set." "Baby on Board." "If This Is Tourist Season, Why Can't We Shoot Them?" If it's important enough to put on your car and wear around for the whole world to see, then it's probably a pretty defining characteristic for you.

I put my copy of the jury questionnaires into the order the potential jurors were sitting and sketched a quick grid on a sheet of blank paper to keep them straight.

Rondo's lawyer, Tracy Drury, was a petite blonde with an elfin face and a rose-colored business suit that looked like it should have been part of a Republican Easter parade. She rose and approached the jury box. Her questions seemed random, but she included each potential juror, sometimes asking about their family and sometimes their background.

There were a couple of jurors I really wanted to keep, like Rodrigues, the twenty-six-year-old black construction worker. When answering questions, he said that he believed "every man's got to watch out for himself on the job" but that "sometimes the boss just doesn't get it, he's not the one doing the work." The female telephone installer next to him added that sometimes it seemed as if "whoever writes these safety manuals has never operated the equipment."

The one juror I wanted to get rid of was Marshall in seat two. He was a sixty-four-year-old ex–Air Force captain who had strutted into the courtroom and taken the first seat in the gallery before anyone else could enter the row. As each name was called, he gave a sweeping gesture to the place in the jury box they should sit. This was a man who wanted to run things; he wanted to be jury foreman.

I handed Tracy a note to ask Mr. Marshall how he felt about personal injury lawsuits. "It's about goddam time these mealymouths started taking responsibility for their own actions," he replied. Then he backpedaled and said he was sure he could be open-minded about the trial. I didn't want him anywhere near the case.

I conferred with Tracy, and we decided to use our peremptory challenges on Mr. Marshall and a businessman who said he thought people were "suit happy these days."

I felt good about the final selection. The men on the jury were predominantly blue-collar workers, a couple of whom said they "did their jobs their own way" and not the way their bosses originally showed them. We had more law-and-order-oriented retirees than I'd hoped for, but that's what you get in Arizona. It's not a place where people are dying to come; it's where they're coming to die. Judge Levy swore in the twelve jurors and two alternates.

When I got back to the office at three o'clock, Jessica glared at me and looked at her watch.

"Another sick day?" she asked.

I looked up in surprise. "No, today was Rondo's jury selection."

"Oh, that's right." She pirouetted on her stiletto heels, pushed past the receptionist, and charged back into her office.

What had I done to piss her off? Sure, I had taken some personal time, but I didn't think it was affecting my work.

I pulled the ever-growing Cates file to the middle of my desk. I wanted the information on tire-tread evidence. There it was, the tire marks at the scene of Lydia Chavez's murder were consistent with the treads of Cates's Cadillac Escalade. It was still new on the night of the attack, with only three hundred miles on the odometer. The report didn't say what color it was, but I was betting it was black and that it had tailed me home on Saturday night.

.   .   .

S ince Jessica was already mad at me for being out of the office, I waited until she left for a meeting before I snuck off to meet Strike. Enrique had copied the most relevant information from Terry Blanken's file, and I wanted to find out more about him. Strike was parked across the street from the Redrock Bank complex, in a patch of shade that only covered the front half of his car. I got in and anchored the loose pages with my right thigh as he drove.

I mentally replayed Strike's story about the Arizona Robin Hood. Maybe it was time to put those horseshoes back on the right way and start moving ahead instead of backwards.

Blanken could certainly be the man I called the Animal. The police records showed that Blanken had been raised in a foster home since he was eight and had been in trouble ever since.

Strike stopped at a red light.

"Why do you suppose Blanken was in a foster home at all?" I asked. It wasn't clear from the notes we had. They just said that the boy's parents left town, leaving him behind. I couldn't imagine abandoning a child like that. Strike grunted.

I looked back at the notes. By the time he was sixteen, Blanken had been picked up five times on Peeping Tom charges. His foster parents had, at first, just thought it was a normal growing-up prank and had not taken it seriously. But when he was sixteen, he had chosen to spy on a judge's daughter and earned himself a year in a juvenile detention center.

He'd been in and out of jail ever since then, once on a vagrancy charge, several times for Peeping Tom convictions, and then the latest, the home invasion and attempted rape when he was twenty-one. At this rate Blanken might want to change his permanent mailing address to the county jail.

"His house is up ahead," Strike said, indicating a square gray building on the right. It was little more than a shack, just unpainted concrete blocks and a tar paper roof. No car in the driveway, and the weeds growing there suggested there hadn't been one for a long time.

Two houses on the block were vacant and looked ready to be condemned. One screen door hung askew, and plywood had been nailed across a broken window.

"Let's see if the neighbors have anything to say." Strike tried the houses on either side of Blanken's. The only response was the angry retort of a massive black dog on a chain.

"I guess we'll have to keep going backwards for a while," I muttered, but Strike overheard me and smiled.

He flipped through the papers I'd been holding. "Look at this. When he was growing up, Blanken's foster family lived near Glenn and Country Club roads, and that means he probably went to Catalina High School. Let's start there."

"That's where Amy and I went to school." Had Amy

known Red Blanken? Had he been stalking her all these years?

I drove past Catalina all the time but hadn't returned for a visit to the school in over fifteen years. The blue and white sign at the entrance still gave the exhortation "Go Trojans!" That soldier mascot had been the butt of a lot of jokes through the years. We went up the broad steps and found the principal's office near the entrance, the same place it had been in my own high school days.

"We're looking for an old Catalina yearbook, please," Strike said. He'd counted back to Blanken's sophomore year, assuming that he had been in a juvenile detention facility for at least part of his junior and senior years.

The blonde looked up from her computer screen and smiled. She was a knockout, and the cat's-eye glasses she wore only seemed to emphasize it. She was all curves and gold and perfume. I glanced at Strike. He looked as love-struck as any acne-ridden teenager.

"That's in the library." She smiled into Strike's eyes and pointed to the right. "Ask for Miss Miller."

We thanked her and headed down the hall. "Put your tongue back in your mouth, Mr. Strike." He almost blushed.

I remembered the librarian from my own days at Catalina, and she hadn't changed a bit. She could have been Miss Gorgeous's grandmother; a soft, sweet-smelling woman with kind eyes and a bear-trap mind. She handed us the right yearbook after a four-second search.

We found Blanken's picture in the sophomore section. He certainly wasn't wearing a mullet in those days; his picture showed a head shaved almost bald. Lips as taut as a tightrope. Terry Blanken wasn't giving the world the benefit of the doubt.

I flipped through the book, looking for any clubs or sports that Blanken might have participated in. Nothing. He was a loner even then.

I flipped farther back in the book. There, amid the timid and arrogant faces of the junior class, was my beautiful baby sister.

Had Amy known Terry Blanken? Even though they were a year apart in age, they would have been at the same school for at least two years. If she had seen him at the rodeo, would she have thought, Ah, there's a face I remember from high school? Is that all it took to approach her and gain her confidence?

I closed the book, my finger still marking the page with Blanken's picture. Miss Miller was back at her desk.

"Miss Miller, do you remember this young man?" I opened the book and pointed to Blanken.

"Oh, young Mr. Blanken. Is he in trouble again?"

20

I drove to work the next day with one eye searching the rearview mirror for a big black SUV that stayed too long behind me. There was nothing.

Jessica announced that she had a hair appointment and sashayed out at three o'clock. I took advantage of the absence-of-boss to do more research on Sharon Hamishfender from Patagonia. An internet search of white-page listings didn't turn up any S. or Sharon Hamishfender anywhere in the country, but there were two listings for Hamishfender in the 520 area code, which included Patagonia.

The first number rang unanswered, but the second one I called was picked up right away.

I tried not to sound like a telemarketer. "I'm a friend of Sharon Hamishfender's. We met several years ago, and I'm trying to get back in touch with her. Are you related to Sharon?"

"I might be. What did you say your name was?"

"Calla Gentry."

"I don't remember Sharon telling me your name before. Where did you say you met her?"

I wasn't going to get anywhere with this protective relative unless I came clean, so I explained why I was trying to reach her.

"I'm Sharon's sister," she said. "She lives in New York now and has an unlisted number that she doesn't like me to give out. I'm sure you understand." I gave her my home and office numbers and asked her to have Sharon call me.

A few minutes later the receptionist said I had a call on line one. The caller wouldn't give her name.

"Ms. Gentry?" she asked.

"Yes, is this Sharon Hamishfender?"

"I don't use that name anymore. It sounds like our two families have a lot in common. Two younger sisters who have been raped, and two older sisters who are the only ones who care enough to do something about it." There was alcohol and veiled venom in her voice.

"Tell me what happened to you. I don't know any of the details."

"It was eight years ago. I got raped leaving work. Two men I'd met inside. I guess I hadn't shown them enough attention."

"You're a dancer, right?"

"Yeah, I was working as an exotic dancer—an ecdysiast, if you prefer—out by Davis-Monthan Air Force Base." The men had both raped and sodomized her. Her words in recounting the story were slurred, but the hatred was not.

"You say your sister was the only one who tried to do something about it. Didn't the police have any luck?"

"I didn't file a police report; my sister did. But I couldn't go through with it." Ice tinkled in a glass as she took a sip.

"Why not?"

"Because everybody else in my family made me feel like it was all my fault. You know how it goes—I had it coming, I deserved it for dancing half naked, nobody would believe it coming from a stripper anyway." She knew the litany of their complaints too well for me to believe that she was past their condemnation.

"But you were raped. They hurt you. Your family had to understand that, didn't they?" I was asking myself the question as much as I was asking her. Why didn't Amy think I would be able to understand? Was she, like Sharon, not convinced of her own innocence?

"I think the way my father put it was, 'What did you expect, wagging yourself in front of a man that way?' That's the last time I ever talked to him. Moved out the next day."

I asked if she could identify the men who had attacked her. She said she could; she even knew their names. I recognized the tightness in her voice: hatred can be a mirror image sometimes.

"Who were they?"

"Real names don't matter. They were just two college

kids. I'd seen them in the club before. Now I just think of them as Mutt and Jeff."

"Do you know the name Terry Blanken . . . Red Blanken?"

"No, never heard of him." She was neither hesitant nor curious in her reply.

"Do you remember Raymond Cates from Patagonia?"

She gave a quiet laugh. "Ray Cates? Sure, I remember him. It didn't surprise me when my sister told me that he'd been arrested for murder."

I picked up a pen to take fast notes. "Why? What do you remember about him?"

"Oh, I remember lots about him. He's four years older than I am, so we never really went to school together. But when I was twelve, he grabbed me on the way home from school and started waving a knife around, saying he was going to cut me if I didn't 'suck him off.' I didn't even know what it meant."

"Did you tell anybody about it?"

"Oh, sure, his family owned just about the whole town. I'm sure they would have taken me real seriously. Or maybe even then I thought it was all my fault."

That was a deep well of guilt she had fallen into. "This may sound like a silly question, but did either of your rapists ever call you Sweet Thing?"

She gave a low laugh. "They called me lots of things, but that wasn't one of them."

"May I call you back if I've got other questions?"

Ice cubes rattled across the wires again. "Call who back? Sharon Hamishfender doesn't exist anymore."

So Sharon knew who her rapists were, and neither one was likely to be the Sweet Thing rapist I was looking for. But I'd also learned that Cates had been a sexual bully during his high school years. Maybe he'd gotten better at it over time.

I replaced the phone on its cradle and thought about the misnamed Thanksgiving Day when Amy tried to take her life. I knew now it was self-accusation that drove her to that haven of liquor, pills, and silence. That same shame echoed in Sharon's voice. In Amy's case there was more than enough guilt to go around, and I laid claim to my share.

Even days after the rape Amy had seemed numb, as if the knife had severed her feelings and instincts as well as her muscles. She must have felt soiled, rent open beyond repair.

Early that morning I had stuffed a turkey, sweetened the cranberries, and put potatoes in a pot of cold water. In other words, I pretended that it was just another Thanksgiving. Amy, like an uncooperative rag doll at a child's tea party, refused to pretend along with me.

"Amy, talk to me. You can say anything."

"There's nothing I want to say."

Back then all I heard was, You can't help me. There's nothing you can do.

"You can't just ask for my help and then turn me away

when it suits you. I want a full-time sister, not the shadow of one."

I had stormed from the room and focused my energy on the advertising job I had ignored for the last three weeks. Stacks of videocassettes from recent focus groups had been delivered from the ad agency and awaited my review. I filled a carafe with coffee and took it back to my bedroom. Then I loaded the first cassette into the VCR and donned earphones to better hear the focus group participants' discussion of a new underarm deodorant our client wanted to introduce. Hours passed as I shuffled through the cassettes and took notes. If Amy didn't want to talk to me, that was fine. I'd show her.

I lost both my patience and my sister that day. The only reason I found Amy still alive was that I had to go to the bathroom.

At the hospital, a caring paramedic tried to explain what had happened.

"It wasn't just the tequila," he said. "With a whole bottle of painkillers like that, she would have been real woozy."

I pictured her there in the bathroom, the air filled with hot moisture from the almost full tub. She would have coughed and swallowed to keep the pills and liquor down, then removed the brace and sling from her left arm and lifted one leg over the rim of the tub.

Maybe she got dizzy. Maybe she got brave. I pictured the slow-motion sequence as she lost her balance, and then, with a crack like thunder, hit her head on the edge of the old enameled tub.

I found her on the bathroom floor. Glass shards from the broken tequila bottle stuck out of her forearms and chest like badges of honor in an army of despair.

And I had been thinking about focus groups for a new deodorant.

There is a legend in Tucson, and probably in most of the desert Southwest, about *La Llorona,* "The Wailing Woman." In a rage of selfishness and jealousy, *La Llorona* kills her children, hacks their bodies into pieces, and throws them in the river. God punishes her by making her haunt the riverbanks until her children's bodies are recovered.

In many ways I had done that same haunting for the last seven years. I was The Mourner. The Ruer. The Regretter. The Wailing Woman who just wanted to put things back the way they used to be.

My hand remained on the cradled phone. I wished that Amy could be whole again. And I wished that Sharon Hamishfender—the real Sharon—were still alive.

❧ 21 ❧

The sky was already slate gray to the east when I pulled up in front of Strike's house, but it was a riot of orange and purple to the west. I had never been to his house before and sat listening to the click of the cooling engine as I took it all in.

Strike rented the entry gatehouse to an estate farther up the hill. He said the rent was reasonable because the homeowners liked having someone with a gun permit live at the driveway entrance.

It was a tiny house made of smooth, worn river rocks and was tucked into the southern slope of a hill in the Tucson Mountains, west of the city. It was maybe twenty by twenty feet and looked smaller than the attached garage at its side. I'll bet that sealed the deal on his choice of rentals—a happy home for his precious Shelby.

His backyard neighbors were giant saguaros, their arms frozen upright as if they were in the middle of a game of Simon Says.

Enrique had already arrived, and Strike opened three beers for us while I checked out the interior. It was only one room, with a stone fireplace along the far wall, an old rocking chair, and an L-shaped banquette that was covered with cushions. Either that banquette pulled out to make a bed or Strike was sleeping with his feet tucked up on a couch that looked smaller than a twin-size mattress. The kitchen was fit into a triangular space at the back of the room, and the door to the bathroom was opposite the drop-leaf kitchen table. It smelled sweet, like the feathery leaves of some herb I'd never cooked with before.

"So, what did you want to meet about?" I asked.

Strike and Enrique exchanged glances, then Enrique took the lead. "We want to start surveillance on Red Blanken."

"Did you find out something new?"

"No, but we think it's possible he was Amy's attacker, and we want to be careful."

What did we know about Red Blanken? A history of sexual crimes, a deformity of the hand, access to a black truck, and a snake knife. "Does he seem a more likely suspect to you than Cates?"

Strike took over. "Cates is in jail; we don't have to worry about him. And I told you at the beginning of this that I didn't think Cates was Amy's rapist. It was just a coincidence that you met him, and it got you thinking about it."

I wasn't sure that I didn't have to worry about Cates. The memory of that black SUV ramming my Jeep was still fresh in my mind.

"Meeting Blanken is just as much of a coincidence, isn't

it?" I asked. "In a period of two months I meet two men who could have been Amy's attacker? What are the odds of that happening?" I was beginning to question my own sanity.

"I've been thinking about that," Strike said. "And it's not that unusual. Until you were assigned to Cates's case, you pretty much had a set routine, went to the same stores, saw the same people at the office. And all that work was on civil cases, so you weren't coming across a lot of people with a criminal history of sexual assaults."

"That we know of." I almost smiled at the thought of the cherubic CEO of Azchemco as a sexual predator.

"Now, all of a sudden, you're going to the county jail; you're attending lineups at the police station. You're being exposed to more possibilities than you were before." Strike closed the curtain behind the banquette. The night air was cooling considerably.

"And you think Blanken might really be the one?"

"He fits the pattern," Enrique said. "He started with misdemeanor sexual crimes, and he's worked his way up. Nothing we've heard rules him out. And I don't like the fact that he and Amy went to school together. Maybe after Amy's attack he worked all the way up to murder. Maybe he did Lydia Chavez, too."

"Do we know where he was the night Lydia died?"

"I'll check and see if he was doing time," Enrique said. "We can't do much more than that. But we can set up a surveillance to watch him. Maybe we'll catch him in the middle of something, maybe we won't. But at least we'll know where he is."

They worked out a schedule between them, and Enrique agreed to take the first shift.

"There's something else, Calla," Enrique said as I started to get up. "It may be nothing, but we want you to be alert. Be prepared."

I sat back down. "For what?"

"Maybe we've been looking in the wrong direction." Enrique drew a black leather belt out of the paper bag he'd hidden behind his chair. The buckle was gold, not silver, but it showed the fanned rays of a sun across the top half.

"Where did you get this? Whose is it?"

"It belongs to a friend of mine, but Strike's the one who noticed the similarity," Enrique said. "And I have to agree with him, it's possible."

"What's possible?"

He folded the paper bag flat and rested the belt on top of it. "It's a highway patrolman's gear. Their badge is based on the Arizona state flag." I visualized that flag design. Liberty blue on the bottom half, thirteen rays of a setting sun on top in red and gold, and a copper star in the center.

Strike nodded in agreement. "They don't usually come in silver, but I found some on the Highway Patrol Association's Web site."

"Amy would have trusted a highway patrolman, wouldn't

she? She would have let her guard down." I dropped the patrolman's belt into my purse.

Calla, good news," Jessica began, barging into my office the next day without knocking. I looked up from a stack of focus group questionnaires and marked my place with a yellow Post-it note.

"I could use some."

"The Rondo jury came back in. They've awarded him seven and a half million." She beamed as if the money was all coming her way. "Drury is sending over champagne."

"Uh-huh." My thoughts were still deep in the subject of Cates's potential jurors. I had put Mr. Rondo's case out of my mind for the last two weeks. It felt like getting a compliment on a dress I'd long ago given to Goodwill. "I guess getting rid of Marshall was a good idea after all. Who wound up being jury foreperson?"

Jessica checked the sheet in her hand. "Harmon. The teacher in seat six." Not unusual. Teachers and scientists often fall into power positions on juries. I hadn't thought the teacher would side with Rondo, but at least he hadn't done him any harm.

"Do they want to do any posttrial interviews?"

"She didn't mention it. I'll check with her this afternoon. My guess is no. She'll take the win and not ask too many questions about why it worked."

My phone rang as Jessica turned back toward to her office.

"It's Enrique. I've got Blanken's dates of incarceration. It looks like he was in prison on that home invasion charge when Christie Parstac and Mary Katherine Carruthers were attacked."

I jotted the dates down in the margin of the questionnaire I'd been working on.

"Hmmm. What do we know about him after he got out?" I was thinking about the attacks on Amy and Miranda, and about the murder of Lydia Chavez.

"We've got nothing on him since then. Don't know where he was."

I thanked him and hung up, then heaved a sigh and threw my pen across the room. I wasn't finding anything to prove that either Cates or Blanken was the author of these attacks. And now I had the disturbing similarity between Amy's description and a highway patrolman's belt. I groaned in frustration.

What if it was Cates? All I could do was my job, as if his trial was any other case. Evaluate strategies and witness credibility; identify the most negative juror profiles to avoid; prepare voir dire questionnaires. Part of my brain still functioned like a researcher—weighing, evaluating, deciding, recommending. But another part of me was in turmoil, wondering if I was helping my sister's rapist escape again.

I retrieved my pen from where it had landed against the

far wall and returned to my questionnaires. We had done more focus groups for Cates, this time trying to pinpoint the case-specific elements that would help us pick a favorable jury. I'd already learned that women were more likely to convict because of the vicious rape and assault involved, but they were also more likely to be positively swayed by Cates's good looks.

Hispanic jurors couldn't be ruled out just because the victim was Hispanic, but potential jurors with higher education seemed to identify with Cates whether they were Hispanic or Caucasian.

I usually loved this part of trial research—ferreting out any hidden attitudes or background elements that would help complete the jigsaw puzzle picture of the best, or worst, jurors in a case. But this time my heart wasn't in it. I couldn't separate my distrust of Cates from the research. Presumption of innocence, my ass.

{ 22 }

L ess than three weeks till Cates's trial date now, and we were preparing to do the mock trial. Normally we used these simulated trials to test possible strategies or fine-tune opening and closing arguments. But this time we wanted to get a read on much more, like the State's circumstantial evidence and Hector Salsipuedes's credibility as a witness.

We had set up the focus group room to look as much like a real courtroom as possible, with a raised judge's bench and separate tables for the defense and the prosecution. A low bar separated the mock jurors from the well of our sham courtroom. One of the lawyers in Merchant's firm had volunteered for the role of the judge in our simulation. McCullough was going to play the part of lead counsel for the defense.

Originally, Gideon Merchant wanted to handle the defense role as he would in the real trial, saying it could help him hone his opening and closing arguments. I finally managed to convince him to play the part of his opponent, a lawyer from the Pima County attorney's office. We always had the most experienced attorney take the role of opposing counsel in trial simulations. That way you make sure you're trying out the strongest possible version the other side could hit you with. It had served us well in trial preparations in the past.

Cates couldn't be in the room, since he was still in jail, but the boyfriend of one of the paralegals from McCullough's office volunteered to sit in instead. He had the same athletic build and sandy hair that Cates did. And we could still show the jurors a videotape of Cates to get more specific reactions to him.

Our "judge" swore in the "jurors," and Merchant and McCullough gave their opening statements. The argument from the prosecution side was simple: We've got the evidence that proves Raymond Cates killed Lydia Chavez. The defense focused on the possibility of mistaken identity and coincidence. "He was eighty miles away having a beer with an old friend," McCullough said.

Merchant began his parade of witnesses for the prosecution. Of course, we didn't really have the sheriff's deputy who had written the parking ticket or their ballistics expert or the bartender from the Blue Moon up on the stand. But we knew roughly what their testimony would be from their written statements, so we used actors and friends in their roles.

McCullough asked questions on cross-examination, just as if it were a real trial. He didn't have any questions for the pseudodeputy who testified about writing Cates a parking ticket. I didn't know how they planned to finesse that one. To me, it was the most damaging evidence the prosecution had.

Then it was time for the defense presentation. McCullough questioned Marjorie Ballast about the tire tread, cat hair, and ballistic evidence. Several jurors were taking notes.

One of McCullough's final witnesses was Hector Salsipuedes, who confirmed that he'd been with Cates eighty miles away at the approximate time of the murder.

We had to assume that the prosecution would find out about Salsipuedes's new truck, so Merchant questioned him about the vehicle. Although Salsipuedes said that it was just a loan and he was paying George Cates back, he stammered and flushed throughout the cross-examination.

Trying to be objective, I thought it had gone reasonably well for the defense. Except for Cates's license plate number on the parking ticket, the State's evidence was not compelling, and several jurors had reacted positively to the notion of mistaken identity. The two lawyers had played their parts well and gave stirring and specific closing arguments.

Unlike a real trial, we split the jurors into three groups to deliberate. It wasn't a verdict prediction we wanted from this mock trial, it was a glimpse of the thought processes that got them there. With three groups we had three chances of hearing different points of view.

I listened in on their discussions. One group particularly liked the mystery boss Chavez was meeting as another possible suspect. Maybe it was too many years of *Perry Mason* reruns where the person who's mentioned once in the first third of the show and never seen again winds up being the killer.

We had no plans to put Cates on the stand in the real trial, but I still wanted to get a sense of how the jury would react to him sitting there next to McCullough at the defense table. So we showed them a tape of Cates sitting at a glossy wooden desk, answering questions from an unseen interviewer about his family, his background, and his favorite foods.

Not unexpectedly, many of the jurors felt comfortable with him — he was nice looking and well dressed, but not in a flashy way. As a rule, jurors are more positively disposed toward good-looking defendants than unattractive ones, except in larceny trials, where good looks work against you.

Two jurors mentioned Cates's trait of tossing his hair back, one of them saying he looked like a pop star preening onstage. We'd have to counsel him not to do that during the real trial.

Hector Salsipuedes was our Achilles' heel. Most of the jurors either didn't like him or didn't believe him. They were suspicious about the new truck, and Hector's shifty responses to the prosecution's questions didn't help.

I wasn't sure if he was salvageable. His defensiveness on the stand would be hard to disguise, and if we did too good a job in coaching him and his delivery became flat and rehearsed, it would definitely look like he was lying.

After meeting him at Cates's house and wondering if he was the mystery driver who harassed me on the way home from Alphabet City, I already had my doubts about him. It's hard to push for improving testimony you think may be false.

By the end of the discussion it was clear that Salsipuedes's poor performance and the incontrovertible evidence of the parking ticket was too much to overcome. All fifteen mock jurors decided Cates was guilty. I looked over at Strike to make sure my Cheshire-cat grin wasn't showing and gave the jurors a silent round of applause.

I had a gut feeling that Cates was guilty of this and other crimes. Maybe the real jury would take care of all my qualms—all those little voices that said he might not be the one.

I've always been afraid of drowning. I know that's a strange phobia when you live in the desert, but there it is. And the fear got worse when I was eighteen and a palm reader at the county fair told me that I would die underwater. So monsoon season always left me kind of shaky.

The first of the summer monsoon rains hit while we were conducting the trial simulation. When I reached the front door of the research facility, thunder boomed like faraway cannon fire, and flat-bottomed black clouds covered the sky. Monsoon rains never really slaked the desert's thirst; an hour from now the streets would have forgotten the taste of that sweet liqueur. But for now the streets ran full from gutter to gutter.

I waded barefoot across the parking lot to the Jeep and inched open the door, hoping that the surge of water wouldn't reach the interior of the car. I scooted in and slammed the door against the fast-moving current at my feet. The engine compartment was still dry, and the starter only ground a few seconds before catching. I'd have to be careful with the brakes; they wouldn't last long in this new urban river.

I waved good-bye to Strike, and we both pulled out of the parking lot, heading north from downtown. My thoughts were miles away, back with the Cates mock jury and their deliberations, or I would have seen it sooner. Just ahead of me the underpass at Stone and Sixth avenues had flooded with the runoff from the storm. It happened often during monsoon season, and if I hadn't been preoccupied, I could have avoided it. But the deep underpass was now a swirling brown death trap, and I was in the middle of it.

I hit the brakes but felt no mechanical reaction from the car. My tires lost contact with the pavement, and the Jeep slammed into the angry overflow.

Pedestrians on the overpass gestured with both arms as if to warn the Jeep away. The marker on the side of the underpass showed the water at eight feet at its deepest level. It sloshed at the top of the wheel wells now and was climbing.

I lunged against the driver's door, but the current was stronger than my panic and the door stayed shut. I was trapped. Water began to wash across the hood.

I pushed all four electric window buttons at once, jabbing and slamming my hand into the controls in frustration. Nothing. I had waited too long, and now the car's electronics were shorted out.

I didn't know if I had enough time for any rescuers to get to me. The water was halfway up the windows, leaking into the passenger compartment. The Jeep drifted toward the deepest area. I tried smashing the glass with anything I could find: fists, shoes, even my cell phone, which splintered and flew apart after the first impact. Nothing.

I scrambled into the rear cargo area and kicked and smashed at the rear window. There was no interior release, and the windows held through the pummeling. My panic rose.

Then a tapping on the passenger-side window. I saw strong sunbrowned hands and pearl snaps on a long-sleeved shirt. The water was at his chest level, and he held a crowbar. I made a lunge for the passenger seat, but he made a "go away" motion, and I scooted back to the cargo area, which was now six inches deep in water. With two shoulder-numbing swings of the crowbar the window exploded and those hands cleared the remaining cubes of glass from the frame. Strike bent down and extended both arms across the seat to lift me out.

S trike arranged for my car to be towed when the water level in the underpass receded. I shivered and apologized for dripping all over the passenger seat of his car. He'd been two car lengths behind me but clearly more alert than I had been because he managed to avoid the flooded area. I'll bet he was rejoicing that he'd had the forethought to borrow Enrique's van today and hadn't put the Mustang at risk.

It must have been eighty degrees, but I couldn't stop my teeth from chattering. When we reached my house, I leaned on Strike and let him open the door.

My glasses had been lost to the swirling water, and I felt a stranger in my own house. Everything was softened and blurred except my nerve endings, which shrieked with delayed adrenaline.

"Come on, out of those wet clothes," Strike said. I let him lead me by the hand like a child. He sat me on the toilet seat while he drew a warm bath, then left the room while I stripped off the soaked business suit and underwear and lowered myself into the tub.

He returned with a glass of red wine and a shy smile. "Here, drink this. A big gulp first. Then you can sip more slowly." The wine worked its magic, calming and warming me. My teeth had almost ceased their staccato complaint.

Strike soaped a washcloth and rubbed my back. I felt like one of Lola Uribe's Pantene babies, so peaceful and safe that I didn't even react to the fact that I was sitting naked in the tub with this man at my side. It felt good to let someone else take control. It had been so long.

"Lean back," he said, bracing the back of my neck with his hand. He let the washcloth wring out over my forehead and hair to get rid of the silty residue from my dunking. A warm flush started in my stomach and moved to my chest. I sat up with a start.

"I think I can take it from here." I grabbed the washcloth with unnecessary urgency. "Go pour yourself a glass of wine, and I'll be out in a minute."

I finished rinsing the dirt away, wrapped myself in a long white seersucker bathrobe, and dug out an old pair of glasses from a bathroom drawer. They were oversized, salmon-colored frames, and I winced when I looked in the mirror. I looked like a hoot owl. When I reached the living room, the sight that greeted me shook away the rest of the shadows, and I started laughing.

"I hope you don't mind," Strike said, gesturing to the sweatpants he'd borrowed from the hook on the back of my bedroom door. He was bare chested, and the sweatpants reached only to mid-shin on his long legs. He looked like a testosterone-riddled teenager whose parents were too cheap to buy new clothes for every growth spurt.

I had forgotten that he, too, would be wet after wading chest-deep in the water to rescue me. "Let's put your clothes in the dryer. That way you'll be able to get back into something that fits you a little better." I stifled another laugh and went to gather his clothes and refill my wine.

I pondered the options of what to do with a half-naked man in my house but ultimately decided just to enjoy the view. It had been a long time since I had sampled even that kind of comfort, since I had thought of someone's skin as anything other than a place to start an IV or watch for signs of bedsores.

We talked about Strike's surveillance of Red Blanken. Strike had tailed him last night to a strip club on Benson Highway and now looked much the worse for those hours of lost sleep.

"He's a real loner when he goes out," Strike said. "Doesn't bring a friend, doesn't start up a conversation with anybody."

I wondered if Blanken had started a conversation with Amy seven years ago. Maybe she had seen his familiar face at the rodeo and let him walk her back to her car. Maybe a high school friendship let him get close enough to turn a chance meeting into a rape.

Was Blanken the one who made my sister want to take her own life? Was it Cates? Maybe it was a man who hid behind the anonymity of a friendly highway patrolman's badge. For all I knew, it was someone who had moved to Detroit or Timbuktu years ago.

23

The morning after the flood I realized that the videotapes and all my notes from Cates's mock trial were ruined, now lying muddy and sodden on the floor of the towed Jeep. I would have to rely on my memory and on other people's notes to re-create the discussion. I took the bus to work.

When I got there, I called my insurance agent, who said he'd send someone out to look at the car later in the day, but it sounded like a total write-off to him. I didn't think submersion in freshwater would do such damage. I was going to miss that Jeep—dents, tired engine, and all—and the insurance settlement wasn't going to be enough to buy much of anything to replace it.

The lady at the eyeglass store said she could duplicate my last pair and have them ready by midafternoon. More good news for my Herculean credit card.

I phoned Giordano and told him about Blanken's high school affiliation. Could he do anything to find out where Blanken had been on Halloween night seven years ago?

Maybe credit card receipts or telephone logs? His response: "Don't get your hopes up."

I didn't tell him about the resemblance of a highway patrolman's belt to the belt I was looking for. Until I found someone on the Highway Patrol who looked like a real suspect—someone with a snake knife or something noticeable about his fingers—it would sound too much like the rantings of a paranoid. I had enough trouble getting Giordano to take me seriously as it was.

Tuesday brought the first news of results from my own sleuthing. The first call was from the DNA lab. They had finished the comparison of the cigarette butts I'd lifted from Cates's house and the strips of Amy's denim skirt from the night of the rape.

"Was there enough DNA on the cigarettes to test?" I asked.

"The samples were fine. Saliva is a great source of DNA, and that's what we found on both the cigarettes and the cloth." The woman's voice was tinny and high pitched over the phone. "There was no match."

"No match?"

All my work to get those cigarette butts was for nothing. Was it even Cates's saliva on the cigarettes? If it was, and it didn't match the saliva on the denim strips, what would that mean? Maybe Cates wasn't the man who attacked Amy. I had to find a way to get a sample of Blanken's DNA.

The second piece of news was better. The Nogales hospital where I'd taken Amy the night of the rape confirmed that a partial rape kit had been done, and Dr. Sanji, the attending physician, was willing to meet with me. I arranged to be there at three o'clock and hurried to get my recommendations for the Cates trial completed. I called Giulia to see if I could borrow her car and hoped Jessica wouldn't notice another afternoon absence.

Giulia's old Buick wheezed and rattled as I eased it up the freeway on-ramp. Like those shopping carts that freeze up when you take them across the yellow lines that define the parking lot, the Buick didn't like leaving the city limits.

Fat raindrops were falling by the time I reached the Nogales hospital. In the desert, if the drops are big, it means it won't rain for long, but you still get just as wet. I pulled my suit coat up around my ears and ran for the front entrance. The receptionist at the information desk paged Dr. Sanji, who told her he'd need fifteen minutes to finish with a patient and then he would come down.

I settled onto an olive green vinyl bench to wait. Two highway patrolmen lounged against a pillar across from the Coke machine. I checked to see if there was anything remarkable about their hands. Maybe I had the "dedo" part right, and the belt had belonged to a highway patrolman.

A siren wailed, and the two patrolmen moved toward

the ambulance entrance off the lobby. They looked happy to be wading into an emergency or disaster.

I've never been comfortable in hospitals. There is an implacable coldness about them, the doctors and nurses steely-eyed in the face of pain and misery. Amy had felt differently about them. For her, the hospital was a door to a new future. She said it made her feel good to help people when they were so scared and alone. I had seen her calm a frightened six-year-old Mexican child by reciting "Este Cochinillo" as she counted "This Little Piggy" on his toes. She would have made a great nurse.

I reached into my pocket and caressed the silver-and-turquoise ring I'd found in Amy's box in the carport.

I ntercom announcements paging doctors to various wards brought me out of my reverie and back to the hospital lobby. Dr. Sanji arrived at a racewalker's pace. I reminded him of our meeting seven years ago, and we agreed to get a cup of coffee. I followed him down a long hallway decorated with children's oversized, unframed watercolors. Sanji hadn't changed much over the years. He was still squat, round, and brown—a toasted marshmallow of a man. He had graceful hands and thin fingers that fiddled with any tool that came to hand: a stethoscope, a pen, and then his spoon once we reached the cafeteria and sat down.

I told him about Amy's suicide attempt and her current comatose state. He shook his head in commiseration.

"I am so sorry to hear this about your sister." If his accent had become more Americanized since I first met him, I couldn't hear it. "I felt that a great evil had been done to her that night. I am sorry we could not help you more at the time." He tapped his spoon on the Formica tabletop in a burst of unexpended energy. I didn't think Dr. Sanji often sat down just to relax.

"It's been seven years," I said, stirring cream into my coffee. "You must have seen thousands of patients since that night. Why do you remember Amaryllis?"

"The name, of course. I had never heard this name before." He smiled. "But I had also just finished my residency, and this was my first month at this hospital. Everything was new to me. I did not know the procedures and protocol. I did not know if it would be proper to authorize a rape kit when the victim did not say she had been raped. I took a chance." His voice was apologetic, but his eyes shone with pleasure at having done the right thing.

I relived the panic and disorganization in the emergency room that night. It was a surprise that he remembered anything about that shift. I took a sip of cold coffee. It hadn't been very hot to start with. "What did you do, specifically?"

"We took vaginal, anal, and oral swabbings, of course, and scraped under her fingernails prior to cleaning her up and suturing her wounds. I did not know if she would later want to press charges, but I wanted to give her that option. We preserved the evidence, but did not send it out for DNA typing. I am only sorry that we did not insist upon photographs and a police report as well." His spoon beat a fox-trot against the saucer while he reviewed his handwritten notes from that night in the emergency room. "There was severe bruising and evidence of ligature around her wrists and ankles. Wounds on her stomach— that U-shaped slash and two puncture wounds. Apart from the broken collarbone, the dislocated shoulder, and the vaginal wounds, of course." He nodded to confirm his recollection, and his knee jittered a faster tempo.

"The cuts on her stomach," I said, picturing the almost Smiley Face gash I had seen, "were they made with the same weapon as the vaginal wound?"

"Yes, I believe so. There was just one knife. I don't know if I made it clear to you that night, but based on the blood smears and tearing of the uterine wall, it appears that your sister was raped after she was assaulted with the knife."

"*Afterwards?*" Someone stabbed her in the vagina with a knife and *then* raped her? I couldn't imagine the rage—or the fetish—that would have been required to perform that act. And even if Amy had gone willingly to the motel room, her willingness ended soon after she got there. There had been no consensual sex. There had been a knife.

I gave him the address of the DNA lab for testing and

told him to have it billed to my overburdened credit card. Maybe I could make a partial payment on the card before their charge came through.

Now I needed to find out whose DNA it was. I had an idea about how to get a sample from Blanken.

And there might be one more piece of potential evidence I could lay my hands on while I was this far south. I took Highway 82 northeast toward Patagonia and the Cates family ranch.

A s I traveled through the ranchland toward Patagonia, the landscape changed from barren piles of rock to rolling hills with verdant groves of tamarisk and cottonwood following the wet streambeds. The tamarisks grew close together, almost leaning on each other. I had been tempted to lean like that on Tonio these last few weeks. It felt as if I'd known him a lifetime already.

I slowed and turned at the arched, wrought-iron entranceway to the Cates ranch and inched my car over the cattle guard and up the rutted dirt road that led to the main house.

George Cates must have heard my approach; he came out from the barn to investigate. He whacked a straw cowboy hat against his leg as if to brush off both accumulated dust and inquisitive callers.

"Hello, Mr. Cates!" I yelled from where I'd parked by

the main house. "Remember me? I'm Calla Gentry. I work with Ray's lawyers."

I saw a spark of recognition in his eyes, but not enough to ignite a pilot light. If he recognized my name, it was probably because he remembered telling Salsipuedes to kick me out of Ray's house in Tucson. He lit a cigarette and squinted at me through the smoke. I bet it was a Camel, just like the cigarettes I found at Ray's house. If I had mistakenly sent the lab a sample of the father's DNA, wouldn't it have shown some sort of parallel or overlap with his son's? I thought that the lab would have told me that. Did that mean that Ray Cates was completely innocent of Amy's attack?

"Kevin McCullough sent me down to pick up some files Ray thought he might have left here or sent here." And I'd love to know why you gave an employee a fifty-thousand-dollar truck, I didn't say.

"Ray hasn't been here since he got arrested. And I don't remember any files." He continued to squint even though I was the one facing the sun.

"It's not a big box or anything. Just two thin files that Ray might have sent. Do you mind if I take a quick look?"

He walked past me and up the two steps to the porch without looking at me.

"There's nothing here, I tell you." He gestured to the spartan surfaces in the living room. I turned a complete circle, taking in the heavy, planked coffee table, the dark leather couch, and the faded Navajo rugs on the floor.

"Maybe they're in his room," I suggested. At that first meeting at the jail, Ray said he often stayed in his old bedroom at the ranch.

Cates senior huffed once but decided to humor me. I followed his broad back down a dark hallway and into Raymond's room. "See for yourself," he said. "Ray hasn't been here since the day they picked him up." The room looked tidy and impersonal.

He had started to close the bedroom door when the phone rang. Cussing under his breath, the elder Cates returned to the front of the house to answer it, unhappy with yet another interruption to his day.

I hurried into Raymond's room. A colorful serape was draped over the bed, and I saw the scars that years of kicked-off cowboy boots had left on the legs of the bed and the bottom of the dresser.

I pulled out the top drawer of the dresser and rummaged through bolo ties, a plastic cup full of Mexican pesos, and a pile of unused matchbooks. The lower drawers yielded only T-shirts, underwear, and jeans. Everything looked washed and fresh; I didn't know if it would be worth swiping something and retesting it for Cates's DNA.

I turned my attention to the closet. Worn denim shirts, khaki pants. A fancy Western suit with curlicues embroidered on the lapels.

A nail stuck out from the back of the closet door with belts hung on it. The bottom one was black leather, three fingers wide, with a radiant silver sun for a buckle. I dropped all the other belts on the floor in my hurry to get at it.

George Cates's heavy footsteps approached. I slung the black belt around my own waist, shifted the buckle to my spine and held my jacket closed over it.

"What are you doing in there?" he asked, seeing me at the open closet door.

"I'm sorry. I must have knocked these loose when I opened the door." I bent to pick up the pile of leather at my feet.

"Leave it," he said. I didn't argue.

I offered him my business card at the front door. "In case you need to get in touch." In truth, I wanted Raymond Cates to know I'd been there.

"Just out of curiosity, Mr. Cates, how did Ray hurt his finger?"

"I slammed the car door on it when he was six."

So he definitely had a mashed finger seven years ago. One more piece of evidence.

Cates's belt was still around my waist when I got in the car, and the buckle dug an arrow of pain into my spine. I didn't adjust it. It would be a long drive, and I needed the painful reminder to keep me alert. I had one stop in Tucson, then I was heading another two hours north to Phoenix and Miranda Lang.

I made sure Amy's ring was still in my pocket. I was going to need it.

24

I pulled into the airport parking lot where Terry Blanken worked. The red, white, and blue pennants that hung over the office trailer made it look more like a used-car lot than a parking facility. The lot was only half full. I guess air travel really was down this year.

A slim black man in a short-sleeved yellow uniform shirt came up to my car. "Are you parking, ma'am?"

When did I cross that invisible line from being a Miss to being a Ma'am to strangers? "Yes." I peered toward the back of the lot, looking for Blanken. My plan wouldn't work unless I got close to him.

"I'll park it for you," the young man said. "Our courtesy shuttle should be back for you in about five minutes."

I spotted Blanken getting out of a blue Thunderbird at the end of a row.

"Oh, that's okay. I'll park it myself. I've got this thing about other people driving my car." As if Giulia's old Buick was the kind of car anybody else would even want to drive. I pulled away toward the far line of cars, and checked my rearview mirror to see the young man alerting

Blanken to my craziness with a circling finger alongside his temple.

Blanken watched my approach and indicated a space for me to pull into. I shut off the engine, twisted Amy's turquoise flower ring to the inside of my hand, and hopped from the car. He didn't seem to recognize me from that day at the police station, and that was fine with me.

"Here, do you need the keys in case you have to move it?" I held the keys out but dropped them just inches away from his outstretched hand. We both bent down to get them, and I scraped across the back of his hand with the sharp-edged ring.

"Oh, I'm sorry, it's bleeding. Here, let me get you a Kleenex."

I took the courtesy shuttle to the airport but returned only twenty minutes later, saying my flight had been canceled. The ring was wrapped in a clean tissue and stowed in a tiny pocket in my purse. They didn't even charge me for parking.

The highway to Phoenix was almost empty, and I had an unobstructed view of the massive black-and-white billboard at Ruthrauff Road: "Pray for Tucson." I thought more jobs, fewer golf courses, and more judicious water rationing would be better for the city than prayer.

Semitrucks passed me with abandon until a Highway Patrol car, piloted by a tall, dark man with sunglasses, tucked in behind me. The trucks slowed down, and we all made a dignified procession north. I drove with the concentration of someone on a learner's permit, trying not to give him an excuse to stop me.

Just past the Casa Grande exit his lights and sirens bloomed behind me. I wasn't speeding. Why was he pulling me over? The semis around us evaporated, happy not to have been selected.

I pulled to the shoulder and searched the dashboard of Giulia's car for the switch to the emergency flashers. I shut off the engine, unbuckled the seat belt, and opened the door.

"Stay in the car," his amplified voice boomed.

I yanked both feet back in the car and shut the door. He made no move toward me, but it looked as if he was talking on the radio. Minutes passed. Now I was more mad than scared. I hadn't done anything wrong.

Suddenly he was beside me, and I hadn't even heard his car door open or shut. He stood close to the driver's-side window, his tall, wiry torso almost pressed to the glass. The rayed sun and copper star on his belt buckle were level with my eyes. I hoped that the identical belt I had in the paper bag on the seat beside me wasn't visible.

"License and registration, please."

I groped in my purse and the glove box for the information, rolled the window down two inches, and passed them through. Reflective, teardrop-shaped sunglasses covered his eyes — I couldn't see much of his face.

"What's the problem, Officer? I wasn't speeding, was I?" No reply.

He jotted down the information from my license but didn't hand me any kind of ticket or warning. A crackle of static and a garbled voice came through the radio mike attached to his shoulder. He clicked the mike and muttered a short answer I couldn't hear, then tossed my ID through the cracked-open window. He touched his fingers to the brim of his hat, said "Ma'am," and hurried back to his car.

The siren wailed again, and tires squealed as he raced north on the freeway. My heart was still pounding, and my mouth was dry. I got out of the car and walked around it in an effort to clear my head. Was this just a random safety check or had someone heard I was trying to track down a highway patrolman with a penchant for rape and violence? If I wasn't speeding, why had he stopped me?

I bent over at the waist, put my hands on my knees, and took a deep breath. I saw Giulia's license plate out of the corner of my eye. The tags had expired two months before. Of course. That was probably the reason he pulled my car over. Maybe there was no highway patrolman attacker at all. Maybe it was all in my mind. I shook my head, started the car again, and headed north toward Phoenix.

I t was almost sunset when Miranda returned home and found me slouched on the bottom step leading up to her condo. "You should have called," she said. "I would have come home earlier."

"I only got here a minute ago." I fanned my face with the crossword puzzle I'd been working on.

"Come on in." We ascended the steps together, and she unlatched the three dead bolts on the door.

She had left the air conditioner running in her absence, and the rush of cool air gave me shivers after the heat outside. She directed me to a nubby white love seat and went to get cold drinks. I admired the art on the walls, mostly modern, representational work, all in hot, vibrant reds and yellows.

When Miranda returned, I handed her the two belts I held coiled around my fist. "Could either of these be the belt your attacker wore?"

Her eyes widened as if I had performed a feat of legerdemain. "Whose are they? Where did you get them?" She wouldn't touch them.

"Take a look at the buckles. Is it possible that one of them is the belt you remember?"

Her hand crept toward the highway patrolman's belt as if it were a sleeping snake. She uncurled it, held it behind her back, and moved both of her hands to cover the buckle. Her eyelids closed and flickered: a REM dream in broad daylight. She did the same with Cates's belt. The tactile memory came back to her like a wave.

"It could be either one of them, but this second belt seems to be more like I remember. Is it Cates's?"

I nodded. We could never use it to convict him. Miranda wasn't sure enough, and there were probably a thousand buckles like that out there. I also didn't know if Red Blanken had a sunburst belt as well.

I wish Miranda had been able to rule out the highway patrolman's belt. Now I'd still have to brace myself every time I spotted one of their officers, and I'd be stealing glances at their hands as they passed by.

One way or another, I was getting closer to identifying that bogeyman under the bed. I wondered if my credit balance would stand up to one more round of DNA testing.

25

August twenty-first. It was the day I'd both dreaded
and prayed for since I'd first seen Raymond Cates
in the Pima County Jail more than two months ago.
He was finally going to trial for the rape and murder of
Lydia Chavez. Jury selection would take only a week or
ten days. Then my forced association with Cates would be
over.

The courthouse was cool, a shocking change from the
stultifying heat outside. My steps echoed as I made my
way to courtroom three. The first batch of potential jurors
milled in the hallway, some looking frustrated to be losing
a day of work, and others peeking into the open court-
rooms; their first look at the physical manifestation of the
justice system. I missed the old, tile-domed courthouse
with its arched, pink stucco walls and pillared walkways,
but they only tried misdemeanors there now, and we were
a long way from that sort of venial sin. We were in the new
courthouse on Congress; a faceless multistory building
with dark ribs and no heart.

Until just this year Arizona juries weren't involved in

determining the sentence for capital offenses. They simply sat in judgment of a defendant's guilt or innocence, and then the judge determined whether the defendant would receive a death sentence, life without the possibility of parole, or life with parole. Of course, the jurors always had to be death-qualified anyway, to eliminate people who refused to vote for conviction because they believed the death penalty was wrong. Recently that death-qualification took on new meaning. The Supreme Court had found Arizona's system unconstitutional, and now the jury had to select the sentence as well.

This was the first time I would have to death-qualify a jury myself. All of my experience had been in civil trials, so Jessica, with heavy sighs and exasperated glances, helped me with the preparations.

It seemed to me to be a system that was inherently disadvantageous to the defense. Not only did the questions get jurors thinking about the defendant's guilt rather than his innocence but death-qualified jurors tended to favor the prosecution in the first place. I would have my work cut out for me if I hoped to find Cates an open-minded panel. But after discovering that belt and seeing Miranda's visceral reaction to it, I wondered how hard I could really work to select a jury in his favor.

If I had an answer on Blanken's DNA from the scratch on his hand, or if Miranda had recognized the highway patrolman's belt, I'd have a better idea of whether I should be encouraging Cates's conviction or not. But when I told

Giordano about the ring and Blanken's skin sample, he sighed. "We don't even have an open investigation into your sister's attack, Calla. You can't go around handpicking suspects and ask us to do DNA testing. That's not how it works." The frustration was clear in his voice.

"Then I'll do it myself." Like the Little Red Hen from the children's story. Unfortunately, I didn't have the finances to back up my boast. The DNA lab had sent back the ring without testing it, telling me they couldn't provide further services until they had been paid for the work they'd already done. The credit card company hadn't processed their previous charges since I was already so far over my limit.

I redirected my thoughts to Cates and the courtroom. We had sent out questionnaires two weeks ago and today would try to sort out the jurors.

I wasn't sure how I felt about the death penalty. In the abstract I knew that I could happily have asked for Amy's attacker to be drawn and quartered, but in reality I thought it would be very hard to be one of those twelve people who sits in judgment and votes to put someone to death.

I recognized Dee Dee Pollock at the prosecution table. With seventeen years' experience, she had tried more capital offenses than anyone else in the county attorney's office. She glanced at her watch and peered at her notes through Ben Franklin reading glasses. I wished that we had used a female to simulate her trial presence during our mock sessions, but we didn't have a woman available whose delivery and instincts were as good as Pollock's. Hopefully, Merchant's performance playing her role had given us a perspective on jurors' reactions to her probable strategy. We didn't have any information on how jurors would respond to Dee Dee herself, but I'd never heard of her losing a jury's trust and confidence.

Merchant and McCullough were already seated at the defense table, with Cates sitting between them. I was glad that the chair left for me wasn't beside Cates. I couldn't have handled the proximity without recoiling, and I knew the jury would see it. Cates looked composed, almost smiling every time he turned to see who had entered the room. He ran his fingers through the long shock of hair tipping down his forehead.

A door opened behind the judge's bench and Judge Robert Gutierrez walked in, followed by a burly, splay-footed bailiff. Gutierrez was small, almost dwarfed by the flowing black robes, but his penetrating gaze belied the childlike image. He never lost control of a courtroom.

It was time for the death-penalty questions. Only those citizens who passed through this screening and were found to be death-qualified would remain in the general jury pool for Cates's trial.

Gutierrez introduced the topic. "Ladies and gentlemen, this trial is going to be in two parts. The first part is the one you're probably most familiar with from television shows, and that's where you hear all the evidence and decide if

Mr. Cates is innocent or guilty." Nods all around. A couple of jurors looked at Cates with curiosity.

"The second part of the trial would happen if you found Mr. Cates guilty, and that's the sentencing phase. Now, of course, the defense doesn't think we're even going to get to part two. They believe you're going to find him not guilty. But, in case you don't, we have to talk about sentencing. Do you understand?" The jurors all nodded. All I understood was that he'd just wiped out Cates's presumption of innocence.

"In that second phase," Gutierrez continued, "you would have three options. A sentence of death, life without the possibility of parole, or life with the possibility of parole. Do you understand these three options?" Nods again, but this time more hesitant.

"So the question is, do you think you could remain open-minded during the sentencing phase, listen to all the evidence, and then realistically consider all three options if you thought it was appropriate?"

A middle-aged woman in the front row raised her hand. "I don't think I could vote for the death penalty," she said. "It's not right to take a life. Any life."

Gutierrez nodded, then asked if anyone else had second thoughts about being able to consider all three sentencing options. A man at the end of the first row raised his hand.

"My name is Randall Manga. I'm in favor of the death penalty. It makes sure they won't do it again, and it costs too much to keep a man in prison."

"I see," the judge said. "But if I told you to listen to all the evidence in part two of the trial and be open to considering all the sentencing options, do you think you could do that?"

"Yeah, I guess." In a pig's eye. I had seen his answers in the jury questionnaire.

When it was his turn, Merchant tried to keep the woman who didn't believe in the death penalty. I agreed with him. She was a perfect defense juror. "Despite your views on the death penalty, could you follow the law and vote to convict if you found that the defendant was responsible for the death of Lydia Chavez?" he asked.

The woman didn't help him. "Not if it meant that he might be put to death. I couldn't do it."

Merchant recognized the futility of further questioning and moved on to the other juror. His back was to me, and he spoke softly to the judge, but I could hear him clearly from my seat.

"I'd like to strike Mr. Manga in seat six. Although he claims he'd be open-minded, it's clear to me that his original answer is how the man truly feels. In addition, if you'll note his written response to this question about lawyers. Quote: 'All defense lawyers use tricks to get their clients off.'"

I checked off one note on my own sheet of lined paper. That was the sentence I had highlighted for Merchant when we were reviewing the forms. It's still a surprise to me how candid some people are when filling out jury questionnaires.

I didn't think their voices reached the jury box, but Pollock's whispered reply was even louder than Merchant's voice had been. "Your Honor, it's perfectly acceptable for a juror to change his mind during questioning. I think Mr. Manga's responses show a person who is open-minded to the death penalty but who would listen to the judge's instructions." I didn't think so.

"Thank you. That's enough," said Gutierrez. "Jurors number two and six, you're excused."

It took almost a week to get enough candidates to begin the final selection of Raymond Cates's jury, and each day I sat with perfect posture and polite attitude only two seats down from a man who might have tried to kill my sister. Outwardly, I presented a hard, professional shell, poring over jury forms, revising voir dire questions, and reviewing trial exhibits. Inside, I raged like a desert sandstorm. I needed evidence.

At the end of the day Friday I hefted my briefcase to my shoulder and said good-bye to McCullough. His disposition was still sunny. "That went well, don't you think?" he asked. I didn't tell him how concerned I was by all the gung-ho, hang-'em-high death penalty advocates we'd heard in the last week.

I stopped at the supermarket on the way home and

picked up milk and bread. It was still light when I pulled into the driveway. I turned the key in the lock and pushed the front door open with my hip.

I stopped. Something was wrong, different. I set down the paper bag of groceries and tilted my overstuffed briefcase against the porch wall. I couldn't see much from here, but the living room was brighter than it should have been, and a breeze drifted from the back of the house, belying a locked and closed room.

I hotfooted it back to the car, locked myself in, and picked up the cell phone Enrique had loaned me after I lost mine to the swirling waters of the underpass. "I think my house has been broken into," I told the 911 operator. "He may still be in there."

They arrived in less than ten minutes. "He could have gone over the back fence," I told them, "but I haven't seen any activity in the side yard and no one has come out the front door." I'd left my phone on and my thumb poised over the send button while I waited.

A female officer took up a position by the front door while her partner went in. He didn't take long; it was only a couple of minutes before he came out holstering his gun. "I can't tell if you've had a break-in or just left your door unlocked." He ushered me into the house and showed me the open sliding glass door to the backyard.

"No. Never. I always close it, and I use this dowel for security." I pointed at the broom-length stick I always dropped into the track on the sliding door. It was propped up in the corner right where I leave it when it's not in use. Had I really forgotten to secure the door?

"Take a look around," the officer said. "See if anything's missing." I kept my hands at my sides and glanced into each room. It was still tidy—well, my version of tidy. Nothing big was missing, but who'd want my television, anyway? It was so old it didn't even have a remote control.

I checked my desk drawer. The papers had been rifled through but it looked like everything was still there. The green satin jewelry box in my bedroom was upended, and my costume jewelry was strewn across the dresser. "Someone's gone through these things, but I can't tell if anything's missing." I didn't keep any cash in the house, and the only valuable jewelry I had was the carved turquoise ring that was in my purse.

He wrote out the details of the call and handed me a copy of the report. "Make a list of anything you discover is missing. The number at the top of the page is what you'll need for your insurance company." I didn't think I'd need it.

When they left, I called Enrique. He was on patrol and not far away so he was there in minutes.

"Do you think you left the door open?" he asked after a quick walk-through.

"I know for sure I closed the glass door and the curtains, but I can't remember if I locked it or used the dowel." That wasn't like me, but my mind had been racing this morning as I headed downtown for what was likely to be our final day of death-qualification.

"If you didn't use the dowel, the lock on that door is easy to jimmy."

"Let's check everything. Room by room." I started in the kitchen. I opened each cupboard. The boxes of cereal and the bags of polenta and sugar looked undisturbed.

Then I opened the utensil drawer. "Enrique, come here." All my knives—steak knives, chopping blade, chef's knife—had been placed in the drawer with the handles toward the back and the blades upright. A quick rustle through a familiar drawer would have resulted in slashed and slivered fingertips.

"I found something, too," he said, coming out of the bathroom. He held three razor blades in a tissue between his fingers. "Buried in the bath mat in front of the sink. That would have been a nasty surprise in the morning." I shuddered.

Then it hit me. I knew what was missing: a black-and-white photo, taken just as she jumped from the tallest rock into the cool waters below at Seven Falls. Her face was alive with joy. It had been signed "All my love, to my best (and only!) sister." I checked the floor and behind the desk to see if it had fallen.

"Why would somebody steal Amy's picture?"

26

I spent the weekend going through every cupboard, drawer, and package in my house. I canceled my bank accounts and credit cards and changed my PIN numbers in case the intruder had taken a moment to look through my records.

I threw out the food in the refrigerator. Whoever had done this had made me afraid to even drink my own coffee. Enrique and Strike took turns standing guard.

By Monday I almost had myself under control. I probably had left the dowel parked by the wall in my hurried departure on Friday and had made the entry easy for the burglar. I wouldn't make that mistake again, and now I was on alert for him. But my mind spun with the possible reasons for the break-in. Nothing valuable was taken. Nothing but Amy's picture, that is.

It was the end of August now, and our newly death-qualified jury candidates had reassembled in courtroom three. Cates looked chastened. I think those long days of hearing how willing these people were to take his life had awakened him to the possibility of failure.

Now it was time to pick among them for the final fourteen who would sit on Cates's jury. The first thirty-four potential jurors sat quietly reading newspapers and taking in their surroundings. That meant enough candidates for a twelve-person jury, two alternates, and the allowed ten strikes from each side in a capital case.

Of course, we were using the Arizona "struck" system, so the entire jury panel would be cleared for cause before either side had to start using their peremptory challenges. Judge Gutierrez conducted that first series of questions to determine if there was a good reason that someone — although already death-qualified — shouldn't serve on this particular jury. Then the lawyers for each side would determine whether to keep them or use their peremptory challenges to remove them.

I've always thought that the way other states select juries is kind of like Dodge Ball, where you have to focus all your attention and energy on one player at a time, without knowing the strengths and weaknesses of the other players on the field. Instead, the Arizona system is more like Red Rover. You get to look over the entire field of potential jurors and plan your strategy for using challenges. And because each side takes turns using peremptory strikes, you know what your opponent is doing as well.

The clerk pulled fourteen names from a basket on her desk, twelve for jurors and two for alternates. The first candidates filed into the jury box, and Judge Gutierrez began.

He tapped his microphone twice, introduced the people at the defense and prosecution tables, and then asked if any prospective jurors knew them or knew Lydia Chavez.

Two hands went up.

An elderly woman on the panel, with hair as fine as the fur on a bichon frise, said she had read newspaper articles about Dee Dee Pollock and therefore felt that she knew her. Gutierrez smiled down into his lap.

He thanked her and moved on to the second juror, a wiry black man with a coin-size, cherry red birthmark on his cheek.

"What's your association with these people?" the judge asked.

"I've done business with Mr. Cates's father for about twenty years now, Your Honor. I've got a hay and feed company on the south side of town. He's been real good for my business, even recommending me to folks."

"I understand, Mister . . . uh . . . Sanders," Gutierrez said, running his finger down the list of juror names. "I think that's a good reason for you not to want to serve on this jury. You're excused."

A young woman with white-blond hair down to her hips replaced him in the jury box.

"Have you or any member of your family ever been the victim of rape? Or has anyone in your family been the victim of a homicide?" the judge asked.

This was the whole reason we had originally asked for individual voir dire. When you start asking sensitive questions about rape and murder, jurors are much less willing to be completely honest when they have to speak in front of a crowd, and we needed to know as much as possible about these people. We had some of the same information from the jury questionnaires, but it was important to hear how they talked about it. Did they feel traumatized? Victimized? Had the police been helpful? Did they now want revenge?

Gutierrez had shot us down on the request, saying that he would be sensitive in his phrasing and would let jurors reply privately if they wanted to. I didn't see a great deal of sensitivity yet.

One hand went up.

She was a plain woman with freckles and light red hair, and she whispered her response while turning her wedding ring around her finger as if it were suddenly too hot to wear. "Do I really have to say it in front of everybody?" she asked, her eyes counting the number of people in the room.

"Would you be more comfortable in chambers?" asked Gutierrez. He had the bailiff bring the juror, the lawyers, Cates, and the court reporter into his private quarters behind the courtroom. When they filed back into the room, McCullough passed me an explanatory note: *Raped by a handyman two years ago. Never told her husband.* I nodded and then heard Gutierrez say the expected words. "You're excused, juror number seven. Thank you."

Three people claimed hardship as their reason for not

being able to serve on the jury. Gutierrez excused an elementary-school teacher and a woman who was the sole caregiver for an Alzheimer's-riddled parent, but did not excuse the Yellow Pages salesman. He said the trial would probably last well past the start of the academic year and the teacher would be needed at school, but that Yellow Pages ads could be sold all year long. New candidates filled the two empty chairs.

The prosecution team went first, and Dee Dee Pollock rose to begin her questioning. She wore high heels to compensate for her diminutive stature, but her voice could have belonged to an Amazon.

"Ladies and gentlemen, my name is Dee Dee Pollock, and I'm a deputy county attorney for Pima County. Do I have your promise that you will give your full attention to the evidence we present and deliberate as fair and impartial jurors in this case?" Each of the jurors nodded, solemn in the recognition of their vow. She looked like the good, avenging angel, and they wanted to be on her side.

"Let's talk about that evidence," she said. "You're going to hear it described as 'circumstantial evidence,' and the judge will tell you that circumstantial evidence can be just as important as direct evidence. Do I have your promise that you can give as much consideration in your deliberations to circumstantial evidence as to direct evidence?" Ah, she'd planted her first seed.

Leaving her associates at the table, Pollock questioned each of the jurors herself, sometimes asking about an opinion, sometimes about their background, and sometimes about any prior jury service. With each juror she ended her questions with, "Do I have your promise that if I prove to you, beyond a reasonable doubt, that the defendant murdered Lydia Chavez, that you can vote to convict him?" By the time she was done, it sounded like the "Hallelujah Chorus."

When it was our turn, Merchant rose from his seat but didn't approach the jury box. Instead, he stood behind Cates and put an avuncular hand on his shoulder.

"Is there anyone among you who thinks he cannot be open-minded in this case, and if the evidence is proved to be flawed, could not find Raymond Cates innocent?" No hands went up.

I flipped the pages of the jury questionnaires into the order the jurors were sitting in the box. Merchant approached juror number one. "Mr. Wheaton, oh, I'm sorry, it's Dr. Wheaton, isn't it?" he said to the young man in the first seat. He looked young enough that I could have babysat him sometime in years past.

"Tell me about your medical practice." Young Dr. Wheaton described his night schedule in the emergency room at Carondolet Hospital, assuring us that he could still be attentive in the trial even if he'd just pulled a night shift at the hospital. Merchant thanked him and moved on. We didn't want any medical personnel on the jury; they had too much inside information about injuries and death and could make it all too vivid for the other jurors during deliberations. The prosecutor was going to be doing her damnedest to do the same thing during the trial; she didn't need any help. I marked him as one of our peremptory challenges.

Patsy Worthington was in seat number three. She was a blowsy, forty-year-old waitress at one of the oldest bars in town. Cigarettes and liquor had added years to a face that had probably never looked young at the best of times. After all this time I bet her feet were molded into the pointy-toed, high-arched shape of the shoes she wore as part of the "elegant" atmosphere at the bar. I passed Merchant a note with the question I wanted him to ask.

"I see you work at Partee's," he said. "Did you ever forget the face of someone you waited on at the bar?" Merchant asked, priming the pump for one of our key defense messages.

Patsy laughed. "Sometimes things get so hectic I don't even look at their faces. One time I took a drink order from my brother before I realized who it was." The other jurors laughed with her.

James Bartholomew was in seat five. Retired from a tire manufacturing company in Akron, he'd moved to Tucson six years ago and lived in a double-wide trailer off Kolb Road. I didn't see anything questionable in Mr. Bartholomew's background to worry us, but I wanted Merchant to gauge his candor, as well as plant another seed for the defense. I passed him a note to ask about mistaken identity.

"Mr. Bartholomew, have you ever thought you recognized someone in the street and then found out it wasn't them?"

"Oh, sure, it happens all the time. Sometimes it's a car I recognize or the back of somebody's head or the way they walk. Sometimes you just see what you expect to see." Bingo. Merchant had hit his mark.

He turned to other jurors. A middle-aged Hispanic woman whose eldest son was a policeman. A stuntman at Old Tucson. A seventy-year-old who managed an apartment building near the university. A thirty-year-old landscaper who said summer was his quietest time of the year because "it's hell to work outdoors in August."

Merchant thanked all the jurors for their time and sat down, smiling at Cates and McCullough as if he'd just come from a birthday party. It was all show, just stage acting to have the jurors think we liked them all and that Cates was part of this big, happy family.

We passed a sheet of paper between the prosecution and defense tables, with each side either accepting a juror or marking a peremptory challenge. I had already talked to McCullough and Merchant about some of the most damaging juror attitudes that we should watch for: a tough-on-crime mentality, a strong antigun stance, or the abject fear of terrorism that had seeped into even local courts since the attacks on the World Trade Center and the Pentagon.

Our team chose to excuse the emergency-room doctor, the Hispanic woman whose son was a policeman, and a scrawny, balding man who said he had moved into a gated community because "you see what the world's coming to."

New jurors took their seats, and Judge Gutierrez said we would continue jury selection the next day. This was going to take some time. Neither side wanted a fair, balanced, and objective panel of jurists. We wanted jurors who could be swayed to our point of view.

After our mock-trial research I had assumed that we would want more women than men on the jury. While they're tougher on rapists, they're easier on murderers.

We now had more men than women, but the men we had were important ones. The stuntman, the landscaper, and the college student could probably all put themselves in Cates's shoes. It was a perfect example of the Similarity Principle: if I can identify with the defendant, then he can't be a bad guy.

I couldn't tell who the leaders were going to be, the ones who could hold out for an unpopular position, who could turn the tide if the jury was indecisive. It was possible that the librarian in seat twelve could rise to the occasion, but if she was the decision maker on this jury, then Cates was in trouble. She sounded more by-the-books, law-and-order oriented than the defense team would have liked. Maybe it would be the young woman from the public relations firm in seat ten. She was used to public speaking and swaying people to her point of view. And I had seen her look at Cates with interest.

I had been careful to keep the jury questionnaires to

myself and not put them on the table, where Cates could see them. It's important to let the jury know that the defendant takes an active role in jury selection, but they get scared if they think a criminal can get a look at their private information, even if their street address isn't shown on the form.

After a full week the prosecutor conferred with her associates and declared herself satisfied with the jury. Merchant, McCullough, Cates, and I held a whispered conference and did the same. Judge Gutierrez looked pleased, saying that our decisiveness would allow him to get home in time for a quick dip in the pool before the baseball game started, and adjourned for the day.

Opening statements would begin Monday morning. My weeks of defending Cates were over. Now it was time to find out if he was guilty.

27

I was watering the rosebushes in the fading sunlight
when the phone rang inside. Maybe it was Tonio. I
raced to the house and panted a breathless greeting.

"It's Miranda Lang. I hope you don't mind me calling
you at home."

I hadn't heard from her since my trip to Phoenix with
the belts. "No, of course not. What's on your mind?"

"I'm in Tucson. Can we get together?" She named a
family restaurant on Campbell, only a five-minute drive
away.

This time I made sure that the sliding glass door was
locked and the wooden security bar was in place. I grabbed
the keys to the used car I'd purchased with the check from
the insurance company. It was a bland car, imported from
some striving Southeast Asian nation, the kind of car you
lose in parking lots. Turning the key in the ignition, I
found myself wanting something a little throatier these
days—clean lines, a big V-8, maybe something a little in-
timidating—but my bank balance would have to change
colors before that happened.

Miranda was already settled in a well-lit back booth when I arrived.

"Cozy in here, don't you think?" She gestured at the surgery-bright lights overhead. "I find that I don't like dark places." She was back in her warrior mode tonight, wearing a sleeveless black turtleneck made out of something that looked like chain mail, and a wide, flat silver bracelet like Wonder Woman's. The muscles in her arms stood out like a relief map of a mountainous country.

When the waitress arrived, Miranda ordered a veggie burger and iced tea. I asked for a coffee and waited for her to begin.

"I don't know why I'm here," she said. "There's nothing I can do about it. But I have to be here to see it." I raised my eyebrows in question. "You didn't see me there today, did you?"

"At the courthouse? No." I paused a beat to consider my words. "But you said he wasn't the one. Why would you want to attend Cates's trial if he wasn't the one who raped you?"

"I didn't say he wasn't the one. I said I wasn't sure." She drew a breath that was a cross between a sigh and a sob. "And then you came by with that belt."

"I thought you weren't sure about the belt."

"I'm not. But I put 'maybe' and 'maybe' and 'maybe' together and it's beginning to sound like 'sure.'"

"Did anybody else in that lineup look familiar to you?

Maybe you thought you'd seen them somewhere before but couldn't place them?"

"I don't know. I couldn't positively identify any of them. Who are you talking about?"

"The guy with the longer hair in back. His name is Blanken, he's got a record, and Giordano thinks he might be the one."

She sighed. "I'm not sure anymore. Do you know what that's like? To have the power to point a finger at someone, change their life forever, and yet to be afraid to do it?"

I knew what she meant. I'd lived with the same feeling since June. "You aren't afraid of using power. Just abusing it by accusing the wrong man."

Some days I wanted to punish Cates or Blanken or this highway patrolman for anything they'd done—an inappropriate remark, a smirk, slamming a door, littering. They were my effigy for all the evil in the world, and they could do the penance whether guilty of the sin or not. I was taking out all my pent-up vengeance on them.

"I know this is difficult," I said, "but I don't understand about the identification. You spent almost two hours with him that night, first in the car, then in the desert, but you're not sure what he looked like. Do you suppose that you've blanked it out? You know, like a protective mechanism when things get too scary?" The waitress brought the food, but Miranda ignored it.

"That cowboy hat covered a lot of his face. And as for 'blanking it out,' I asked Giordano the same thing," she said. "We even talked about hypnosis. But he said that my testimony might not hold up in court now that I couldn't identify anyone in the first lineup. And nobody really trusts a witness ID after hypnosis." She bowed her head in resignation. "But I'm going to sit in that courtroom every day. I'm going to hear every detail. If it's Cates, I don't know how, but I'll know for sure. Maybe his voice, maybe some detail. I'll know, even if I can't do anything about it."

"If it's him, we'll get him. I promise you. And if it's not, we'll find out who did it. He won't get away with it." Although I directed my words to Miranda, I sent them on silent wings to Amy as well.

I was going to tell Jessica that I needed vacation time but didn't want to tell her it was to attend Cates's trial. Our role in his defense was at an end unless they wanted post-trial research, and we wouldn't normally attend the entire trial. I couldn't explain to her why I had to be there, but, like Miranda, I had to see it for myself. I had to decide for myself if he was really guilty of this murder. If he was, it would be another brick in the wall for me—another reason to believe he had attacked Amy as well.

"Go ahead, Calla," Jessica said. "Take as much time as you want because you're not coming back here. You're fired."

"For what?"

"I just had a visit from Detective Giordano from the

Tucson PD. He says you pointed him toward Ray Cates for attacking another woman. He's our client and still on trial!" Her voice held outrage and fear for the financial jeopardy I'd put her in.

I should have realized that Giordano would call her. In fact, I should have expected it weeks ago. He was probably checking on my story. Had I really been assigned as jury consultant in Raymond Cates's defense? Was Jessica aware of any other association I had with Cates? Had I ever mentioned his name or his family before?

"You've been out of the office so much recently that I can't count on you. And even when you're here, your mind isn't on work. I wouldn't be surprised if Whitcomb, Merchant filed a lawsuit against you. Breach of confidentiality. Libel. Slander. You'll be lucky if you keep the shirt on your back."

She hung up before I could reply, but I don't know what I would have said anyway. She was right. Now I could probably add legal fees to the pile of unpaid bills.

I had no job, but I certainly had somewhere to go: back to Raymond Cates's trial.

Monday morning Judge Gutierrez had other court business to attend to, so by the time the bailiff called for order and the jury was seated, it was already ten thirty and the courtroom was packed. Reporters had been on hand early for the best seats. The Chavez family had come in from Bakersfield and taken the first row of seats behind Dee Dee Pollock. Cates senior sat behind McCullough.

Now that my association with the defense team was over, along with my job, I looked for a place in the gallery. Miranda Lang gestured me to an empty seat beside her in the back row.

Pollock tapped the stack of papers in front of her into alignment, then stood and approached the jury box. "Lydia Chavez was a beautiful young woman with a sweet baby boy and a whole, full life ahead of her. On the night of April first, this man, the defendant"—she flung an accusatory arm in Cates's direction—"met her in a bar, bought her drinks, then took her to the desert and raped and killed her."

She walked back to the prosecution table, lifted a glass, and took a small sip of water, then turned back to the jury.

"He put the gun inside her vagina and pulled the trigger." A stunned silence, then nervous throat clearing. "He ... put ... the ... gun ... inside ... her ... and ... he ... pulled ... the ... trigger," she said again, as if each word carried the weight of the world on its small rounded shoulders.

Her reiteration worked. No one was taking notes. They didn't need to. That phrase was carved into their memory. She'd said it out loud, and it became real.

"How do we know this? There was no one there in that empty desert except Lydia and her killer, so no one saw him do it. That's not unusual in a murder case. Most murderers don't wait until there's a crowd around. And he had the presence of mind to get rid of the gun, so there's no comparison we can make to a specific weapon."

Merchant bristled in his seat, trying to decide whether to object to the "presence of mind" comment, then thought better of it and folded his hands on the table.

"But he wasn't as smart as he thought," Pollock said. "He left behind evidence. And people noticed. And that's what's going to get him in the end.

"Over the course of the next few days you'll hear evidence that three people in the bar that night saw this man" — she pointed again — "with Lydia Chavez. They'll also tell you that they left the bar within moments of each other." She started counting on her fingers, starting with an index finger for the witnesses she'd just mentioned.

"Then there are the tire tracks at the murder scene. You'll hear that the tread marks are not only consistent with his tires but that the tracks are spaced exactly as far apart as the wheels on his car." Now she had two fingers raised.

"You'll also learn that the defendant owned a gun — an unusual gun — just like the one that killed Lydia Chavez." Three fingers.

"And you'll learn that similar orange-colored cat hair was found on his clothing and on the body of Lydia Chavez." Four fingers.

Her fingers curled down, and she wrapped her thumb around them, forming a fist. "And most importantly, you'll learn that we have proof that the defendant's car was at the murder scene within an hour of the time Lydia Chavez lost her life. How do we know that? Because an alert sheriff's deputy gave it a ticket for parking outside the marked visitors' parking area at Gates Pass."

I remembered McCullough's comment in my first meeting with him. "That parking ticket is why they focused on Ray so quickly when the body was discovered."

"You put all that evidence together, and it's no longer circumstantial," Pollock continued. "It's not a coincidence. It's not a mistake." She thumped her fist on the railing around the jury box, sending three jurors backwards in their chairs in surprise. "It means he's guilty of the sexual assault and murder of Lydia Chavez." She glared at Cates, spun on her heel, and strode to the prosecution table, her head held high.

I nodded my congratulations. Exactly the right tone of outrage and horror, and a simple description of the evidence she wanted the jurors to follow.

Gideon Merchant, hampered by thirty pounds of excess weight, struggled to rise. He looked more grandfatherly today, a tweed jacket over gray slacks. He didn't approach the jury box but placed his hand on Cates's shoulder and rocked in place.

"Ladies and gentlemen of the jury, your task here today will not be as difficult as my esteemed colleague from the county attorney's office suggests. Your decision will be easy. You'll decide that Raymond Cates is not guilty because he did not commit this crime."

He unbuttoned his coat, stuck both hands in his pants pockets, and walked toward the jury box.

"You will meet Hector Salsipuedes, an honorable and hardworking man, who will tell you that Raymond Cates couldn't have killed Lydia Chavez, because he was sharing a beer with him eighty miles away near Patagonia when she was killed.

"And you will hear from Ms. Vicki Tenning, a friend of Ms. Chavez's, who can confirm that the man Ms. Chavez was drinking with was not Raymond Cates.

"You will come to understand that all the State's evidence—their supposed witness IDs and parking tickets and bullets and cat hair and tire treads—are all coincidences or plain and simple mistakes. Nothing more.

"We don't pretend to know who was in the bar with Ms. Chavez that night. You'll hear in the next few days that she left word with a friend that she was meeting a potential new boss there. Who knows? She was young and attractive. Maybe it was just a potential new boyfriend. But listen well, and when you've heard all the evidence, you'll know that it wasn't Ray Cates."

He paced back to the defense table and put both hands on Cates's shoulders again. "This is a terrible crime, but it was committed by someone else. The prosecution's evidence is just coincidence, and the witnesses are mistaken. Listen carefully to what both sides have to say, and I know you'll come back with a verdict of not guilty. Not guilty because he didn't do it."

If I were awarding points, I would have called it a draw after round one. But heavyweight bouts usually last longer than one round. And I didn't know whom to bet on.

28

When court opened on Tuesday morning, I was already seated next to Miranda in the third row of the gallery. I was torn between needing to be in the courtroom—to bear witness to this—and needing to be out looking for a job. It took my breath away to realize how close I was to bankruptcy, and money worries clouded my every thought. What would that mean for Amy? Would I have to put her in a state facility?

I tried a mental exercise that had sometimes worked for me in the past. I closed my eyes and visualized coins and dollar bills tumbling farther and farther away, as if tossed by a strong wind coming from behind me. I let them drift off. Then I let the sounds of the courtroom grow louder and brighter in my ears until the money had disappeared. Gutierrez rapped his gavel twice, and I opened my eyes.

The prosecution began its case with Sheriff's Deputy Paul Thompson, who had investigated the crime scene.

Thompson had been called to the scene at one fifty-five a.m., when two tourists out for a midnight stroll had found the bloody, mangled body of a woman hidden behind a knee-high shelf of rock at Gates Pass. He described the position of the body, faceup with naked legs spread wide, her bound arms tucked to her chest as if she was cold. After the evidence techs had gathered hair, blood, and fiber samples, they turned the body over and unearthed the bullet lodged in the wet sand beneath her.

As part of the early investigation, Thompson said, he put in calls to the Tucson PD and the sheriff's office to follow up on any vehicles that had been seen in the area that evening, and he put a rush on the identification of tire marks left at the scene.

Merchant only had a few questions for him on redirect.

"Deputy Thompson, you were at both the crime scene and the Cates family home outside of Patagonia, weren't you?"

"Yes."

"And did you wear the same clothes — slacks, shoes — in both locations?" Thompson nodded, but his mouth turned down.

"You'll have to do more than nod, Deputy."

"Yes, sir."

"And you drove the same car?" Again a nod, then a "Yes."

"No more questions." Merchant was just planting a seed. He was saving his real ammunition for the testimony that more directly pointed at Cates rather than at the crime.

Pollock's next witness was Sheriff's Deputy Ernie Niles,

who had written the parking ticket for Cates's car that night. He told the court how he had found the black Cadillac at ten forty-five on the night of April first, more than twenty feet outside the marked parking area at Gates Pass, where cars were not allowed. He had written a ticket and was prepared to have the car towed if it was still there when he made his next pass.

"What was the license number of the car you ticketed?" Pollock asked.

"Arizona plate, 376 NVT."

"Did you find out who owned that car?"

"Yes, it's registered to Raymond Cates at a Patagonia address. That's why we went looking for Mr. Cates the morning after the body was found."

"Please put an *X* on this diagram, showing us the position of the car at ten forty-five." Niles rose from the witness box and wrote an *X* in orange Magic Marker a hairsbreadth away from the stick figure of a body that Pollock had drawn on the chart.

"How far away from the body would you say that is, Deputy Niles?"

"About forty yards. Both the vehicle and the body were outside the parking area on the east side of the pass."

The black-and-white diagram sprang to life in my head. Could the officer have been that close to Lydia and her killer but not seen them? Was she still alive? Did the killer have his hand plastered to her mouth to keep her from screaming? Or was she already dead while he hunkered down behind a rocky shelf or a mesquite, holding his breath until the officer turned away?

Merchant rose and approached the deputy. "I only have a couple of questions for this witness." A couple of questions? This was the heart of the prosecution's case. If he didn't discredit Niles, I thought the jury would vote to convict, just like the people in our mock trial.

"Were there any other cars in the lot when you ticketed the Cadillac?"

"Yes, sir. Two sedans and a truck."

"And did you investigate those drivers as well?"

"No, sir, they weren't ticketed. They were parked legally."

"Nothing more for this witness," Merchant said with a dismissive flip of his wrist. If he wanted to make it look like the parking ticket wasn't important, it wasn't working. The jurors began to frown when they looked Cates's way now.

The revenge seeker in me smiled, thinking that we now had evidence that put Cates at the scene of a crime. That's more than I had been able to do with Amy's attack. It was a lucky break for Cates that he no longer used vanity plates like the RAM 'EM designation on his pickup truck seven years ago. If Officer Niles had ticketed a black Escalade with a license plate as unique and memorable as RAM 'EM, the jury would be asking to take a vote right now.

At the end of the afternoon's testimony I gave Miranda

a hug, picked up my purse, and moved to the aisle. When I turned to the back of the courtroom, I caught the profile of a tall, thin highway patrolman leaving the room. His size and coloring were the same as the patrolman who had pulled me over on the way to Phoenix. What was he doing here? Nothing in this case involved the Highway Patrol. I pushed past two aisle-standers and was rewarded with "Well, of all the nerve" over my shoulder. I didn't slow down. When I reached the courtroom door, I looked both left and right. Lydia's mother stood with a group that must be friends or family. Three journalists laughed at a joke only they would understand. And there, entering the elevator, a tall man in a patrolman's uniform put his sunglasses on as the door closed. I'd lost him.

Wednesday brought the testimony that Miranda and I dreaded most. My stomach was sour with coffee, and I hadn't been able to eat anything. When I greeted Miranda at the door to the courtroom, her palms were as sweaty as mine.

The Pima County coroner was a wiry, light-skinned Hispanic man with wavy hair that was graying at the temples. He seemed completely at ease in the witness chair, and spoke concisely but with barely veiled emotion about the damage that had been done to Lydia Chavez. He described the ligatures around her wrists, the laceration on her chest, the broken jaw, and the path of the bullet as it carved new canyons of pain inside her. When he amplified his testimony with graphic full-color photographs of the victim, the jurors recoiled, trying to keep the gruesome damage at arm's length.

"Can you confirm that Lydia Chavez was alive when the gun was put inside her and fired?" Pollock asked.

"Yes."

Miranda stood up to excuse herself and tripped over three pairs of feet to get to the aisle and head outside. I wanted to follow and help her, but knew I had to stay to hear every word. I leaned forward and focused all my attention on the coroner's litany of horror.

"When do you estimate the time of death to be?"

"Ms. Chavez died between nine thirty and eleven thirty that night."

In my mind each of the prosecutor's questions became a new chapter in Amy's attack as well, each reply a caption to the illustration of my sister's damage. I saw her face in each photo. I measured her pain with each piece of evidence.

Something in this testimony pulled at me, something I was supposed to hear. What was it that caught and held at the back of my mind?

Merchant and McCullough had decided not to cross-examine the coroner, and he rose to leave the stand. While his testimony brought the rape and murder to lurid life for the jury, there was no evidence from him that tied directly to Raymond Cates. No semen, no fingerprints, so no reason to do battle when, as Merchant had suggested in his opening argument, "This is a terrible crime, but it was committed by someone else."

Pollock introduced her ballistics expert, David Queen, who testified about the unusual caliber of the bullet used to kill Lydia Chavez. He was jowly without being fat, and his plummy English accent made him sound as if he had two more degrees than anyone else in the courtroom. Marjorie Ballast had warned us that he would be a formidable presenter. "Every word out of his mouth sounds like it ought to be carved into a building somewhere," she had said.

Queen had a blown-up photo of a bullet on an easel next to the witness chair. "The bullet exited through the victim's back and lodged in the sand beneath her. Since it didn't hit any bone inside her or any rocks in the soil, it was still in one piece and we could take an accurate measurement of the caliber of cartridge used."

"And what was that caliber?" Pollock asked.

"A .41 Magnum, just like the gun owned by the defendant, Mr. Cates."

McCullough leaped to his feet to erase that "just like the defendant's gun" line, but Queen outmaneuvered him.

"Of course it's just like the defendant's gun," Queen repeated. "The only .41 Magnums with five lands and grooves and a right twist, as shown on this bullet, are the Smith & Wesson Models 57 and 58. The defendant owns a

Smith & Wesson Model 57." It sounded as if he was correcting a child's math homework.

McCullough asked about the number of these guns in Arizona. "Assuming that the killer was even an Arizona resident!" Like he was offering to fight with one hand behind his back.

"They've been around for more than twenty years, so I'd estimate something like two or three thousand were sold in Arizona."

"Did you or the sheriff's office at least check on the whereabouts of the owners of each of those other several thousand Smith & Wessons?" Pollock was on her feet objecting before the words even left McCullough's mouth.

"My apologies, Your Honor," McCullough said. "I forgot myself. I guess I was just asking myself the same question that's probably on the jury's mind right now." He had learned a few things about showmanship and shenanigans from Gideon Merchant.

Dee Dee sputtered a renewed objection, and the judge glared at the defense table. "That's enough, Mr. McCullough. The jury will disregard Mr. McCullough's last statement."

Three jurors jotted notes on their pads. It didn't look like a game of Hangman. McCullough had made his point.

29

Tonio and I met on the courthouse steps, but I wasn't sure I could eat anything after the morning's grisly session. As we moved north on the narrow sidewalk, I filled him in on the morning's testimony and on spotting the highway patrolman in the courtroom the day before. He said he'd ask Enrique if there was any way we could get a roster of the officers patrolling I-10 the day I was pulled over, but who also might have been at court yesterday. I breathed a sigh of relief, and Tonio guided me around pedestrians and parking meters with a hand on my elbow.

We took a table on the front porch at El Charro. I ordered a *topopo* salad, and Tonio chose the citrus-marinated ceviche. I could only pick at the salad.

"How do you think it's going?" he asked.

"I can't tell how the jury responded to Deputy Thompson's testimony, but there was nothing really controversial in there. Niles's parking ticket sure woke them up."

Strike nodded, but seemed uneasy about my comment on Deputy Niles's testimony. He spooned a scallop onto my plate without my asking. "How's Miranda taking all of this?"

"I hope she'll be okay. She couldn't sit through that graphic description of the murder."

Strike pushed his plate away. "There's something I've got to tell you. It's nothing illegal, but it's been bothering me. I found the mystery boss. You know, the potential real estate job Chavez was looking for."

"Who was it? Did he see Lydia and Cates at the bar?"

"Name's Tim Badger. Works for Argent Realty on Speedway. He was interviewing Lydia as a receptionist. And, no, he didn't see Lydia or Cates."

"What did he see?"

"Nothing. He got the bar wrong. Or Lydia did. He was at The Blue Grotto, not the Blue Moon. Over a mile away, and he's got receipts to prove it." He dipped his fork in the seafood but didn't taste it.

"Merchant's going to have to do some backpedaling," I said.

"That's what makes me mad. McCullough isn't going to introduce him. Says it isn't relevant if Badger was in another bar a mile away."

I was fuming. "What right does he have to withhold evidence?" I downgraded McCullough's stock in my mental portfolio.

"He's just trying to keep the specter of some other bad guy—another suspect—out there."

"Why didn't Badger come forward?" I asked.

"He saw that someone had been arrested. Thought it was all over with and he wouldn't have to get involved."

"Can we do anything about it?"

"Not if I want to keep working for this law firm." Strike took a long swallow of iced tea. "It may be legal, but that doesn't make it right." It sounded as if he was already weighing just how much he wanted to keep working for Whitcomb, Merchant & Dryer.

We finished the tea and walked back to the courthouse. Strike still seemed preoccupied and said he had other business to attend to. I had a crossword to keep me busy until the judge returned, but once I figured out the joke in the puzzle, I didn't want to finish it. In every themed clue you were supposed to leave one square blank, to represent the word "nothing." An eleven-square answer that was supposed to be a "description of a Seinfeld plot" became "a show about (nothing)." A nine-letter answer for "just business" was "(nothing) personal." I felt as empty and full of nothing as those gaping, blank squares.

I n the afternoon the prosecution moved on to the cat hair evidence. Their expert witness was Sara Davidson, the criminalist from the Department of Public Safety who had done the hair analysis. She testified that the sample of cat hair taken from Lydia's body was consistent with the sample taken from Cates.

I remembered Pollock raising her fourth finger when

she talked about the cat hair in her opening statement. It was right before she curled her fingers down and made a fist to slam her evidence home with the jury.

Merchant didn't seem at all daunted; he pranced up to the witness box. "So you can tell that these hairs came from Ms. Chavez's cat, is that right?"

Davidson shifted in the chair and looked past Merchant to direct her answer back to the prosecution table. "No, I said the cat hair found on the defendant was consistent with the hair from Ms. Chavez's cat."

Pollock gestured under the table for the witness to look at the jury, the way all expert witnesses are taught to testify. Jurors give more credence to witnesses who look right at them. "He looked me in the eye when he said it," some jurors comment.

"Did you do a DNA comparison between the two samples?" Merchant sounded as if he would actually be interested in the answer.

"No. This was shed hair. No follicles."

"I see. So you can say you have two samples of yellowish hair from a cat or cats, is that right?"

"Yes."

"Imagine that. Two yellow cats in Tucson," Merchant muttered as he turned back to the defense table. A woman in the front row of the jury shook her head in a "tsk, tsk" motion.

"Oh, one more question, Ms. Davidson. Did you take hair samples from Deputy Thompson's clothing or car?"

Davidson looked confused. Why would she take samples from the deputy? "No." She drew out the long *O*.

"Then you can't say whether Deputy Thompson was the one who carried the cat hair from the victim's clothing to Mr. Cates's clothing, isn't that right?"

"The deputies and crime scene analysts are very careful not to contaminate or move evidence."

Merchant wanted to drill his point home. "You don't know whether Deputy Thompson was the carrier of the cat hair, do you?"

"It's not likely, sir. But—"

"Just answer yes or no."

"No."

The bullet and cat hair evidence were beginning to look coincidental rather than incriminating. But I didn't see how the jury could look past the parking ticket that placed Cates's car at the crime scene that night.

Pollock decided to move on to the tire tread evidence. Under cross-examination, this expert from the sheriff's department didn't fare well with Merchant either. He admitted that the tracks at the murder scene were from tires so new that there were no unique wear or cut marks that could be linked to Cates's tires. And under heated questioning he also said that several other brands of SUV might have used the same kind of tires and had the wheels a similar distance apart.

Then Merchant decided to push his luck. "You can't even say when these tire marks were made, can you? Mr.

Cates might have been there earlier in the day, or even two days before, isn't that right?"

The analyst smiled. "Except for the fact that it rained the night of April first. Any tracks that were there before seven o'clock that night when the rain started would have been washed away."

Merchant looked as stunned as the man who picks the wrong card in a game of three-card monte. A furious red flush rose from his neck to his cheeks. He turned away from the jury box.

"Nothing more for this witness."

Pollock wanted to press her advantage. "So does this mean that those tracks must have been left between seven o'clock that night and the time the body was discovered?"

"Yes."

The same three jurors who had taken such deliberate notes about the parking ticket wrote this down as well.

30

Thursday was as steamy as a romance novel; a cotton wool feeling with every breath. I sat in front of the swamp-box cooler to dry off after my shower, then pulled a gray blouse and slacks from the closet. The coloring of the female peacock rather than the male.

My new car stuttered to life. At least its air conditioner worked well.

I reached the courtroom before trial started for the day and had stopped in the doorway when I was jostled from behind. I swung around and ran face-first into Kevin McCullough.

"Hey, Calla, nice to see you," he said. "You come to watch the show?"

"Yeah. It seems to be going well for you."

He didn't seem poised to sue me for libel and slander. I'll bet Jessica never even told him about Giordano's visit or about firing me. She probably wanted to sweep it discreetly under the rug.

I envied McCullough his calmness and ease, if not his ethical treatment of the mystery boss as a potential witness. This was still just a job to him. A chance to shine and be center stage, certainly, but also a way to use his skills to make money. And if he had to bend a few rules to win, he had no compunction about doing so. It was just like that "nothing" puzzle. A nine-letter answer for "just business"? (Nothing) personal.

For seven years I had vacillated between forgiveness and revenge, denial and acceptance, and back again. If Raymond Cates was found guilty of the Chavez murder, maybe I could begin to put my life back together. It would mean that a bad man was put away—maybe even the man who had hurt Amaryllis.

Dee Dee Pollock entered the courtroom at a fast trot, approached the prosecution table, and began a whispered conversation with her colleagues. Her face was tight with urgency. Merchant preened when he came in, and grinned like the smart kid in the front row with all the answers. Something was up.

After a hurried discussion at the prosecution table Pollock and Merchant went into the judge's chambers at the back of the courtroom. They came out with Judge Gutierrez a few minutes later, and he called for a recess, saying we would resume the following morning. I waited until the courtroom had cleared, told Miranda to wait for me out front, and sidestepped down the line of chairs toward Kevin McCullough.

"What happened?"

"Just about the best thing Cates could have hoped

for," he said, stuffing his files back in his briefcase. "The body of a woman was found this morning at a picnic area at Madera Canyon. She was shot with a .41 Magnum."

I shared the news with Miranda on the front steps and, as she turned to go back to her car, I called Enrique. "Is the sheriff's office looking at Red Blanken for this murder in Madera Canyon?"

He sighed. "It's an ongoing investigation, Calla—"

"C'mon, you and Tony Strike were the ones worried about him in the first place. You have to tell me, please."

His voice dropped to a whisper. "We're way ahead of you. The foster family he spent the most time with owns a cabin in Madera Canyon. And we found a witness who thinks he saw a light-colored Taurus parked next to the victim's car on the highway that night."

I wondered if an innocent-looking Highway Patrol vehicle might have been parked near her car sometime that night as well.

S trike and I sat on the living-room floor with our backs up against the couch. It was lunchtime, but neither of us was hungry. The local TV channel broke away from its regular programming to give us the details on the new murder. Strike leaned forward and turned the volume knob to the right.

The hair-sprayed reporter stood with her back to the barbecue pits and concrete benches of a public picnic area in the woods. Crime scene tape was strung like a Maypole decoration and waved in the breeze.

"Sunrise this morning revealed the gruesome remains of a partially burned and half-naked body here at a picnic area at Madera Canyon, forty miles south of Tucson. Bonnie DeGroot, a twenty-nine-year-old Sahuarita resident and mother of two, was raped and then killed by the gun that was shoved inside her. The county coroner reported . . ."

"A bit sensationalistic for daytime television, don't you think?" I asked.

"Not for the channel that measures Tucson traffic congestion by counting the number of cars in the Krispy Kreme drive-thru," he replied.

I swallowed a grin and turned back to the reporter. DeGroot's car had been found out of gas on Sahuarita Road, only four miles from her home. Her husband called the police at nine p.m. when she hadn't returned from her workout at the gym. Her body had been doused with gasoline and set ablaze, and the fire had alerted forest rangers in the predawn hours. Her arms were underneath her, and the fire hadn't reached them. The reporter said an "anonymous source close to the investigation" had leaked the information that DeGroot was tied with the same kind of cord and the same knots as those used on Lydia Chavez.

"Were either you or Enrique following Blanken last night?"

"No, we got our signals crossed. We each thought the other was on it. God, I hope Bonnie DeGroot didn't pay the price for that."

I hoped not, too.

"What else did McCullough and Enrique say?" Strike asked over the reporter's nasal voice.

"Enrique said the sheriff's deputies thought there were so many similarities to the Chavez case that they put a rush on identifying the bullet. The results came in—a .41 Magnum like Cates's gun—just as we were about to start the session today. By now they've probably done the comparison to the bullet found under Chavez."

"Blanken never used a gun before in any of his attacks, did he?"

"Not that we know of," I said.

"Merchant must be laughing."

"I suppose so. I'll bet he tries to get this new murder introduced as exculpatory evidence during the defense presentation. Or maybe he can get them to drop the charges altogether. If it's the same gun, don't they have to end the trial? They'll know the killer is someone else."

Strike leaned forward and shut off the TV. "Pollock can always say that Cates discarded the gun and someone else picked it up. That's probably the dance she's doing right now."

"Not if the cords and the knots were the same."

"That does make it trickier," he admitted.

I thought the prosecution had intended to wrap up its

presentation today, but I didn't know how the news of DeGroot's murder would affect that decision.

Pollock and Merchant both had decisions to make, but I knew what I had to do. Realign my world to conform to the fact that Cates hadn't killed Chavez or DeGroot and probably wasn't Amy's attacker either.

I felt like a Magellan who had just discovered that the world was flat after all. I had built a shaky house of logic that said that the Chavez trial would also tell me if Cates was Amy and Miranda's Sweet Thing rapist. It wasn't any kind of real proof. But if he was convicted of one rape and attack, then it was more likely he'd committed another as well. It would make my catalogue of belt buckles and black trucks and damaged fingers seem downright prescient. And he would serve his time for one crime, but I would know that he was paying for three.

Now my assumptions seemed absurd. How dare I have magnified those tiny crumbs of coincidence into proof against him? I had taken my sister's nightmare ramblings and turned them into a gospel. I had taken a truck and a belt and turned them into a gallows and noose.

It was like waking up from a dream of flying. Suddenly grounded, weighted down by the reality of another, almost identical murder, I could no longer sustain my belief in his guilt.

I exhaled, blowing away the suspicions of Cates I'd held on to these last three months. I had been caught up in a dream of revenge against him. Now that dream could focus on a highway patrolman or a man with cherry red fingers and a turquoise snake knife.

31

The court session didn't start on time the next morning. Gutierrez was closeted with both teams of lawyers until almost ten thirty. I wasn't sure what had been decided behind those closed doors, but it didn't look like Merchant was able to get the State to drop the charges altogether. Maybe the judge had been swayed by the hypothesis that Cates had thrown the gun away and a copycat killer had found it.

Dee Dee Pollock had dressed in her most formal and funereal garb. She wore a black business suit with its high collar buttoned all the way to her earlobes, black stockings, and alarmingly high heels. She called the bartender from the Blue Moon as her first witness of the day.

The checked shirt he wore did nothing to dispel the Howdy Doody image his square jaw and red hair suggested. He told the same story he'd told Strike earlier: Cates was an annoying and impatient customer who had accused him of shortchanging him. He would recognize him anywhere, and he swore that Cates didn't leave the bar until after nine thirty. Merchant tried to cast doubt on the identification.

"How crowded was the bar that night?"

"It was pretty busy. NCAA finals and all."

"Had you ever seen him before? Did you know what kind of drink he preferred when he came in?" No. "So this was the first time you had seen this gentleman. Did he pay by credit card or maybe introduce himself?" No. "So you have no proof that it was Raymond Cates." No.

"Have you ever seen this gentleman before?" Merchant asked, gesturing for a man in the middle of the second row of the gallery to stand. The bartender shook his head.

"Are you sure? What if I told you that he was in your bar last week and that he gave you a bad time because you only gave him change for a ten when he gave you a twenty?" Very sly, Mr. Merchant.

Pollock jumped to her feet in objection. "Your honor. Is defense counsel testifying himself? If he wants to introduce this testimony, he can call the witness when he presents his case." The judge agreed, and Merchant apologized to the court.

"I have no more questions for this witness," he said. This time "witness" became a four-letter word in his mouth. Merchant would never have to call the mystery customer to the stand. He'd already made his point with the jury. The waitress on the jury nudged the stuntman sitting next to her.

Pollock moved on to the eyewitness testimony from the

bar patrons that night. We had taken depositions from them, so I knew what they were going to say. They had picked Cates out of a lineup, they were sure he had been in the bar between eight and nine thirty, and they were sure that he was sitting with Lydia Chavez for part of that time. Gideon Merchant rose and began to hammer at the certainty of their identification.

"Had you ever seen Ray Cates before that night, Ms. Wilcox?" he asked the pretty thirty-year-old who had identified Cates. She wore low-heeled pumps, a silk skirt and jacket, and a string of pearls, as if she expected Publishers Clearinghouse to drop by any minute.

"No," she replied with a shake of her head. "I'm certain of it."

"And yet I see here that you attended the Symphony Gala four years ago, where an evening with Tucson's most eligible bachelors was put up for auction." He held up a program the size of a paperback book and tilted his head like an owl that hears a sound in the woods. "Raymond Cates was one of those bachelors."

Her mouth flopped open, but no sound came out.

Merchant bored in. "Didn't you see someone in the bar that night who reminded you of Raymond Cates, a man you'd met at a charity function four years earlier?"

The public relations specialist on the jury looked from Yvonne Wilcox to Cates and back again, then made a note on her lined yellow notepad. Score one for the defense.

Merchant also created doubt with the next witness,

Gary Gilbert, a construction worker who said that he had been sitting next to Cates at the bar during the early part of the evening. He said Cates had spilled a beer on him as he got up to move to a table.

"How much did you have to drink that night, Mr. Gilbert?"

"Just beer."

"Not *what* did you have to drink. I asked how much."

"Three or four."

Merchant consulted a notepad in his hand. "Are you sure it wasn't five or six, Mr. Gilbert?"

Gilbert looked down at his shoes. "Maybe."

"When did you tell the police that you could identify the man in the bar?" Merchant asked.

"It was four or five days later. I just got back from a fishing trip," Gilbert replied. His callused hands looked out of place attached to a body in a button-down shirt and tie.

"And what made you realize that you knew him?" Merchant asked. He stood halfway between the defense table and the witness chair, so his voice boomed over the courtroom.

"It was when I saw his picture in the paper," Gilbert muttered.

"What was that? You'll have to speak up, young man."

"I said, when I saw his picture in the paper."

Merchant let that sink in for a moment. "I see. You had five or six beers. Then, five days later, you saw this man's picture in the paper as a suspect in a murder case. Then you went to the police and said, 'I sat next to this man in the bar.' And then you picked the same man out of a lineup?" He sounded more incredulous with each question.

"Yes." Gilbert's voice was smaller now. Once again the lackluster student without the answers.

"What a surprise," Merchant said with a barely concealed sneer before he turned back to the defense table.

Pollock aligned the stack of papers on the table in front of her and rose. Her back was straight, and her voice was strong. "The State rests, Your Honor."

As much as Merchant must have hated to leave the State's evidence at the forefront of the jury's mind over the weekend, there was no time to begin with his first witness. Judge Gutierrez reminded the jurors not to read newspaper reports of the case or discuss the testimony over the weekend, and adjourned at four o'clock.

I gave Miranda a hug and merged with the departing spectators. Merchant's defense of Cates was going well. I didn't think Cates would be spending many more weekends in jail.

32

After visiting Amy on Sunday, I met Giulia at her trailer for a late breakfast. I smelled the chorizo all the way from the car, and my mouth was watering by the time the screen door slapped shut behind me.

"That smells great. Breakfast burritos?" I asked.

"Remember how you used to love them when you were a kid?" She stirred the sausage in the pan and added the eggs. A pile of grated cheese on the cutting board waited its turn.

We listened to a woodpecker try to tear the metal trailer apart as we chewed. "If evolution is the survival of the fittest, then that bird's not going to be around long," Giulia offered. "Not very bright."

I filled her in on the trial, on Merchant's handling of the witnesses, and on the jurors' reactions to the evidence. She listened but seemed to hear more than my words. When I paused, she said, "Calla, what are you doing in that court-room? Your job doesn't require you to attend the whole trial. What aren't you telling me?"

I took a sip of coffee. "I lost my job."

"Lost your job? Why, that good-for-nothing, lousy . . ." She gave Jessica several new honorary titles in her fury.

"It's not Jessica's fault. She's afraid the law firm is going to sue us for my meddling in Cates's life outside my role as a trial consultant. I can't blame her." I explained about Giordano's visit.

Giulia snorted her disapproval, whether of Jessica, Giordano, or me, I wasn't sure. "What are you going to do now?"

"I don't know."

She picked up our plates and scraped them clean at the sink. Over her shoulder she said, "Can you remember what the flight attendants on airplanes say before take-off?"

"Have a nice trip?"

"I'm serious. What are the instructions?"

I didn't know where she was headed, but I played along. "Well, they demonstrate how to put on a seat belt, for all of those air travelers who have never been in a car or on an amusement ride."

"Don't be funny. What else?"

"They say to obey all lighted signs and placards. Who talks that way, anyway?" I asked as an aside.

"Never mind that. What else?"

"They say an oxygen mask will drop from the ceiling in the case of sudden loss of pressure. . . ."

"Go on."

What was this? I knew Giulia had something in mind,

but this was like playing verbal charades. "They say to put your own mask on first before helping those around you."

"There. That's it. That's what I wanted you to remember."

"Put my own mask on before helping the person sitting next to me? I don't think any of us needs oxygen, Giulia."

"But we do need help. And you won't be able to help us until you help yourself."

I fought against the gloomy picture she was painting. "Giulia, I'm fine. I have a job . . . well, I'll get another one. I'm healthy. I have friends. I have you."

"You've been looking out for everyone but yourself for the last seven years. How long has it been since you got laid?"

"Giulia!"

"You need to take your life back. That's all I'm saying. Do something for yourself. Be happy. You know I love you, but right now you're just like Amy. It's a life of suspended animation." She had moved behind me and massaged my shoulders with long-practiced love.

I changed the subject, and she let me, but Giulia's words echoed in my ears. And *La Llorona* wailed.

On Monday, Merchant started the defense presentation with what he probably thought was his strongest point, the alibi from Hector Salsipuedes. If even a few jurors believed him, it could swing the verdict Cates's way. I couldn't concentrate on Merchant's words; I still heard Giulia's verdict of "suspended animation" in my head.

We hadn't overly prepped Salsipuedes, in the hope that his answers would still seem genuine and not stilted, but nothing could overcome his bad case of nerves. He shook like a puppy in a thunderstorm.

Merchant led him through the evening hours—what he'd done, when Cates had shown up, which car he had been driving, where they'd gone—then handed Salsipuedes over to the prosecution for cross-examination. Hector's eyes tracked Pollock's approach.

First she hammered him on the time, since he didn't wear a watch. Then she attacked his sobriety, questioning how many beers he'd already consumed before he saw Cates. He was bearing up well until she started asking about the new truck. We were right to try to prepare Salsipuedes for this line of questioning. Clearly, when the prosecution had learned about the truck, they, too, thought the gift was more than coincidental.

"Isn't it true that Raymond Cates's father gave you that truck so that you would provide an alibi for his son?" she asked, her voice raised to stentorian levels.

With each demur, she phrased the questions more aggressively: "Do you expect us to believe . . ." and "Why did you register the truck in your mother's name? . . ." and "How are you—making less than seven thousand dollars a year—supposed to pay him back? . . ." and "Let me

remind you that there's a penalty for perjury, Mr. Salsipuedes."

Maybe he really was going to pay Cates back for the
truck. Or maybe it was a thank-you for being a good employee and for standing up for his son, just like George
Cates said. Merchant's cross-examination had convinced
me that the witnesses who identified Cates in the bar were
mistaken, but I wasn't sure that the jury would agree with
me. Salsipuedes's delivery made it look as if his testimony
was bought and paid for. He hung his head as he left the
stand.

Merchant called Vicki Tenning, the witness he mentioned in his opening statement who would say Lydia
Chavez was not sitting with Cates in the bar. I hadn't
heard her testimony before, but Merchant had described
it as "a Tiffany-wrapped package for the defense." She
was an elementary-school teacher who lived in Lydia's
neighborhood. She said she was in the Blue Moon Bar
that night and saw Chavez there.

"I know Lydia," she insisted. "We waved at each other
when she came in. But the man she sat down with was not
the defendant. That man was much darker and stockier."
Merchant got her to say that she thought Lydia was drinking heavily and seemed to be having a good time, touching
the man on the arm and leaning into him.

With this testimony and Hector's alibi, the jury would
surely have enough doubt to return a verdict of not guilty.

Louise Ure

Especially if they ever heard anything about the new murder.

Pollock strode to the stand. She did not seem as convinced as I was. "How's your vision, Ms. Tenning?"

"It's fine."

"I see on your license that you're required to wear corrective lenses while driving," Pollock continued.

"I do have glasses, but I don't really need them."

"You don't have glasses on here today in court. Did you wear your glasses at the Blue Moon Bar that night?"

"I don't remember. Probably not. I don't wear them much if I'm not driving."

Dee Dee asked a man at the back of the courtroom to stand. "Tell me what magazine he's holding up, Ms. Tenning." The *TIME* magazine logo looked as big as a pizza box to me, but Tenning couldn't see it. "No more questions for this witness."

Merchant stood behind the defense table. "The defense calls Rowena Purcell." I raised questioning eyebrows to Miranda, who shrugged her ignorance of the name. A stocky black woman with close-cropped hair and long earrings took the stand.

"Please tell us what your job is, Ms. Purcell," McCullough said.

"I work in the communications department of the sheriff's office. We handle the radio calls from officers in the field."

"And on the night of April first, did you take a call from Deputy Niles?"

She looked chagrined. "Yes, I did. He requested the registration information on a car he was ticketing at Gates Pass."

"Did you have any difficulty with the license number he provided?" McCullough seemed almost kindly with his questions.

"It's kind of a joke in our group. Ernie—Deputy Niles—is dyslexic, and sometimes he gets the numbers mixed up."

"Did he mix up the numbers on that call?"

"Oh, I wouldn't say he mixed them up," she said, looking over to Pollock at the prosecution table. "But we did have to go through the numbers three times before it came back registered to a Cadillac Escalade."

I looked for the jurors' reaction. Several were shaking their heads as they jotted notes on the lined legal pads that they'd been given. Merchant had diminished the power of that parking ticket with one simple sentence: "We had to go through the numbers three times."

Merchant waited a beat for the information to sink in, then recalled the Pima County coroner to the stand. I guessed that he had been granted the right to bring in the new murder as exculpatory evidence.

"I direct your attention to last Friday morning. Were you called to a crime scene in Madera Canyon?"

"Yes."

"Please tell us what you found there."

The coroner was as straightforward and comfortable as he had been in his earlier testimony. I've often thought that the State's forensic specialists, even though they are part of the prosecution team, are the most objective participants in a trial. They're not testifying, the evidence is.

He described the broken, mangled body of Bonnie De-Groot, positioned facedown in the picnic area with her feet spread like a starfish across the sand. He said her hands were tied in front of her and he described the rope and the knots. It sounded just like Deputy Thompson's testimony about Lydia Chavez.

"Did you find a bullet at the scene?" Merchant asked.

"Yes, a .41 Magnum."

"And have you compared this bullet to the bullet used in the murder of Lydia Chavez?" This was it. The big question. The one that would let Raymond Cates go free.

"Yes. Both bullets have five lands and grooves with a right twist and similar markings. I believe the same gun was used in both murders."

I exhaled a breath I didn't know I was holding. Merchant stepped back to the defense table.

"The defense rests, Your Honor."

The young woman from the public relations agency was in seat ten in the jury box and was one of the last to file out. She turned and looked squarely at Cates, eyes wide and unblinking. She wasn't waiting for deliberations. She'd already made up her mind.

33

My nerves were as taut as high wires in a strong wind. I couldn't wait anywhere near the courtroom, so Aunt Giulia, Selena, and I met for a picnic at Sabino Canyon. The day was egg-cooking hot, but black clouds were building on the horizon. We parked at the circular lot near the visitors' information center and gathered our supplies. I looked over the big Plexiglas map that was posted on the patio. Bird Canyon, Rattlesnake Canyon, the wriggly dimensions of Sabino Canyon, and the remote Seven Falls area almost four miles farther away. The spiny mountain ridges between them were as well defined as a half-closed fan.

We hiked in a half mile to the picnic tables next to the Sabino Creek. Ash, cottonwood, and willows provided the shade that the stately saguaros did not.

When I was a girl, the Sabino Canyon Recreation Area had not been this developed and tamed. There had been scratchy dirt trails to the cooler glens and waterfalls, but no asphalt roads and motorized trams as there were today. Back then you could find privacy and peace in the sheltered canyons. Now, on just about any Sunday afternoon, you were likely to see old friends and make new ones on the crisscrossing trails that led to government-approved picnic areas. Seven Falls, unreachable by road, remained wilder and more primitive.

"Watch out for snakes," Giulia warned. Her bony, big-knuckled hands unwrapped foot-long sandwiches piled high with cold cuts, jalapeños, and iceberg lettuce. "They like the warm concrete here around the picnic area." Selena set out the black-eyed-pea salad called Texas Caviar.

Miranda had gone back to Phoenix, and I was glad. I would do everything I could to help her find the Sweet Thing rapist, but it wasn't likely that it was Cates. We'd start with Red Blanken and then find out more about highway patrolmen who might have been in both Nogales and Tucson.

"Tonio is waiting at the courthouse," I said. "He'll call us if the jury comes back in." I gestured at Enrique's loaner cell phone clipped to my belt. Giulia parceled out the sandwiches, but no one ate.

"What if they find him guilty?" Selena asked.

"They won't. Not after finding Bonnie DeGroot's body."

"But a not-guilty verdict wouldn't necessarily mean that he didn't attack Amy," Giulia said.

"In my mind it does," I said. "I wouldn't even have noticed him or thought about Amy's rape if it wasn't for this murder charge against him. I mean, why would I ever have picked him out from all the men in Southern Arizona with a damaged finger and a black truck?

Giulia huffed at my response.

"It's like your crossword puzzles, Giulia. What's a four-letter word for 'press'? It could be 'urge.' But it could also be 'iron.' You have to fill in some of the other squares before you know. And even if you filled in the second space with the letter *R*, you still wouldn't know which word it was. 'Urge' or 'iron'? I'm reconciled to it now. I let a damaged finger and a black truck make me think I had the answer, but I didn't. All I had was a four letter word and that *R*."

We stared at the food and the two big blowflies that hovered at eye level. A rain-heavy cloud passed overhead, leaving us in shivery shadow.

I checked out the want ads on Thursday morning. Lots of opportunities for pipe fitters and hotel maintenance staff. Nothing for a near-middle-age researcher with a love of Mexican music and crossword puzzles. Where was that perfect job—the one that said "magnificent salary, no special skills, and no heavy lifting"?

The call came in after lunch.

"They've just alerted the attorneys. The jury is coming back," Strike said. I couldn't tell if this was good news or bad. They had been deliberating for less than two days. I exchanged my T-shirt and shorts for more businesslike attire and left for the courthouse.

I found a parking place in a lot only two blocks from the courthouse and hurried up the south steps and into courtroom three. The chair next to me was empty, as if the other spectators had allowed me a cocoon of privacy. When the jury filed into the room, the stuntman and PR specialist stared at Cates. The librarian looked away. I realized I was grinding my teeth.

"Has the jury reached a verdict?" Gutierrez asked.

"We have, Your Honor." It was the public relations rep in seat ten. The verdict slip made the rounds from her hands to the bailiff, the judge, then to the clerk, who read the words.

"We the jury, duly impaneled and sworn upon our oaths, do find the defendant, Raymond Cates, not guilty of sexual assault and not guilty of murder in the first degree."

34

Tonio and I marked the end of the trial with a bottle of Two-Buck Chuck at the little wishing shrine, *El Tiradito*. The shrine, an L-shaped, adobe-walled alcove off Main Avenue, was close to the courthouse and seemed an appropriate place to celebrate the end of my association with criminal litigation. Sprays of plastic flowers and votive candles in tiny glass jars were wired to the stucco walls of the building. Tattered notes of thanks and prayer were tucked into the cracks.

Nobody knows how or why the wishing shrine was created, but legend has it that a handsome young Mexican man was found stabbed to death on that spot decades ago, his shiny silver pistol still tucked into the waistband of his pants. His body was never claimed by family or friends, so the neighbors, regretting that he had died alone and unloved, began to bring candles and flowers in remembrance. He was *El Tiradito*, "the Lost One," "the Castaway."

"Look at this one." I squatted next to the makeshift altar and smoothed a frayed yellow note that had been left at the wall. "'Thank you, God, for my remaining testicle.' Must be a cancer survivor. And this one: 'Please send Jaime home to us.' Well, this is certainly the place to pray for lost things."

My own faith was no longer as strong as that of the note writers. The left-right punch of losing my parents and Amy's rape had taken away any vestige of belief in a kindly, protective Creator or the power of prayer. I thought of myself these days as a Roaming Catholic. Still willing to go to the magic show but watching for the sleight of hand all the same.

Tonio sat on the sidewalk with his legs stretched out in front of him and his back braced against the stucco wall.

"How're you feeling, Calla?"

I shook my head. "Confused. I really got caught up in this. I spent three months believing Cates killed Lydia Chavez and trying to prove he attacked Amy, when he shouldn't even have been a suspect in either case. I can't trust my own instincts anymore." I stood and stretched my back, loosening the kinks.

Strike skipped a piece of gravel off the sidewalk. "I told you early on that I didn't think Ray attacked Amy, but I admit that I thought they had the right man for the Chavez murder. You can't blame yourself for bad instincts. Mine were bad, too."

"Here's to justice." I raised the bottle of wine to my lips in a toast.

I looked back over my shoulder at Strike. "Tonio, I

never would have known this much about Amy's attack except for you. The motel clerk. The probability that she knew her attacker. That it might have been a date rape. I've learned some things I didn't want to know.

"And I learned a lot about myself. I knew that what happened to Amy had rocked me, but I didn't realize how much. I think I need to give myself the same advice I gave Miranda. 'Go talk to a professional about this.'"

"Whatever you need"—he rose to his feet—"I'll still be here."

He folded me in his arms, and I breathed in the smell of sagebrush and safety.

I had overheard the interviews with the jury foreperson on the courthouse steps after the verdict had been announced. She looked as comfortable as if she was giving a press conference for one of her firm's corporate clients.

"There were several of us who understood right away that this was a case of mistaken identity," she had explained. "Especially after we heard about this latest murder. And that parking ticket was just an error. The license plate number the deputy wrote down must have belonged to another car."

I should have given her more credit for being able to see through the coincidences and mistakes in the evidence. Even during the interviews I saw the glances she was giving Cates, the small smile of complicity she offered when asked if she had ever mistaken a person for someone else. She had the strength of personality to convince others if she knew she was right, but she hadn't had to do it. The rest of the group understood as well.

The librarian was probably a holdout at first. A mouth held as rigid as the spine of a book. A tabbed and color-coded mind that would have believed the evidence never lied. I'll bet she was the reason the jury took two days in their deliberations.

"Want to come over tonight?" I asked. Tonio nodded and grinned. When I reached down to grab his hand, I saw a flash of white shirt from the corner of my eye.

There, on the corner of Main and Cushing, Terrence "Red" Blanken leaned against a lamppost and cleaned his nails with a long-bladed knife.

I looked away before he saw the recognition in my eyes. "Tonio, there in the white shirt. It's Blanken."

Strike spun around. "Where?"

"There. By the lamppost." I kept my head down.

"There's nobody there, Calla."

I looked left and right. "Where is he? He was standing right there!" I pointed at a businessman walking past. He looked alarmed at my raised voice and pointing gesture.

We ran back to the corner and checked both directions. No white shirt. No knife. Great. First the highway patrolman in the courtroom and now Blanken. It wasn't just my instincts that couldn't be trusted, it was my sanity.

"Let's give Giordano a call anyway," Strike said, taking the cell phone out of his pocket. "Maybe he ducked into an alley. The police need to know he might be around here."

We stopped to buy a bottle of champagne on the way back to the house, and Tonio decided to forsake the errands he was going to run to stay with me. I wondered if he thought that seeing Blanken was all in my imagination. I wondered the same thing. Maybe I'd just substituted one bogeyman for another. He made sure the house was empty and all the doors locked as I'd left them before he let me in.

He took the sports section out to the patio, and I straightened the room and plumped pillows so the house would be fit for company.

I had some duck in the freezer that Enrique had passed along from a weekend hunt. I ticked through the other ingredients I'd need: brown sugar, garlic, cayenne, ancho chile powder. Extra jalapeños. I'd be eating beans and rice for a month after this meal, but it would be worth it.

I started mixing the sauce; the duck would need to braise for almost three hours, and at this rate we wouldn't be eating until late. With the pan bubbling in the oven, I redirected my attention to the house, stacking and storing the information from all the rape interviews and wiping the counters in the bathroom and kitchen. I felt like a schoolgirl on a first date.

Strike had helped me with the investigation of Amy's rape and helped me understand her lies. Well, not lies really, just the half-truths of self-preservation. Maybe he could help me through this next phase, too. The one where I tried to get back my faith in mankind and tried to put the past behind me. I had promised Amy I would find the man who did this to her, but what good would it do now? It wouldn't bring my sister back to me.

"Tonio? I'm going to take a quick bath. Help yourself to something to drink if you want."

I luxuriated in the sweet-smelling suds and tried to put all thoughts of patrolmen, Blanken, rapes, and murders out of my head. I had just wrapped myself in the seer-sucker robe when the doorbell rang. I yanked the bathroom door open and raced through the living room. Wet mist billowed out around me.

"Want me to get it?" Strike called from the backyard.

"Nope, I've got it."

A quick glance through the peephole showed a man with sandy brown hair, but I couldn't see his face. I opened the door as far as the chain guard would let it. Cates was slouched against the doorjamb and raised his right hand to push his hair off his forehead. I yelped and backpedaled across the room. I guess my body wasn't as conditioned to his innocence as my head was.

"Sorry, you startled me." I unlatched the chain and let him in.

"I can see that." His appraisal took in my bathrobe and towel-wrapped hair, and he pushed a foil-topped bottle of champagne in my direction. "Here, I brought you this. Thought maybe we could celebrate."

"That's really nice." Now I was even more ashamed of my reaction to him at the door. "But I'm sorry, I'm not

really ready for company right now." I gestured at my tur-
ban headdress.

He looked past me to see Strike opening the sliding
glass door.

"Hey, Ray. Congratulations," Strike said.

"Thanks. It looks like I've caught you at a bad time. I
wanted to come by and drop this off for you." He handed
me the champagne. "Take it, with my thanks. You did a
good job with the jury and everything." He backed up two
steps on the small front porch.

"You're welcome. I'm glad it all worked out."

I closed the door as he walked away, berating myself for
my selfishness. He could have stayed and joined Tonio and
me. But seeing him at the door with the outline of that big
black Cadillac behind him brought back all the distrust
from my summer-long spree of suspicion. I'd need more
than one day to get used to seeing Raymond Cates out of
jail. Aside from that, I kind of wanted Tonio all to myself.

"That was nice of him," Strike said. "We should probably be throwing him a party, not the other way around."
He stowed Cates's champagne on a shelf in the refrigerator and opened the one he'd bought.

Later, when we'd finished the duck and one bottle of
champagne, Enrique called to ask if I wanted any company.

"What did you tell him?" Strike asked when I hung up.

"I told him I already had some." I opened the second
bottle of champagne.

35

W ho do you think you are? Xena, Warrior Princess?"
Giulia stubbed out her third cigarette in thirty
minutes, grinding the butt into the ashtray with
vigor. "You expected to do all this without the authorities?"

She had always been an unrepentant smoker. I remember chiding her for her smoking when I was a child,
coughing and blowing the wafting nimbus away with an
energetic hand. "Calla, there are three things in this world
that smoke," she said. "Dragons, chimneys, and your Aunt
Giulia. Get used to it." I came to love the smell of fresh to-
bacco when she opened a new pack and took the first cigarette from the box.

"You and Tony Strike have done a great job of digging
up details about Amy's attack. It's enough to get the authorities to start a formal investigation," she said.

I stirred milk into my coffee and shook my head. "It's
nothing more than we had seven years ago. And it's not
enough. Look at Cates's trial. They said they could place
him at the scene, and they had tire marks, cat hair, and a

bullet from a gun like his. All that evidence against an innocent man. I won't be a party to doing that to someone else."

"We've got science on our side. They can compare the DNA samples you've got to their statewide database. There's no arguing with DNA," she said. "Unless you're from Los Angeles, of course." She took another deep hit off the cigarette. "Promise me something. Let's go down and see that county attorney in Nogales—what was her name?"

"Margaret Lance."

"Lance, that's right. Now that Cates's trial is over and you don't have to worry about your confidentiality agreement, let's lay out for her what you've found and ask her how to proceed."

I reluctantly agreed although my heart said we didn't have enough to rouse the interest of the justice machine.

A twenty-minute storm had cooled the air, and the drive to Nogales was redolent with the smell of creosote and wet sand. We had all the windows open so we could enjoy the desert renaissance and so that Giulia could smoke. I kept an eye on the rearview mirror for highway patrol cars.

After ten minutes of silence Giulia said, "How about a puzzle where every answer is at least five letters and contains only one vowel?"

"Like *church*? *String*? *Prompt*?"

"Yep, but maybe more esoteric. More like *myrrh, schism, gnarl*. Maybe *angst, phlegm . . . scrod*."

"I think it would be easier to solve than it would be to plot out," I said, imagining a *Fantasia*-dance of consonants teetering across the page.

"I know what you mean. That's what's kept me so quiet over here." We lapsed back into silence, each musing about vowel-challenged words. My thoughts went to Amy, who still slept. Ah, another five-letter word for Giulia's puzzle.

We were the only visitors in the echoing lobby of the Santa Cruz County complex. After introducing ourselves to the receptionist we only had to wait a few minutes to see the county attorney. Giulia greeted her like an old friend. "My niece has told me so much about you, I feel like we've already met."

I began by confessing that my hypothetical "friend" was actually my comatose half sister. Lance nodded with understanding. I think she had suspected all along that it was either a relative or myself I'd been describing. I told her everything, from the nightmare ride to the hospital the night of the rape to Amy's description of the coral and turquoise snake knife, the black truck, the suicide attempt, and my guess as to the meaning of "day-doh." I described our investigation at the No-Tell Motel, the new DNA evidence from the denim strips, and the rape kit from the hospital. I told her about getting a sample of Red Blanken's DNA but not having enough money to test it and about my recent association with Raymond Cates's defense team.

"And Pima County is looking at Red Blanken now for the murder of Bonnie DeGroot."

The only thing I didn't tell her was the information about the other rape victims. I didn't think I had enough evidence, and I didn't want to get Enrique in trouble for telling us about them.

She took fast notes and asked lots of questions. Then, after several minutes of silence as Lance checked and cross-checked her notes, Giulia asked, "Is this enough information to open an investigation of my niece's attack?"

Lance sounded as if she were weighing her words on the scales of justice. "Look at it this way. First, a lot of this is just hearsay—the truck, the finger, the belt buckle, the knife. Second, the DNA evidence you have from the clothing could go a long way toward confirming the attacker's identity, but the defense would argue that the evidence has been in your possession for seven years and may not be reliable."

I bristled at that last remark. "They would say that I tampered with the evidence?"

"Maybe. Even if we got a match to someone in our database, they could say the results were unreliable because there was no documented chain of custody. Or the sample had degenerated in the heat of the garage." She shrugged as if all the explanations made equal sense to her.

"You aren't even going to run a DNA comparison to Blanken?"

"And third," she continued as if she hadn't heard me, "we've got this time lag working against us. The rape was seven years ago. Amy never filed a police report. And even you admit you haven't been able to dig up any witnesses. There's not much evidence here."

I sputtered like a gaffed catfish. I didn't think all our work could be so easily dismissed.

Giulia took it more in stride. "You're saying that you won't start an investigation?"

"Not right now. Santa Cruz County is barely operating within its budget as it is; I have to save our office's time and money for cases I think I can win. Let's see what Pima County comes up with against Blanken. Then maybe we can consider adding on charges." Lance put her slim hand over Giulia's knobby fingers on the desk. "I know it seems harsh, but those are the kind of decisions I have to make. I'm sorry."

We thanked her but didn't mean it and left the office in silence. Giulia's back was straight and steady, but she leaned on my arm as we descended the front stairs on the way to the car. I walked as if in a fog—all my hopes and plans blurring before me.

"Let's go find a hole-in-the-wall," Giulia said when we reached the sidewalk. I questioned her with a glance, then nodded my understanding.

.   .   .

I 've often thought that the city of Nogales is like an old man with a stroke. On the U.S. side of the border he shows his age but still has strength and energy. On the Mexican side his stroke is evident. Within a hundred yards of the border crossing there are one-legged urchins hawking overpriced packets of Chiclets, streets with pot-holes as wide as the cars traversing them, and gaggles of out-of-work laborers lounging and drinking at the cor-ners.

Originally, our hole-in-the-wall had been La Caverna, on the Mexican side of the border. My memories of it were still strong, even though it had erupted in a fero-cious grease fire that closed the restaurant more than fifteen years ago. It was truly a cavern, as the name im-plied, and a cool place of refuge from the dusty, sweating streets around it. Romex wiring, like hardy metal vines, crawled to hammered-tin sconces set against the stone walls. It was icebox cool, underground-spring wet, and margarita-blender noisy. The house specialty had been *sopa de cahuama*, green turtle soup, a taste to heal all wounds.

Now all the current cavern dining was done at the new La Roca, just steps from the original caves. Deciding to treat ourselves to the luxury of a new hole-in-the-wall, we parked on the U.S. side of the border and crossed over on foot. A three-block walk took us across the railroad tracks and down shop-lined Elias Street. Many of the little *tiendas* sold identical Mexican crafts and souvenirs, colorful sera-pes, woven leather belts, and *nacimientos*, those distinctively Mexican nativity scenes. We paused at the windows of El Changarro, next to the entrance to La Roca, and drooled over their dream-inspired weavings and carved wooden statues.

La Roca was quiet and cool: an oasis from Sonoran Mexico, even after only three blocks. We both ordered the garlicky *camarónes al mojo de ajo* and watched the roving band of mariachis curl around the tables. They wore their pants appropriately tight over cannonball bellies, and when they raised the violins to their chins, the silver buttons down the side seams of their pants gleamed in the light.

"You know that vowel-less puzzle?" Giulia asked after the shrimp arrived, "It's kind of like finding Amy's rapist. We have all the words ready, but the hard part is putting it all together."

I nodded, thinking that "empty" was another word to add to the list, but I didn't say it, as the strings and horns of the mariachi band approached the chorus of "Volver volver" at a volume appropriate to a broken heart.

36

On Wednesday morning I had a meeting with Amy's doctors. They were full of news about recent successes with electrical stimulation of the brain. Rewiring the circuitry, they called it, as if Amy was a kind of faulty television. We'd been through this before, and just like every other time, I let my mind wander to the possibility of happy endings. I'd read about some of these successes, and about comatose patients who spontaneously awakened weeks, months, even years after their trauma. I had to continue to believe.

Strike, Enrique, and I had agreed to meet at Alphabet City at noon. I was the first to arrive and joined Selena and her twin sons as they sat down for lunch.

"Want one?" she asked, doling out the sandwiches.

I declined her offer, and Selena turned her attention to pondering a new menu.

"What letter will it be?"

"O," she replied, her mouth full of peanut butter.

"My, we're feeling brave. Oysters and octopus?"

"Maybe oysters. Omelets. *Olla podrida*, of course; that kind of stew pleases just about anyone."

I read the potential menu over her shoulder. She'd already crossed off the oxtail soup but left okra, osso buco, and oatmeal cookies as possibilities.

"Give me a *ch* day any day," I offered. She gave me an exasperated smile and returned to her list.

Enrique's arrival was followed by a blast of hot air through the door. He wiped beads of sweat from his forehead. "Isn't it supposed to cool off in the fall?" There had been no rain today, but the salmon-bellied clouds crouching over the Tucson Mountains at sunset last night had promised relief soon.

Enrique ruffled his nephews' hair and grinned when he saw his little sister's scratchy notes on the menu. "Olives and onions and orange marble cake," he chanted in a sing-song voice.

We all turned our heads at the sound of the revved engine out front. "Sounds like Strike is here."

Strike slid sideways through the partially opened door, kissed me on the forehead, and took the last empty seat at the table. Selena took in the kiss with rolled eyes and an elbow dug into her brother's side.

"It's on the radio," Strike said. "The sheriff's office just picked up Blanken. They found him at a campsite up near Mount Baldy in Madera Canyon." Enrique got up to phone his office for more details.

I breathed a sigh of relief. "Have they charged him with DeGroot's murder yet?"

"No, they're still calling him 'a person of interest.'"

"The only thing about him that 'interests' me is whether he attacked Amy and Miranda. But at least I won't have to keep watch for that Taurus in my rearview mirror." I felt buoyant. It was all I could do not to start dancing, munchkinlike, singing "Ding-dong, the witch is dead."

Smiles blossomed around the table. Cates had been found not guilty, and Blanken was in police custody. Now, if I could only shake the specter of a vicious highway patrolman.

"What did the Santa Cruz County attorney say?" Strike asked.

"She says we've got plenty of nothin', but that may change now that they've found Blanken." I filled them in on her reasons for refusing to start an investigation of her own.

Maybe it was time to let the authorities handle it. I could give Giordano or the sheriff's department all the evidence we'd collected, tell them our guesses about Blanken or the highway patrolman, and just walk away and get on with my life.

"What are you going to do, Calla?" Selena asked.

"Some meditation."

. . .

B y the time I left town and headed southeast toward
Patagonia, long shadows raced ahead of my car like
a shy friend playing tag. I was going to return Cates's
belt and put this hunt for rapists behind me. Strike had
accused me of "buying a dog and doing all the barking
myself." It was time I let the police and sheriff's offices
do the barking.

Giulia's well-meant advice whispered to me. "Put your
own oxygen mask on first." She was right. I needed to put
Amy's attack behind me. It would always be part of me,
like my English-Italian heritage, my love of crossword puzzles, and my dislike of exercise — but it would no longer define me. I had to create a new life for myself and not be just
a mute witness to my sister's pain.

I promised myself that when I got back to town I'd look
into state financial aid again, to see if they could help with
Amy's care. And I'd find a job that was light-years away
from the world of criminal defense.

I swung under the wrought-iron arch at the entrance to
the ranch and inched up the dirt road toward the house in
low gear. Lights were on downstairs, and a television
laugh track leaked through the open window. Ray Cates
came out on the porch and stood silhouetted against the
light.

"I'm glad you're here," I said. "I wanted to return your
belt to you." I put one foot on the first step and reached toward him with the belt in my outstretched hand.

"I was wondering about that. My father said you had

been here." He tucked the belt though a single loop on his pants and buckled it.

"It was stupid. I'm sorry. I wasn't thinking very clearly."

"That's okay. No hard feelings." I don't know what he thought I'd wanted with the belt, but I was glad he wasn't asking for an explanation. He picked up a cowboy hat from the benchlike swing beside him on the porch. "I was just going out for a beer, maybe get some dinner. Would you like to join me?"

"No, thanks anyway. I really ought to be getting back." With no clouds on the horizon to give us a Kodachrome sunset, the darkness was already settling in.

"It would mean a lot to me. I've felt like a real pariah these last few months, and now you're making me feel like more of one." He shuffled the hat in a circle between his hands.

"I don't mean to do that. Sure. Shall I follow you?"

"It's just up the road." He eyed my car in the deepening gloom. "But I'm not sure your axle would clear some of the ruts the monsoons left us with in this part of the county."

"Okay, let me get my purse." I pulled my bag from the passenger seat and walked toward the black Escalade. I heaved myself onto the running board and then into the car. It was new enough to still smell like leather. I dug around in my purse until I found the cell phone and pushed the power button to see if I had enough juice and a clear signal for a call.

"Who are you calling?" he asked as he started the car.

I laughed. "My babysitter." I dialed Strike's home number. Whether he took me literally or figuratively, Cates nodded.

Strike didn't answer, so I left a message at the beep. "Hi, it's Calla. I'm down in Patagonia and I ran into Ray Cates. We're going out to get a drink and maybe some dinner. I'll be back in town before midnight." I peered at the dial pad to locate the end-call button.

"Everything okay?" Cates asked.

"Sure. Where are we headed?"

"Just up the road to Patagonia. There's a great little Mexican restaurant there."

"Hope it's not too fancy. I'm not dressed for a night on the town." I looked down at my jeans and huaraches.

I finally found the end-call button and pushed it. I hoped Strike didn't mind hearing part of our dinner planning as a message from me.

"Tell me about yourself," Cates said. "I sat next to you at that table for weeks, but I don't know anything about you."

It made me think of Giulia's comment, that I had no life, no identity except as Amy's sister and caretaker. In Cates's eyes, I began and ended as his jury consultant. I was still somebody else's apostrophe. "Let's see. I'm a third generation Tucsonan—"

"So am I. My grandfather moved here from Virginia."

"My mother's family came from Italy. My father's from—"

"How would you feel about a steak dinner instead of

Mexican food?" he interrupted. We had passed through the little town of Patagonia and were on the north side of the city, headed toward Tucson.

"Sure. That would be great."

"Have you been doing this trial consulting long? Do you like it?"

I didn't want to tell him I'd been fired. It would have made me look stupid and him feel guilty. "I've only done it for six years, and to tell you the truth, I'm thinking about changing careers."

"Oh?" He looked over with interest.

"How far is the restaurant? Would it be easier to go back for my car and I can follow you?" If I'd known we would be heading north, I would definitely have taken my car. As it was, I could look forward to a heavy, red meat dinner and a long drive back home trying to keep my eyes open.

"Not far. And I'm enjoying the company."

"Okay. Me, too."

Cates tuned the radio to an oldies station, and Wilson Pickett crooned "In the Midnight Hour." My thoughts returned, unbidden, to the rapes I'd investigated. What was it that had tickled the back of my mind in the courtroom? That one sentence that I knew was meant for me to understand.

Stop it, I told myself. If you're going to get past this, you have to quit miring yourself in sadness. Get on with your life.

"I've always liked an oldies style of music," Cates said. "In fact, I think my favorite music is from my father's era. You know, a big band sound. Blaring trumpets, drum solos that go on for days."

"I like my parents' music, too. But for me that's the *rancheras*. Old-fashioned Mexican love songs."

"I like that. It fits you."

Did it? I hadn't associated myself with a love song for a long time. And what about all the women I'd met in this rapist hunt? Christie Parstac, the student nurse who had been picked up in a bar but couldn't identify her rapist. Mary Katherine Carruthers, who created the only safe place she could, behind barred windows and guard dogs. Sharon Hamishfender, the dancer who was punished for ignoring the advances of two men in a bar. I hoped there would be love songs ahead for all of them. Maybe mine would include Tonio Strike.

"You like your steak rare?" Cates asked, taking me out of my dour reflections.

I laughed. "It's been so long since I treated myself to a really good steak that I can't remember how I like it. How much farther is it now?" We had passed Sonoita and were still heading north toward Tucson.

"I'm sorry. Are you getting hungry? I thought of another place I'd rather go. They make the best steaks in the state. Forty-eight ounces, mesquite grilled."

"I wish you'd told me. It would have been easier to take two cars." If this restaurant was close to Tucson, then maybe I would have Cates drop me off at home after dinner and I'd ask Tonio to pick up the car with me tomorrow.

Cates continued to talk about his favorite foods and restaurants. I remembered hearing some of the same comments from the get-to-know-you tape of Cates we'd played for the jurors in the mock trial.

"I think my appreciation of food is tempered by my wallet," I said. "Someday, when I have lots of money, I'm going to eat nothing but truffles and sea bass and saffron and champagne."

"We can do that tonight if you want," he said with a smile.

I grinned back.

The lights of Green Valley and Sahuarita were off to our left. Bonnie DeGroot's hometown.

Twenty minutes later we approached the outskirts of Tucson, and Cates took the Vail Road exit instead of continuing on into town on I-10, then swung east of the city on Old Spanish Trail. I remembered some great steak restaurants out this way, and my stomach grumbled in complaint.

He laughed when he heard the rumble. "Not much farther now."

"That's great. I think I've decided on the forty-eight ouncer, rare, with baked beans and cherry pie and ice cream."

"Sounds like you're working up an appetite."

The radio had moved on to Sinatra and "I've Got You Under My Skin." My mind twisted the lyrics from amorous to literal.

What about their skin? Amy and Miranda both had thin cut marks on their stomachs. Certainly not life threatening, but why were they there at all?

"Earth to Calla. Earth to Calla."

"I'm sorry. I'm not very good company, am I?" I tried to pay attention as Cates described his plans to go down to Mexico for more cattle for his father's herd.

We crossed over the dry Tanque Verde Wash. Palm trees lined the street and cast spearlike shadows from the moon and the yellow streetlights. They looked like visiting out-of-state relatives to the paloverdes and eucalyptus around them.

Put your own oxygen mask on first, Giulia had said. I took a deep breath as an example. I could do it. I could turn my life around. Maybe I would buy a bright red shirt—something to make me stand out in a crowd. I might even try lipstick—put on a happy face.

A Happy Face? I thought back to the autopsy photos I'd seen of Lydia Chavez. Razor-like cuts marked her chest as well, like a turned-down mouth and two angry dimples. A frowning face? And Amy's cuts made a prototypical Smiley Face?

The scars on Miranda's stomach were three separate cuts, like a widely spaced colon and then a close-parenthesis mark. Turn it on its side, and it was the same as the other two.

Now I knew for sure. The same man had tried to kill Miranda and Amy, and he had succeeded in killing Lydia Chavez.

"We're almost there, Sweet Thing."

37

M y heart dropped into my stomach.

Like Miranda, I was in a car heading out to a restaurant where no restaurant existed. Like Lydia Chavez, I was in a remote and empty landscape with a man I thought I could trust. Like Amy, I had thought I was safe. I'd found the Sweet Thing rapist.

I couldn't let him see my fear, and I had to get away.

"I just remembered I promised Tony Strike I'd meet him tonight." I reached for the cell phone.

"Put that away," he said quietly, ripping the phone from my hand. He made sure it was turned off and jammed it into the pocket of his khaki pants. "I thought you were going to help me celebrate." He turned and grinned at me.

"That phone message I left was for Strike. He knows I'm with you. You won't get away with it this time."

"Doesn't worry me a bit. I'll be able to prove I was in Tucson or I was getting my rocks off with a whore in Nogales. Or maybe I was on a boat in the Gulf of Mexico. They'll have even less proof this time. I'm getting smarter." He tapped his temple with a forefinger.

I cradled the seat belt release in my hands, ready to make a move. We were on Sabino Canyon Road now. The road ended just up ahead at the public parking area that led to the trails through the mountains. Hot, late-summer air whistled through the open window. I watched the isolated homes of adobe, stucco, and glass blur past me. No lights. No one I could go to for help. The engine roared as he pushed the massive SUV up the final grade toward the canyon. With a crunch of gravel he swung into the circular lot for visitors' parking. There were two cars in the lot but they were empty, probably left overnight by hikers who planned multiday trips into the rugged Pusch Ridge Wilderness nearby.

Cates grabbed both my wrists with his right hand and yanked the sun-buckle belt around them, passing the tongue of the belt through the buckle so he could use the strap like a leash. "Come on, I'll show you how I want to celebrate."

I kicked out, connecting solidly with his right kneecap. He howled and grabbed his leg, freeing my arms. I took advantage of his pain and clawed at the door handle. I was halfway out the door when he grabbed the waistband of my jeans and hauled me back. My huaraches couldn't get a grip on the asphalt, and I slid closer to him. Finally I managed to get my elbow outside the car and used it to pry myself out of his grasp.

I threw the car door closed behind me. "I slammed the car door on it when he was six," Cates's father had told me when I asked about his son's damaged hand. I hoped that I had done it again.

A dim glow radiated from the visitors' center, but this late at night there was no activity to accompany the light. Moonlight sparkled off shards of mica in the desert rocks.

I ran toward the darkness of Bear Canyon Trail, wrapping Cates's belt around my fist like a gladiator's gauntlet.

I t had been a long time since I'd spent a moonlit night in the canyon. Now I would have to call on all the resources of my past, remember every stone and twist in the path, to renew my acquaintance with the canyon that I'd known in my youth.

Cates's car door closed with an angry clap. Evidently, I hadn't hurt him enough to stop him.

Maybe he hadn't seen which trail I took. Three paths led away from the parking lot, and each of those branched out like veins within a quarter of a mile. Bear Canyon was the southernmost of the trails. I moved as quietly as possible, careful to plant my feet and not dislodge pebbles or scare night creatures into flight.

I couldn't hear any motion behind me, so I thought I had bought myself a few minutes. I picked up my pace from a creep to a crawl. The path was narrow, and mesquite trees brushed my face with their soft, feathery leaves. I gave an involuntary shudder. On my left was the moonlit path leading to the picnic area where Selena, Giulia, and I had waited to hear the verdict. I didn't take it. I would have felt too exposed.

Canyon tree frogs croaked lonely serenades around me, then went silent. Suddenly footsteps crashed in the brush behind me, and I took off running. The trail rose and fell in gentle waves, but my feet stumbled over even the smallest pebble. I fell to one knee and scared the whitetail deer that leaped out of the thicket as much as he scared me. If Cates hadn't known where I was before, he did now.

I made as much noise as possible in case someone else was in the canyon. "Help!" I yelled. "I'm here! I need help!" No answer but the running footsteps behind me.

The terrain changed to loose rocks and steep hillsides on my left. I had no sense of how far I had run, but my lungs burned with the hot, dry air, and my legs, unused to adrenaline or exercise, shook with palsy.

When I splashed into four inches of water in the creek, I knew I was lost. I found another trail on the far side of the creek and began to climb up the rocky hillside. I gripped the craggy edge of a boulder with my right hand, but my woven leather shoes slipped on the volcanic stone, and I dangled like a kitten caught on a string.

Talonlike fingers grabbed my ankles, and I shrieked. Cates yanked with the strength of the rightfully accused and tossed me to the ground. He dropped to his knees and caught my flailing hands between iron fists. I bucked and scrambled, my grandmother's voice ringing in my ears:

"Calla, you're not much for pretty, but you're sure good for strong."

His hands lost their purchase on my wrists, and I skittered away toward the creek. Thank God for those low-center-of-gravity Italian genes.

Cates gave another lunge, this time pinning my legs and grabbing my hair. He dragged me to the shallow water and pushed my face into the silty runoff. It was only a couple of inches deep. If I could turn my head to the side, I would be able to breathe. And if I couldn't, then that palm reader's prediction of a drowning death would soon come true.

Cates was stronger than my resolve. I sputtered and flailed as the pressure on the back of my head increased. I scratched and clawed at his hands, and my glasses flew off, lost in the darkness. Like a beetle in resin, I was held immobile between the stone of his fists and the trickle of water that would kill me.

It took all of my courage and the last of my breath, but I quit fighting and let my arms float free. Cates did not let up, continuing to grind my face into the wet sand. I let my arms drop to my sides and took a firm grip on the sun-shaped belt buckle. When I sensed the slightest release of tension from above, I flipped over like an angry cat and raked at his eyes. The metal gouged his face, and the wet leather strap snapped like an insult. He gave a bellow of pain and surprise and put his hands to his face. I didn't wait, racing blindly away from the creek to lose myself in the trees.

Without my glasses the night was a blur of shadow and shape. I was facing the rising moon when I started on the trail, but it was now well above the horizon. I didn't know which direction to turn.

Maybe I could follow the direction of the creek. No, the creek ran to the southwest, back in the direction of the visitors' center and the parking lot, and that was the direction where Cates waited.

I felt my way farther up the canyon. If I was right about the trail I was on, it only went one place: Seven Falls.

38

I paralleled the dirt trail, moving more toward the absence of shape than from one place to another. To my damaged eyes a dark shape could be a shadow or a stone, and absence of darkness meant either a clear part of the trail or the possibility of a silent stone to step on. A rounded shape could be a boulder or a brittlebush, a tall shape a man or a saguaro. I blinked and squinted, but it didn't help.

The moon cast a yellow and black tapestry across the desert floor. I inched farther up the mountainside from one pool of lighter shade to another, slipping on loose shale, panting with fear and once walking smack into a jumping cholla cactus that hooked its wiry barbs into the tender flesh at the base of my ear. I swallowed my cry of pain and brushed away the blood that oozed from the thorny gashes.

In the daytime Seven Falls is a popular gathering spot, a year-round receptacle for the sweet rainwater that washes down off the Santa Catalina Mountains. Flat, house-size boulders provide natural stepping stones for the cascading water, and an afternoon of lolling in the narrow canyon can bring respite and release. But under a full moon and populated only by residents who crawled, it would be a nightmare landscape.

I found that I fell less often if I stayed on my knees. So, like those other canyon dwellers, I crawled, a blind penitent in the desert night.

I couldn't see my watch, but by my reckoning I had inched across the canyon floor and hillsides for almost three hours. Three hours and almost three miles farther away from help. I took a deep breath and leaned back against a still-warm boulder.

The deep canyon had not yet accepted my presence and had not resumed its cacophony of desert sounds. The wind sighed softly, rubbing creosote branches together and perfuming the air with the promise of rain. It was a shadow-filled world, the full moon now overhead. The dark monoliths of giant saguaros stood like a surrendered army.

Suddenly Cates was in front of me, close enough that even my dull eyes could see the rictus mouth and the thick spittle on his lips. He bunched my shirt into his fist, pulled me toward him, and threw me across the desert sand. Mica and shale ground into my cheek and my knees. I flailed my arms to the side but found only a cholla cactus that dug achingly into my palm like a self-adhesive grenade. I gasped with pain, scooted back into a seated position, and tried to dislodge the spiny cactus from my hand.

Cates was breathing hard. I couldn't see his face. Without my glasses my world had narrowed to one of sensation and sound. There was no shape, no definition that was clear enough for me to recognize and avoid. I was held captive in a gauzy, blurry world of gray and black, unable to find an exit route or a weapon, or even to avoid an onrushing fist.

I cowered there in my seated position, his hot breath on my cheek.

"I got a big kick out of you coming by to give me back my belt." He panted the words into my ear. "But I couldn't trust you to drop the whole thing. Someday . . . somehow . . . you'd start thinking about this belt again. And you'd start asking questions."

He pulled his belt from where it lay by my side, wrapped the leather around his hand, buckle-side out, then gripped my left hand like a manacle. "Let's see how you like the feel of it."

Said with such complete confidence and composure. A personal mantra I knew he had used before. My teeth began to chatter, and I pain-flexed my right hand, still held in the iron grip of the cholla cactus.

All the rage I had felt for the last seven years boiled up in me. The loss of Amy's smile, of her laugh. Seven years of cringing and living with my elbows tucked in. With a wordless grunt, I lashed out at the sinister shadow that hung over me and ground the cholla into his eye.

He roared with pain.

I ignored the cactus spines imbedded in my palm and scrambled backward over sand, shoe-size rocks, and brittle thorns. Even with one damaged eye he still had some vision. That was more than I had. I had to hide.

I groped my way across the sand to the flat boulders Seven Falls was famous for. The water level probably wasn't high, but a thin stream below me cascaded from one stony shelf to another. There didn't seem to be any place to hide along this flat, open plain of rock, so I continued moving, crablike, reaching out with a Braille hand to read the geography of the canyon with each step. I sensed a darker shadow, an overhang of stone, perhaps, above me. I would still be in the open, but in a darker patch of open. A dark nest that was as warm as a cooling oven.

"Motherfucking son of a bitch," I heard behind me as he continued to pull the razor-sharp spines from his face. "You'll pay for this."

His steps came toward me, deliberate with menace and finality.

"You're going to regret this," he promised. "I'll make it last. I'm going to take a long time to kill you."

I heard a soft rattle beside me. I froze. I couldn't see it, but I recognized that deadly maraca sound. On warm summer nights the rattlesnakes come out to bask on the still-hot flat rocks of the canyon. By the sound of him, we had interrupted the nap of a sizeable adult diamondback. The hollow rattle painted a picture in my mind—an elongated, gray diamond design as intricate as a woven basket, a forked tongue tasting the air for prey.

Don't move, don't breathe, I cautioned myself. Two predators: one beside me and one in front. If Cates continued his angry march in this direction, the snake was just as likely to lash out at the closer of its two targets. Me.

My legs ached with the held position and the desire to run. I grabbed a small, sharp-edged stone with my thorny hand. I may have lost my sense of sight, but I still had hearing. And Cates's fury had robbed him of that.

I listened for his steps across the stone, hard-soled cowboy boots slipping on the smooth surface. He growled and cussed in pain. When I sensed he was just an arm's length away, I threw the stone toward the snake and rolled to my left. The rattler, recognizing the danger of another predator, struck twice at the target in front of him.

The sky was changing to a hint of navy blue on the eastern horizon with the promise of a new day, even if it was still hours away. Without my glasses I still could have found my way back down the trail in two or three hours, but I chose not to.

I wanted to watch him die.

I scooted far enough away to know that I would no longer be disturbing the rattlesnake, and far enough to know that Cates couldn't reach out for me. I hung my head and listened to the progress of his pain.

He wailed terror-pitched high notes against the ache in his groin and his hand. The snake had first struck high on the inside of Cates's leg, piercing the thin khaki cloth and hanging there momentarily with his fangs caught in the fabric. When Cates reached down in reaction to the hot-poker sting of the bite, he struck again.

I listened to Cates's ranting as the delirium grew worse. First he complained of the pain, then became dizzy and weak, his vision blurring to a cottony myopia I could identify with.

"It's your family crest, isn't it?" I said. "The Sleepy C brand. Just like the archway at the entrance to your ranch. I even saw you drawing it that first day at the jail." I remembered the sketch I'd thought was a landscape of freedom: the dip of a valley and two high-flying birds. "That's what the cuts mean. You had to mark these women. Show them how powerful you are. And you did it by carving your brand into them."

He grunted. Neither an acknowledgment nor a denial.

"You called my sister Sweet Thing, too." He looked at me with curiosity, perhaps not realizing it was this signature phrase that had condemned him. "Amaryllis Del Arte. That's her name. Not Sweet Thing."

"Huh." This time recognition of the words, but too much pain for more than that.

Sweat poured off his face. When the convulsions started, I knew it was close to the end.

A darker shadow moved across the moon.

"Ray, it looks like you can't do nothin' right," Salsipuedes said.

39

"Where did you come from?" Fatigue was making me stupid and slow, and my words sounded as if they came from underwater.

"Ray called me on the cell phone when you got away from him," Salsipuedes replied, then turned his head to Cates. "Sorry it took me so long to get here. I made it from the ranch pretty fast but had some trouble finding you in these hills."

"Ray is the one who raped my sister," I told him. "And Miranda Lang. He probably killed Lydia Chavez, too. I've got proof now." Maybe I could appeal to Salsipuedes with the truth. He was certainly loyal to the Cates family, but I didn't think he would have provided that alibi if he knew Cates was really guilty.

"Naw, that was me. Ray's never been able to finish anything on his own."

My head jerked up. "You?"

His lip curled into a sneer. "Yep. Ray's never been able to get the job done. Calls me every time he gets himself in trouble. Calls me his 'cleanup man.'"

My mind was reeling. I was hunting for one man and thought I had the proof against him. Now I knew that Cates was the lesser of two evils. He was still the vicious sexual predator Sharon had known in her preteen years, but he'd found himself a stronger arm, a more virulent evil, in Salsipuedes.

"And my sister?"

"Yeah, Ray recognized that picture I took from your house. So that little slut in Nogales was your sister, huh? Ummmm, pretty little thing. She picked Ray up—did you know that? Slow traffic leaving the rodeo, so she yells over to him and asks if he wants to stop and get a cold drink. I was in a truck right behind him. Got to watch her in the bar sucking on that soda straw like it was a cock."

Oh, Amaryllis, you thought you brought this all on yourself.

"She was something." He was happy to reminisce. "They had a drink, and then, when Ray got her in that motel room, I came in and tied her up. Let him do what he wanted to."

He came back to the present with a lazy blink of his eyes. "Take off your shirt."

I knew now the terror that Amy had felt in the motel room. That moment of incredulity that Miranda had described when her attacker lashed out at her. That gut-wrenching sense that you were not going to live through the night and there was nothing you could do to stop it.

My fingers fumbled at the buttons on my shirt, and Salsipuedes, in a fit of pique or excitement, ripped the last two buttons off and grabbed the cloth. He unleashed the blade of a slim knife, its razor edge as long as my hand, and began slicing the white cloth into ribbons. He wrapped three strong strands together and bound my hands in front of me.

He glanced at Cates. "Hang in there, Ray. I'll get you out of here. But first I have a little partying of my own to do."

I scooted back out of his reach, listening for the deadly rattle of the snake, but I didn't dare hope it would save me twice tonight. Salsipuedes took one step forward and dragged me back by the wrists.

Cates's breathing was shallow now. I didn't think he'd survive a trip back down the canyon. But I also didn't think Salsipuedes really wanted him to.

"You don't care if Cates lives or dies, do you? You can just go back to being George Cates's best cowhand and almost son." I sneered the last two words, hoping to disturb his serene confidence.

He turned his head toward Cates's supine form. Cates wasn't moving. "Naw, it suits me just fine if he dies here with you and everybody thinks it's over. Ray's always fucked up anything he tried to do. He's been trying to prove he's a man his whole life, and he can't even do that right. Can't get it up. Has to use a knife or a gun instead of his cock—and then he can't go through with the killing. It's been up to me for years. But I did it for Mr. Cates, not for Ray."

And George Cates rewards you for it. "What about Lydia Chavez?"

"Oh, yeah." He smiled as he remembered. "I thought for a while that deputy was going to remember the old ranch truck in the parking lot there. Ray and I were hunkered down behind the bushes just a few yards away from him. She was still alive then . . . for a little while longer, anyway."

I didn't have to ask about Bonnie DeGroot; it was clear who had killed her. Salsipuedes probably expected a pat on the back from Cates senior for ensuring a not-guilty verdict. And for convincing me of Cates's innocence.

I groped around me for anything I could use against him. Nothing but plum-size rocks and sand. My knees shook. I didn't know if my legs would support me if I tried to stand.

"And Miranda Lang?"

"Which one is she?"

"She was at the mariachi concert."

"Oh, that was just Ray. I had nothing to do with it. Guess that's why she's still alive. He fucked that up, too. Like his daddy always says, 'Ray, you're not man enough to piss standing up.'"

He grabbed my leg and tied a strip of cotton around my left ankle. I jerked my right leg as far away as I could.

"My sister is still alive. I guess you don't always clean things up," I taunted.

Salsipuedes squatted in front of me and waved the knife

in a figure eight. "You're right. I thought she was dead. Ray sliced his brand and used the knife inside her just the way he likes to do, so when I came in for sloppy seconds, I didn't even think she was breathing."

"That's about your speed, raping a dead woman. That's probably the only way you can get it up." I picked up a small, flat piece of shale between my bound hands and hid it beside my knee.

When Cates had come after me, I had the advantage of silence. His bellowing rage and pain had deafened him to the sounds around him. Against Salsipuedes I had nothing, and his calmness made him a much more dangerous enemy.

The fist came out of nowhere, connecting with the left side of my face. He grabbed my bra and pulled me toward him, but the clasp broke, and he lost his grip. I scuttled crab-like toward the edge of the falls.

"I'll show you what I can do to a live woman."

He crept toward me, first toe then heel, like an Indian stalking a deer. I leaned back and felt the rocky edge of the precipice. There would be five shelves of rock below me to escort the water down the canyon. Five shelves that were beyond my reach.

Salsipuedes sprang, tackling me as I tried to move to the side. He ground my face into the wind-cleaned rock, and his weight bore down from my shoulders to my knees. The sound of the waterfall was buzzing in my ears.

I had to get behind him. I twisted left and right, then

bucked him off like a wild horse. The knife clattered onto the rocks below. He was only inches away and still face-down.

I gripped the sharp-edged shale between my bound hands and looped my arms over his head. The stone was not big enough to be a real weapon, but held by two mana-cled hands, it might become a blade. I clung to him and sawed back and forth at his throat. I retched with the dark, salty smell of blood that cascaded over my hands but held on with all my strength.

Now it was his turn to buck against a deadly restraint. He clawed at my hands and twisted like a speared snake, but I held on. Then I pulled back as far as I could, pulled my knees up against my chest, and pushed.

His body swung backwards over the cliff face, but my manacled hands around his neck kept him from falling the whole way. To a bystander I would have looked like his savior, like a mother clinging to a falling child.

He gasped and scrabbled behind him, trying to find purchase on the top of the rocky ledge. A dark shadow of blood now coated the front of his shirt.

He pulled me closer to the edge. I inched forward to take the weight of his body off my wrists, then craned my head as near to my hands as I could reach. My bloody el-bows scraped across the rocks. One inch. One more inch. Salsipuedes's head, circled by my arms, was as close as a lover's. I bit hard into the cloth handcuffs and gnawed, chewed, and pulled. I ripped my head to the left and heard the cloth tear free.

Salsipuedes's body hit three of the five jagged shelves before he finally reached the rocks below.

I sat bare chested in the desert night like the warrior princess Giulia had accused me of emulating.

Salsipuedes was still alive; his pleas for help echoed from the canyon floor. I must not have cut deep enough into his throat to do much damage. I crawled back to where Cates lay, pulled the cell phone from the pocket of his pants, and watched the predawn desert lighten to dove gray around me.

It took Tonio and Enrique over an hour to reach me. When they arrived, Cates was still alive, too, but his breath was filled with a liquid rasp.

"I'll call in a helicopter," Enrique said.

"Let's wait," Tonio said, looking at me for confirmation. I nodded. He had given me his blue plaid shirt to cover my nakedness and now shivered in his sleeveless undershirt.

Enrique looked back and forth between us, weighing the options, then sat cross-legged on the ground. Strike sat down behind me, folded me in his arms, and wrapped his legs around me like a cradle. The chorus from "Volver, volver" swirled through my head—return, return to your arms once again.

"I guess it took longer to find you here in the hills than I realized," Enrique said, gesturing at the cell phone. He knew the authorities would be able to tell when I had called for help. But they couldn't tell what time Strike and Enrique had arrived.

We watched in silence as Cates drew his last breath.

Salsipuedes called out that he needed help and that he wanted a lawyer.

I stood, brushed myself off, and put a hand on Strike's back to use him as a guide dog for the trip down the mountain. A blurry sun rose over the jagged ridge of Seven Falls.

Epilogue

I nestled Amy's soft hand in mine.

Tonio had come to the nursing home with me and had cooed encouragement to Amy as he brushed the hair off her face. I was wrong about him at first. He's definitely a hopeful romantic. I saw him now outside the window, framed by a curtain of jasmine and bougainvillea as he lounged against the passenger door of the Shelby.

"I don't know where to start," I told my sister's sleeping form. My thoughts swirled from Cates's last moments at Seven Falls to the night of my sister's suicide attempt to the comfort I had come to know with Anthony Strike.

I could have told her about Cates's final transit in the early dawn hours from the rocky plateaus of Seven Falls to the parking lot near the visitors' center. The black body bag was suspended from the helicopter by four strong steel cables. It swayed with the downdraft from the blades.

They brought Salsipuedes out first. His back was broken in the fall, and he screamed whenever the rescuers touched him.

I could have described all the too-late investigation that had proved Salsipuedes's participation in the attacks. It was all there, if we'd just known where to look. Deputy Niles remembered a beat-up old pickup truck parked legally at Gates Pass the night that Lydia Chavez died, but he couldn't confirm that the license number matched the old truck from Cates's ranch. Providing an alibi for Cates cut two ways; it gave Salsipuedes an alibi, too.

Most important was the DNA evidence. As Giulia said, "We've got science on our side." If only we'd had it on our side sooner. Salsipuedes's DNA matched the semen left in Bonnie DeGroot. He had killed DeGroot in an attempt to be "cleanup man" once again, to be the "good son" to George Cates, and to guarantee Ray a not-guilty verdict. Chavez's body held no semen. The authorities speculated that he either wore a condom or he didn't come. Salsipuedes did not confirm it.

But his DNA also matched the saliva from the denim strips of Amy's skirt and from her rape kit. Salsipuedes, the loyal retainer and handyman, had indeed taken his pleasure in Amy's pain. But that DNA evidence would have proven his guilt only if I'd known who to match it to. He'd never been arrested before; his DNA would not have been in the sheriff's database.

Salsipuedes cut a deal. He pleaded guilty to both murders and to the attack on Amy in order to avoid the death penalty.

We found out that Cates senior had smoked the cigarettes I found at Ray's Tucson house. He had come to look for the gun he presumed would set his son free. Mercedes, the cleaning lady, was embarrassed not to have seen the ashtray sooner.

George Cates had never known the truth. "I admit, I never thought Ray amounted to much, and Hector has always watched out for him," he told the newspapers. "But I never thought it had gone this far." He thought Salsipuedes was telling the truth with his alibi, and he had rewarded his courage by buying him a shiny new truck. Now George Cates wandered his ranch alone, like a lost calf.

I could have told Amy about the gifts that arrived anonymously. The lush oil painting from an art gallery in Phoenix depicting the joyously upraised face of a mariachi in full voice. He was brandishing his guitar like a trophy. The police had found a sharp-sided chalcedony ring at Cates's Tucson house. Now we knew for sure that he was Miranda's Sweet Thing rapist. They never found the turquoise knife.

Flowers arrived, but there was no name attached. Maybe from the new Sharon Hamishfender or whatever she was calling herself these days. The note said, "Thank you for standing up for all of us." I could have told her it wasn't courage at work, it was an instinct to survive—fueled by the bitter acid of revenge.

I suppose I could have told Amy about the call from Jessica, asking me to come back to work. Apparently,

Whitcomb, Merchant & Dryer was not anxious to file a lawsuit against me for breach of confidentiality. I didn't respond to Jessica right away. I told her I needed time to think about it.

Kevin McCullough was grinning like a baboon the afternoon he stopped by my house. He said that the law firm was getting calls from all over the country. They were legal heroes for having secured a not guilty verdict for a killer. Business had never been better.

I wasn't feeling as successful. Like that vowel-less crossword puzzle, all my investigation had done was to give me the words, not the solution. In the end, the only evidence I had against Cates was the Sleepy C brand he carved into his victims' skin and the taunting refrain, Sweet Thing. Not enough to sway a jury. Not enough to even sway a county attorney. But certainly enough to rock and sway my world.

I scratched at the bandages that still circled my hand. The gashes from the cholla cactus were healing, but they would leave fishhook scars across my palm. It looked like I'd have a brand as well.

Cates's words—Sweet Thing—used to have such different connotations for me. They would have been said in dulcet tones, pleasant to the ear, soft as a mother's breath on a baby's cheek. A phrase for families—for lovers—for those generous and giving in spirit. Now they were the hard-edged words of death, bleak despair, and pain. He